Someone to Kiss

Jamie Anderson

Someone to Kiss

First published by TRM Publishing, 2022

To my parents and brother
My biggest supporters and greatest teachers

New Year's Eve

Ten Seconds to Midnight

She was drunk—not "super-fun life of the party" drunk. And not even "hugging everyone and telling them she loved them" drunk. She had crossed the line into "sloppy, slurring, feeling sorry for herself and trying to pick up random guys" drunk. She was pretty sure she had told someone she would do "literally anything" for a shot of tequila.

She rested her head on her napkin, her cheek pressing into a sticky smear of wedding cake icing. How on earth did she get here? Forty-three years old. Single. Sitting alone at midnight at a New Year's Eve wedding. Her head on the table while everyone around her hugged, kissed and danced to "Auld Lang Syne." Feeling an odd sense of comfort from the sharpness of the plastic bride and bride she had stolen off the wedding cake, squeezing it in her hand like it was her last piece of sanity.

She never used to care. She liked being single. Loved it. Doing what she wanted to do, eating what she wanted to eat, watching what she wanted to watch on TV—never having to compromise. A queen-sized bed all to herself, cereal and a diet soda for supper—not being accountable to anyone.

But tonight, her cheek crusted with cake icing, she wondered if she'd been lying to herself all along. Maybe she did want someone to share her life with. Someone to stand by her side and help her make decisions, to share her joys and help her through her sorrows. Maybe she didn't want to be alone after all. Maybe she did want what all of these happy, dancing, blurry people had already found. Maybe she did want someone to kiss.

As she slid off her chair and rolled under the table, she made a promise to herself: next year, things would be different. Next New Year's, she wouldn't find herself curled up on a dirty floor, head on a balled-up chair cover, bare feet blocking the entrance to the men's washroom. This year would be different. This year she would put in the effort. She would actively seek out love. When next New Year's Eve rolled around and the clock struck midnight, she'd have someone of her own to kiss. She could do this! Her plan started now…

…Okay, her plan would start tomorrow.

Chapter 1

January 1st

Oh, God! I'm dying.

It was 8:00 a.m. on a Friday, the first, fresh day of a brand-new year, and I couldn't get off the couch. I whimpered as I reached for a glass of water that wasn't there. The inside of my mouth was like paste. I desperately needed liquid. My cat, Mittens, curious at the noises I was making, pawed at my face with his tiny, spikey claws.

Mittens was an asshole.

"Go get me some water," I said, only half-joking. Mittens jabbed me in the eye.

How much had I drunk last night? I rolled over on my side, wanting to go back to sleep and forget I was alive. But knowing from experience that my pounding head wouldn't let me, I continued to roll until I was on the floor, pressing my face against the cool hardwood. My stomach lurched as I pushed myself onto my hands and knees and crawled toward the kitchen. I breathed deeply, paused just long enough to drink a glass of warm water that was sitting on the kitchen table, poured Mittens' dry cat food onto the floor and promptly threw up in the cat dish.

There you go, Mittens, I thought as I flattened myself onto the ceramic tiles, reaching for a floor mat to fashion into some sort of pillow. *That's what you get for being a dick.*

I woke up three hours later with pain shooting through my hip. I guess that's what happens when you are in your forties and you wake up on the kitchen floor. I moved my head from side to side, testing the waters, and waited for signs of nausea. Determining that I felt slightly better, I boosted myself up to a low squat and managed to stand with the help of a slightly wobbly kitchen chair.

"I'm sorry, buddy," I said as I scooped Mittens up in a hug, burying my face in his soft fur. "It's not your fault I'm a disaster." He squirmed out of my grasp with an unforgiving (and well-deserved) yowl. I cleaned up the mess I'd made, opened a can of his favorite cat food and plopped it in his dish, trying to win back his love. He waited until I looked away before he dug in with gusto. He wasn't going to let me off that easily.

I walked into my living room. Fancy clothes were strewn all over my mismatched couch and armchair, shoes tucked under my favourite crochet blanket like they were taking a nap. *Where on earth is my phone?* I thought before spotting my fancy wedding clutch lying on the floor under my TV stand. I emptied its sticky contents onto the table, eyes watering from the smell of spilled tequila. Drink tickets stuck to my phone like wallpaper. I scraped them off with an equally sticky coin.

Dead.

I found the charger nestled amongst the cat toys, plugged in the phone and was greeted by an unusually long symphony of alerts. My stomach sank. Either someone had died or something I did last night had ignited a social media firestorm. I honestly didn't know which option I dreaded the most.

My phone vibrated and I turned it on speaker, not wanting to feel its stickiness against my face.

"What in the actual hell, Kate?" It was Julie.

"Did you just wake up?" I asked, eyebrows raised.

"Obviously," she said, groaning softly as she stretched. "It's eleven a.m."

"Before you judge, let's revisit an image I saw on Facebook this morning." I could hear the hint of a smile in her voice.

Even though we were best friends, Julie and I were almost polar opposites. Case in point, she would sleep until noon any chance she got. Despite the fact I was still a lump on my couch, I was usually up early on weekends. Since the advent of three-day hangovers in my thirties, I'd shelved the partying and sleeping-in part of my life in favour of weekend productivity.

"Hold on," I said as I went through the alerts on my phone.

I scrolled through texts, Facebook messages and Instagram posts. Pictures of me as I danced alone wearing someone else's shoes; as I tipped back a wine bottle, red wine dribbling down my chin; as I hugged a random elderly lady; as I sat on the floor, my mouth wide open in manic laughter; as I hugged another random elderly lady; and— the grand finale—as I slept under a table while someone pulled down my dress to cover my now-famous ass.

I trudged back to the living room and sank into the oversized sofa. It was decided: I would never go out in public again.

"So, are you going to tell me what happened?" she prodded.

The weird thing was I couldn't for the life of me remember what had set me off. The last time I'd let myself get that unreasonably trashed was decades ago—back when my self-confidence was much more easily bruised and I would try to make myself feel better by pounding cheap beer and hitting on guys at clubs, convincing myself that they found super-sloppy-drunk women attractive. (Spoiler alert: they didn't.)

"I honestly can't remember." I tipped over onto my side and perched the phone on the pillow.

"I've been there plenty of times," she said. "Take me through the day and we'll piece it together. Plus, I want to hear about the wedding. I still think I should have been your date, even if it was for work."

I closed my eyes and tried to clear the fog pressing against the sides of my head. "Cody and Nate were late, as usual," I started. "So I sat by myself scrolling through Facebook and sneaking looks over my shoulder. I hate being alone at weddings. I swear, I was the only one there who wasn't part of a couple."

"Sounds about right," she said without sympathy.

"They got there right before the ceremony started, pushing into the pew, not even waiting until I moved my legs. Nate tripped over my purse and Cody fell onto my lap before rolling over to sit beside me."

"Smooth," she said. "They couldn't have waited five seconds for you to move?"

"To be fair, they wanted to get in before Terry arrived so he wouldn't see where they were sitting."

"Good call."

While not my greatest friends in the world, Nate and Cody were the colleagues I hung out with the most. Nate was tall and dark, blessed with a dad bod and receding hairline. Cody, who I was closer with, was your stereotypical pretty boy. They were contradictions physically, but they more than made up for it with their bond of emotional immaturity. We didn't have a lot in common, but we were staunchly united in our absolute hatred of our boss, Terry.

"How was the ceremony?" Julie yawned.

"It was really nice," I said. "You know I love weddings. They're so full of romance and possibility."

"I've seen your wedding book," she said. "It's embarrassing."

I laughed, a sound that was more bitter than joyful. "Well, you're not the only one who feels that way. I may have mentioned it halfway through the ceremony, which was clearly a mistake."

"How so?"

"I believe Cody's exact words were: 'Aren't you in your forties? Maybe just get a few more cats.'"

"Well, we both know Cody's an ass."

"Yeah, that's the part I don't like about being treated like one of the guys. I'm just one of their buds, so I must not have feelings. I mean what he said is true, but it seems less real when I say it inside my head."

I'd watched the rest of the ceremony mostly dry-eyed, feeling sorry for myself. The only tears shed had been those for my wasted years.

"You have plenty of good years left," Julie said, reading my mind as usual. "Don't let those idiots make you feel bad about yourself."

"Too late," I said, the hangover fuelling my pity party. "I'm a forty-three-year-old, lying on my couch, hungover after a wedding. A wedding that wasn't mine. A wedding for someone who could literally be my child."

"So, was that when you decided to get incoherently drunk?" Julie asked.

"I don't think so." My head throbbed as I tried to remember. "When we got to the dinner, we went straight to the free bar, skipping the buffet entirely."

"Well, that's disappointing," Julie said. "I mean, not the free bar, obviously, but the best part of small-town Saskatchewan weddings is the buffet. Think of all the grandmas, aunts, sisters and cousins who gave up their weekend to make delicious cabbage rolls and perogies for you and you didn't even eat them. What a waste!"

I groaned, both because I knew she was right and because my stomach was not ready to think about food. "I know, it's shameful. I hadn't eaten all day, so I was pretty drunk by the time the dancing started and I knew I had to slow down." Having once been a hard-core partier, I'd known when I'd reached my limit. And when I'd passed it. And once that had happened, there was no going back.

"If you'd started slowing down, how did you end up under a table?"

A faint spark pushed its way through the blackout, jolting my dozing neural pathways.

"Cody and Nate were on Tinder!" I shouted like I had just solved the puzzle on *Wheel of Fortune.*

"As one does at weddings."

"I was curious and peeked over their shoulders to watch. The girls were so much younger than them; all of them seemed to be in their twenties."

Julie, who was an online dating pro, made a noise that was both a scoff and an affirmation.

"When I brought that up, they both laughed and looked at me like I was an idiot. 'I would never date anyone my age,'" I said, mimicking Nate, if Nate had an annoyingly high-pitched voice.

Then I was Cody, chin tucked in as I pushed out a mocking baritone: "'If I had a choice between dating a young, pretty goddess with a tight ass or an older, opinionated "woman" who was constantly telling me she needed to have kids before all her eggs dried up, I would probably pick the first one.'"

"I think he might have been overgeneralizing based on experience," Julie said.

"That's what I said! 'Look, no offence, Kate,'" I continued as Cody, "'but I don't *have* to date chicks my age, so why would I?'"

Julie laughed. "No offence?"

"Hey man, I'm only forty-three," I'd said and crossed my arms, pouting.

"Exactly," he'd replied, like I'd just proven his point.

And that was when I'd done my first tequila shot.

Chapter 2

I hung up with Julie, wanting to continue feeling sorry for myself on my own.

But could you blame me? Being a single woman in her forties sucked. And the problem was exactly the kind of conversation I'd had with Nate and Cody.

"Right, Mittens?" I said as he jumped into my lap and nudged his head under my arm, wanting a scratch. I happily obliged, relieved to be forgiven again for being a shitty cat mom.

If it was socially acceptable, I mused—or, more accurately, admirable—for a man to walk into a room with a pretty young thing ten or twenty years his junior, why wouldn't he skew that way?

Single men my age were often divorced or coming out of a failed relationship and were typically looking for a bit of freedom. They wanted something fun and sexy, like a new car. They wanted a Corvette, not a minivan. I used to be a Corvette, or, at least, some kind of average-looking sedan. Guys would sometimes buy me drinks and ask for my number. They would call me and I wouldn't answer. I was ghosting before ghosting was a thing. Now I couldn't remember the last time a guy had bought me a drink. No one ever asked for my number. No one even noticed me. I'd turned into a ghost myself.

Despite joining in on the scoffing about how stupid it was to be getting married on New Year's Eve, I'd secretly been happy. At least it meant I'd have something to do. I spent most of my New Year's Eves depressed and alone on my couch watching a movie, wishing I had a significant other to spend it with. The only significant other I'd had for over a decade was my TV.

I scrolled through the pictures on my phone one more time, purposely reminding myself what a mess I'd been so I would never do it again. Despite the vast majority of them being mortifying, a few pictures had come out all right. I'd pulled my curly brown hair back in a messy up-do with a few ringlets framing my face. My control-top pantyhose had done their job, hiding the soft parts under my slim-fitting emerald-green dress that brought out the flecks of gold in my hazel eyes. I mean, I was no Julie, but I looked pretty good. I zoomed into my face and immediately changed my mind. When had I started looking my age?

I needed to eat something. I opened the fridge and thanked drunk Kate for not eating the last two pieces of bread when she'd stumbled through the door last night. Toast it was. Breakfast of champions. Although it was now well past noon, so I guess it would be a late lunch of champions.

As I sat on the couch with the toast on my lap and a pitcher of water on the coffee table, the rest of the night came and went in pieces. Unsettling images flashed through my head like I was remembering a trauma.

Flash: Dancing with Nate to "Cotton Eyed Joe," grabbing his beer and pounding it like it was a glass of water.

Flash: Sharing glossy pink lipstick in the bathroom with a woman I'd never met.

Flash: Shivering outside on a bench, asking if I could have a drag of someone's cigarette.

Flash: Concerned, blurry faces—someone pulling me off the ground and bringing me back inside, the smell of vomit following close behind.

I tried, unsuccessfully, to swallow a bite of dry toast and my stomach heaved.

I hate this, I thought. Who did this to themselves? I would never feel normal again.

Swallowing the toast and the last piece of dignity that seemed to be lodged in my throat, I forced myself to feel the shame. I forced myself to feel the nausea and regret so overwhelming it hurt to breathe.

Never again will I do something like this, I promised myself. *Never again will I lose control.*

I pushed myself off the couch, walked into the kitchen, and picked through the mess from my purse. I wiped off the sticky coins and credit cards and grabbed a handful of soggy drink tickets and a napkin that had somehow managed to stay dry. I was about to crumple all the detritus into a ball to throw into the garbage when I noticed the napkin had writing on it. My stomach sank. Had I asked for someone's phone number?

I peeked at its contents through half-closed eyes, almost expecting to find "For a good time call…" but it was something else. Something I'd written. A poem? I could barely make it out, but it looked like I'd signed it at the bottom.

I smoothed out the napkin on the table, pulling the corners tight so I could read through the wrinkles:

I, Kate Graham, solemnly swear (something I couldn't read) *find someone to kiss.* (Something I couldn't read) *end of this year or die trying. Forty-three is the new* (something I couldn't read). *So there. Cody sucks.*

(My signature, barely.)

The memory came back to me as I read. In my sappy, sloppy, lonely drunken stupor, I'd promised myself that next New Year's Eve, I would no longer be single. Next New Year's, I'd have someone to kiss.

I smiled and let out a breath. Thank goodness that was all it was. Something silly and self-serving. At least it wasn't something I needed to follow through on. Like dinner tonight or, God forbid, another wedding.

I washed my hands and forced myself to finish my toast, trying not to gag. I actually felt a bit better. I was still mortified, of course, but I felt less like I wanted to crawl back to bed and die.

I reached down to cup Mittens' furry little face in my hands.

"It's your lucky day, buddy. I'm all yours."

He climbed into my lap and I readied myself for a day of getting nothing accomplished. I automatically reached for the remote and turned on the TV. *I would never leave you, Netflix. You and Mittens are my only true loves.*

I mindlessly flicked through my options, unsure what I

wanted to binge on, my brain fixated on what I'd drunkenly written. *Stupid napkin promise,* I thought. I would never find someone anyway. Nate and Cody were right: my ship had sailed. No man of worth would want to date someone whose glory days were behind her—skin sagging and body soft, hair where hair shouldn't be. If I was meant to be with someone, I would have met him by now.

But then I paused. Since when did I back away from challenges? (Most of the time.) Since when did I let drunken juvenile conversations make me feel shitty about myself and question my worth? (Quite often.) Since when did I even care about what other people thought? (Almost every day.) Still, why shouldn't I have someone to kiss? I mean, yeah, I might not have been in my prime, but I was certainly not ready to give up. I was only forty-three, not ninety.

I would do it, dammit. I would prove all the ageist naysayers wrong. I would give it a shot. A real shot. A more-than-two-weeks shot. I *was* going to find someone to kiss. I sprang off the couch, sending Mittens scampering in a confused burst of fur. I was ready to get started. Ready to seize the day...

...Right after I threw up.

Chapter 3

January 2nd

I'd always thought online dating was stupid. I still thought it was stupid, especially after watching two idiots on Tinder at a wedding. Scrolling through people like they were items on sale. Judging by appearance alone. Trying to find the perfect fit with only an image as your guide.

"It's like shoe shopping," I said to Julie as we were chatting that afternoon.

"It's not at all like shoe shopping." I could almost hear her rolling her eyes over the phone. "You build a profile so you can scroll through other people's profiles and then you pick the ones you like."

"So, if I think he's too short?"

"Don't pick him."

"And if I don't like his style?"

"Don't pick him."

"So, basically like shoe shopping."

"Fine." She sighed. "It's like shoe shopping. But when your shoes arrive at your condo, you can't get drunk and sleep with them. Well, I mean unless you're into that kind of thing, I guess."

Another big difference between me and Julie was that Julie's view on men was that they were put on this earth purely for her entertainment. Every weekend, she would find a guy on Tinder to hang out with or "hang out" with and, come Monday, it would be like he had never existed. It wasn't like she lied about it, though, or pretended she was looking for a relationship. She always let them know she was only looking for fun. Most were happy to oblige. Julie was drop-dead gorgeous with very little effort. I would definitely have hated her if I didn't love her so much.

It was because of Julie that I had been such a party girl in my twenties. We would be at a different bar or club every night. We'd both had jobs but would somehow manage to go out, get wasted and come home in the wee hours of the morning. We'd sleep for a couple of hours, go to work and then do it all over again. If I were to do that now, I would almost certainly die.

Some might wonder how we could have afforded this on our meagre "just entering the workforce" salaries, but it turns out that girls in their twenties don't have to buy a lot of drinks, especially if one of them is smoking hot. I had been happy to follow along and take what I was given, slow dancing at the end of the night pressed up against the sweaty chest of every hot guy's less attractive friend.

At closing time, we'd usually leave with a random group, go to someone's place, drink more and dance more and party until the sun came up.

Our recklessness was terrifying, but we never got into trouble. No one ever got hurt; shockingly, that thought never even crossed our minds. The most important thing was that we were having fun. We didn't have a care in the world back then. We had no responsibilities and, more importantly, no hangovers. The world was our oyster and we lived our lives to the fullest. I look back on my early twenties with both fondness and horror.

Now, on the rare occasions when Julie and I went out, when guys came over to chat, they came over alone, and while they weren't rude, they didn't make much of an effort to include me in the conversation. I might as well not even have been there.

As we talked on the phone, I walked up to the oval mirror by the front door and stared, trying to see what others saw; trying to understand why, since I'd entered my forties, I seemed to have disappeared. *I'm still here,* I thought as I ran the tips of my fingers over the tiny lines above my top lip, over a small crease in my forehead, over the faint shadow of a laugh around my eyes. *I look like my mom,* I thought. And then: *I wish my mom looked more like Julie.*

Which was why I'd called Julie in the first place: I needed help. I'd been single for so long that I hadn't put much effort into not being single. I'd never tried online dating or gone to a speed dating event. I'd never even smiled at a guy who hadn't smiled at me first. Julie had done all of those things. Many times.

"First, we need to set up an online dating profile," she said, not one to waste time.

I sighed. "Do I really need to?"

Chapter 4

All scoffing aside, I knew many people who'd found their partner online. I'd met a lot of them and most of them were pretty amazing. Despite this, the whole thing made me uncomfortable and I had no idea where to begin.

While I waited for Julie, I browsed the plethora of online dating sites I could join. There were so many options. Should I pay? Should I join a free one? Would I consider myself a cougar?

I could tell Julie was pumped about coming over to talk about her passion. I hadn't planned on telling anyone I was doing this, but I also didn't want to jump into it completely clueless. I was glad I was going to have an expert on my team.

She arrived two hours later, bursting through the door with a bottle of merlot. When Julie entered a room, she *entered a room*. There was no mistaking who the alpha female was when she was around. She was so full of energy that the air would practically vibrate. You couldn't help but sit up and notice. We were the perfect complement to each other. She was the energetic extrovert and I was the calm introvert. She brought me up when I needed a boost and I could settle her down when things got too intense. When we were together, we automatically balanced each other out.

Julie stomped off her boots and brushed the snow from her perfectly styled long blonde hair. Putting the wine down, she unwrapped a soft pink scarf from her long neck. She unbuttoned her grey, fitted, knee-length coat to reveal a fashionable pair of ripped jeans and a cream-coloured sweater that hugged her flawless hourglass figure. Her green eyes were flashing, cheeks rosy from the cold. She looked like she'd just stepped out of a Hallmark Christmas movie.

I, on the other hand, was clad in a pair of worn-out men's pyjama pants and an old cardigan that probably used to be white.

She handed me her jacket. "Is that peanut butter in the corner of your mouth?"

My tongue poked out to check. "Maybe." I wiped it off.

"I have wine," I said as Julie bounced into my kitchen, tipped up on her toes and took two wine glasses off the top shelf.

"My wine is better." She dug into my kitchen drawer for a corkscrew, opened the bottle and poured herself a generous glass.

"No, thanks," I said when she pointed the bottle in my direction. She shrugged, brought her glass and the bottle into the living room and joined me on the couch, jostling me in the process.

"Careful, I still feel a bit nauseated," I said with my hand over my mouth. Two-day hangovers were the best.

She laughed and plucked the laptop from my hands. Despite the fact that Julie had gone to her own party on New Year's Eve, she appeared to be as fresh as a daisy. The extreme unfairness of this did not escape me.

"What?" I asked as she stared. "Let's do this." I gestured to the laptop. "Show me how you work your magic."

She continued to stare, tilting her head and raising her eyebrows. Apparently she wasn't going to let me off that easily.

"Fine." I sighed. I pulled the crumpled napkin out of one of the pockets of my pyjama pants and handed it to her.

She looked at it. Turned it upside down. Looked at it again. "You're going to have to explain this one to me verbally," she said and handed the napkin back.

I flushed, snatched the napkin away and put it back in my pocket. "I made a pledge to myself to…"

"To…?"

"Ugh. To find someone to kiss, okay?" I pretended to pick some fluff from the sleeve of my cardigan. "I made a pledge to find someone to kiss before next New Year's. I'm lonely. I want someone to share my life with." A wry smile tugged up the corner of my mouth. "I guess I just needed to get really drunk and show the world my underwear to figure that out."

"Finally!" Julie shouted, and I jumped. "I've been waiting so long for this! I know you were happy single, but I also know you have a ton to offer someone else. I'm so excited that I get to help you!"

"You don't think it's stupid?"

"Why would I think it's stupid? Just because I don't

21

want a relationship doesn't mean I don't think anyone else should have one. You're a catch!"

"Oh. Okay. Cool then." I perked up, now eager to begin.

"Keep that napkin with you at all times," she said. "It can be your motivator. And I'll be your accountability buddy. This is going to be so fun!"

"Yeah!" I cheered. Her enthusiasm was infectious.

"So," she started, "the most important thing to know is you have to pay if you want quality. The only problem is quality is often hard to detect."

"Sounds great so far." I rolled my eyes.

"I'd recommend a free site to start, just to get your feet wet, and if you're lucky, it won't be just your feet." She winked and nudged me in the ribs.

"Gross."

She opened one of the many online dating apps on her phone. "With any online dating site, you can basically break the types of men into five categories. And you can tell which category they fit into by their pictures."

"Okay, ready." I sat up.

"For what?"

"I'm going to take notes." I grabbed my notebook, a highlighter and a few coloured pens.

She sighed. Julie was the most unorganized person I knew, and she owned it with pride. She would never let anyone see her taking notes about anything, especially online dating. I really didn't care though. I liked notes.

"Fine," she huffed. "I'm going to talk normally though, so you better write fast."

"Sure thing, boss." I tipped her a mock salute, pens at the ready.

She ignored me. "First, there are the hunters. Obviously, these are the ones with the pictures of themselves in front of dead animals."

"I'm sorry, what?" I cringed. "Guys post pictures of themselves posing in front of dead animals?"

"Sadly, yes, more often than you'd think. Stay away from these ones unless you're super into hunting, which I know you're not. The fact that they actually think a picture of a dead animal is appealing to anyone, let alone a woman, is honestly beyond my comprehension."

"Noted." *Men are dumb*, I wrote in my notebook.

She gulped her wine. "The second type," she continued, "are the ones who have one or more profile pictures of their bare chest." She showed me her phone as she scrolled through what seemed to be an endless list of guys. "Look." She clicked on one of the images. "His profile has four pictures of him flexing in front of the mirror and zero pictures of his face. These guys are either arrogant or just want sex. I've found it's usually a combo."

"Okay, got it. We don't like these guys," I said as I wrote.

"No, *you* don't like these guys. I like these guys just fine," Julie said.

I laughed.

"The third type are the ones who have at least one profile picture of themselves and a baby or a puppy. They're trying to tell you that they're sensitive, and that's okay, sometimes they actually do like babies and puppies, but you still need to be careful. Sometimes guys like this are deliberately deceptive because they're looking for a certain type of woman. A good rule of thumb is that if their profile says they 'give great massages' or 'love to cuddle,' they're going after a specific type of woman. A specific *naïve* type of woman."

"I like massages and cuddling."

"Exactly. The fourth type are those who are into polygamy, threesomes, bondage and other—let's say 'alternative'—sex stuff. It's cool if you're into that, but—"

"I'm not."

"Yes, I'm aware. I was going to say, it's pretty easy to pick these ones out because they're usually quite honest on their profile. They're actually the most honest ones." She emptied her glass and reached for the bottle. "Do you have any snacks?"

"Sure do." I threw her a protein bar that I had set aside.

"Ugh, I mean actual snacks that people like."

"I have rice cakes."

"Forget it, let's move on. Fifth on the list are your *Dungeons and Dragons* types. These guys love all kinds of games and are usually super into cosplay or LARP. Or both. They often have at least one picture of themselves in some sort of costume and their profiles say things like, 'embracing my inner nerd' or 'fan fiction is my jam.' These guys aren't really my type, they're generally pretty shy, but they're also harmless. Kinda like Ben."

"What if I like fan fiction?" Dating someone like Julie's older brother Ben wouldn't be that bad. Yes, he was a bit awkward, but he was also one of the nicest people I had ever met. I was grateful to consider him a friend.

"Well, then maybe you should put a little star by this one with one of your pink pens."

"Are you mocking my pens?"

"All right," she said, ignoring me again, "let's start on your profile."

"I'm writing my own profile." I grabbed the laptop from her.

She glared at me over her wine glass. "I strongly suggest you don't."

"But it's *my* profile."

"I know what men are looking for." Her voice started to rise. "I've been doing this for decades."

"Yes, I'm aware, and I appreciate your knowledge, but while your profile is effective at getting you the types of men you want, it will not get me the types of men I want. They're very different and even you can admit that."

"Fine." She threw her hands up in a gesture of surrender. "I'm going to search for some snacks."

I'd been dreading this part. There weren't many things I disliked more than talking myself up. But if I was going to do this right, I would have to put in some effort. I wanted my profile to be funny, light, genuine and honest. Well, I wanted it to *sound* genuine and honest. But from what I'd seen so far, if I said I didn't like camping, living life to its fullest, or the Saskatchewan Roughriders, I might as well not even bother.

"No one reads profiles anyway," Julie said as if she'd read my mind. She set a glass of wine down in front of me.

I opened my mouth, intending to decline the wine—again—but took a small sip instead.

"What we really need to do is get some killer pics," Julie continued. "Do you have any from the wedding where you're not lying in a puddle of your own vomit?"

"Wait a minute, back up," I said. "What do you mean no one reads profiles? Isn't that where you get the chance to show what kind of person you are?"

She gave me a look one would give a puppy barking at its reflection in the mirror. "You're adorable. Yes, if they get that far, but they won't get to the written part if they're not enticed by your picture."

The few flattering pictures of me at the wedding had someone else in them, so we went through my Facebook and Instagram to find some "killer pics." We found a picture of me at a party seven years ago and a picture of me shoving a donut in my face.

"This is going to have to do for now," she said with a snort of disgust. "How do you not have any pictures of yourself?"

"I don't like pictures of myself. I always end up looking super awkward. Do I really have to put in where I live?" I asked, quickly changing the subject.

"Well, it does help with the dating part if you're matched with someone who actually lives near you."

"What if I just put Canada?"

"That's a pretty wide berth." She laughed.

"Fine," I said. "But if the largest city in our province hasn't netted me a soulmate up to this point, I find it hard to believe it's going to now."

"It's actually the second largest city in Saskatchewan."

"Not helpful," I said. "What do I need to do next?"

She watched while I entered the rest of my information into the website questionnaire. I'd decided to pursue men who were between thirty-five and forty-nine (against my better judgement), at least my height (5'6"), and who didn't smoke. According to Julie, I should have put twenty-six to forty-nine because twenty-six was "definitely not too young" and I should "live a little for the love of God." I'd wanted to put forty to forty-nine, so we'd compromised.

I'd read somewhere that most men aimed low when choosing their preferred age range and women aimed high. I wanted to meet a man who was around forty. But if what I'd read was accurate, a man in his forties would want to meet a woman in her twenties or thirties. Considering what Nate and Cody had said at the wedding, this appeared to be true. Which basically meant I was screwed.

"Have any twenty-six-year-old guys asked you if you know their mom?" I said to Julie and smirked.

"Hilarious," she deadpanned. "You'd be surprised how little in common you need to have a good time. Now, write your brilliant profile."

Chapter 5

Thirty minutes later, I was ready for Julie to take a look. She was pretty tipsy by this point, so I wasn't that concerned. One good thing about Julie was that the more she drank the more agreeable she got. And she was also very safe. Knowing she'd had too much wine to drive, she'd called her brother Ben to come give her a ride home. And also to bring us pizza. It was way past supper time by this point and we were starving.

He now sat beside her, a slice of peperoni in his hand and an encouraging grin on his face. I handed the laptop over to Julie and grabbed a slice for myself, licking a dab of tomato sauce off my fingers. Regina might not have been the world's best tourist destination, but it could easily be argued that it had the world's best pizza.

"Looking for Mr. Right?" Julie grimaced as she read my opening line. She glanced at Ben for backup, but he held up his hands, wisely refusing to get involved.

"Well, I am," I said, crossing my arms.

"No. Change that right now," she ordered.

"Why don't you just read the whole thing and save your judgement for the end?"

"Change it and I promise to wait until the end to judge anything else." She handed the laptop back and plucked a crispy corner piece from the ham and pineapple side of the pizza box.

"What's wrong with wanting to find Mr. Right?" I asked.

"Well, for one, it's a cliché. For another, it makes you look like a newbie. Also, stay away from, 'just trying this out' or 'seeing what's out there.' Guys will pounce like a coyote on a scared little bunny and rip you to pieces."

Ben laughed, wiping his hand on a napkin and adjusting his wire-framed glasses. "That was unnecessarily graphic." He sat back, looking relaxed in his uniform of faded jeans, a plain T-shirt and a hoodie.

I covertly deleted *just trying this out* from my summary paragraph. "Okay, ready?"

"Go." She sat forward in anticipation.

"Looking to meet my partner in crime."

"No. I said no clichés."

"Looking to meet—"

"No."

"Looking to share?"

"Sure." Julie shrugged non-committedly.

"Looking to share my life with—"

"No."

"*Why not*?" I threw my hands up.

Ben snorted with laughter.

"Sharing your life with someone sounds *too* committed. You'll scare most of them off," she said.

"Looking for someone to share my next adventure with?" I tried.

"That's actually not bad, keep it."

I tipped my head and examined what I had written. "I probably shouldn't end with a preposition. I'll rewrite it."

Julie threw her head back and laughed. "You most certainly can end with a preposition. This is online dating, not a university entrance exam. Keep going."

"Self-summary: I like travelling, going for walks and hiking. To be physically attracted to someone is important, but equally important is a sense of humour, honesty and an open mind." I paused and looked up. Neither of them said anything, so I continued.

"What I'm doing with my life: I work full time and like to hang out with friends. I enjoy going out, but I'm just as happy to curl up with a good book."

Julie leaned forward to grab her glass. She saw me looking at her and waved her hand. "Continue."

Ben busied himself pulling at the sleeves of his hoodie.

"Favourite movies, books, shows, food: I love a good chick flick but also would be up for seeing a fun adventure movie. I read pretty much anything, but I especially love thrillers and romances. I don't watch a lot of TV but enjoy a good drama. I like all foods—"

Ben snorted.

I stopped. "What?"

"Kate," he said, "you watch a lot of TV."

"I know, but I don't want to scare them away."

Ben ran his hands through his hair. "I just find it ironic that you list 'honesty' as being important in your opening paragraph."

"Well, maybe once I start dating someone, I won't

watch as much TV as I do right now. So, it's basically the truth."

"Basically," Ben said, hiding a smile.

Julie rolled her eyes. "For the love of all that is holy, please keep going. I'm almost out of wine."

I cleared my throat. "Okay, where was I? Food: I love all kinds of food, especially Italian.

The five things I could never do without: Family, friends, coffee, chocolate, and my cat, Mittens. At the end I added: You should message me if you're in my age range, you don't smoke and you love animals." I set my laptop down on the coffee table. "What do you think?"

"Well, it's kind of vanilla," Julie said.

I slumped back into the couch.

Ben frowned at Julie then turned to me, his expression softening. "I think it sounds great. I'm still not a hundred percent certain why you're doing it though."

Julie nodded in my direction. "Show him the napkin."

"Julie!" I glanced sideways at Ben and lowered my voice. "I didn't want anyone else to know."

"I can still hear you," Ben said. "We're in the same room."

"The more people who know the better," Julie said. "Accountability is key. I know you; you won't do it if it's just for you."

I sighed and gave the napkin to Ben.

He looked at it, then looked at me, then looked back at the napkin. "Am I supposed to be able to read this or…?"

I sighed and plucked it out of his hands. "It's a pledge I made to myself. On New Year's."

"Oh." He looked down at my lower half and blushed. "Right, New Year's."

Now it was my turn to blush. I guess Ben had been part of the lucky group who got to see me in my underwear before my attempt to delete everything off social media. Great. I continued to explain the rest of the pledge while Ben tried to look anywhere else.

"Cool." He smiled when I was done. "Good luck."

"All right, I'm out." Julie stood and stretched. "Let's go, Ben."

"But wait, what do I do now?" I jumped off the couch and followed her to the door.

They put on their jackets and tugged on their gloves, bracing themselves for the bitter cold.

"Post your profile, close your laptop and don't open it until tomorrow," Julie said while we walked down to the lobby. "You're new blood and you'll get a flurry of messages from the dudes who sit on the site all day waiting to ambush the untouched. Give me a call tomorrow afternoon and I'll help you wade through them."

When we got to the lobby, Julie opened the door and turned her face against a burst of cold air. "Also, download the app on your phone. But don't open it until tomorrow." She hunkered down against the wind and pushed toward the car through knee-deep snow, muttering something about choosing to live in a place so cold it made her face hurt.

I looked at Ben, my eyes wide with fear and uncertainty.

"I'll be right out," he called to Julie before stepping back inside and shutting the door.

"Remember when Julie first started bringing you over when we were kids?" His kind smile instantly calmed me down.

I laughed. "It took you months to talk to me."

"Exactly." He stuck his hands in his jacket pockets. "Because of my anxiety, it took me a while to feel comfortable talking to someone new, but eventually…"

"We became really good friends," I finished.

"The same thing happened when I went away to university. You and Julie thought I wouldn't last a month."

I was stunned. "How did you know we had our doubts?"

"I'm socially awkward, not stupid." He laughed. "I know how much Julie took care of me. I didn't know if I would make it either. But I did, and I made a lot of friends."

He'd made it a good two years. I still didn't fully know why he'd come home.

"I missed you when you were gone," I said, eyes lowered.

He opened his mouth to respond, but all that came out was a loud, obnoxious car horn.

"I think Julie is getting impatient," he said. "Anyway, my point is, once you start meeting people, you'll get the hang of it. I'm sure…" He paused, searching for the right words, his face saying something I couldn't quite decipher. "I'm sure you'll find what you're looking for."

Chapter 6

Julie

Julie slipped into her small apartment and set her keys on the wooden stool by the door. She brushed a loose piece of hair from her face and sighed. Thank goodness for the wine or she wouldn't have been in any shape to be out in public.

The things I do for Kate… the things I don't do for myself, she mulled.

She slid off her jacket, threw it on a chair and opened the door to her bedroom. She'd chosen to avoid it when she'd gotten up that afternoon, leaving her pick of the night still snoring under the comforter. It was still a mess—clothes scattered everywhere, used condoms on the floor. The bathroom was also empty, and still messy.

Looks like Buddy decided to take a shower before he left. And used three towels. Which are now on the floor. Classy.

What had she expected? He'd found her on Facebook—a friend of a friend. She didn't even remember his name.

Normally, she didn't let guys stay over, but this one had fallen asleep immediately after they'd finished, and for the life of her, she couldn't wake him up. She'd ended up sleeping—if you could call it that—on her couch, curled up under a jacket. Thank God he was gone.

She walked into her dark bedroom. The smell of stale smoke and sweat made her stomach lurch and she cracked open the window. The biting chill took her breath away, but at least she could breathe again.

Stumbling over a pair of heels, she ripped off the sheets and threw them into the overflowing laundry hamper in the corner. She'd deal with the condoms later.

Her once-glowing face sagged with defeat as she reached for the top shelf of her closet and grabbed her favourite old comforter. She held it to her face and breathed deeply, trying to return to the comfortable security of her childhood—wrapped up in the warmth, watching TV with Ben. Feeling loved. Feeling safe.

She collapsed onto the bare mattress, the pounding in her head softening to match the beat of her heart. She couldn't remember the last time she'd felt safe like that. She couldn't remember what it had felt like before her world had crumbled—before being awake hadn't required being drunk.

Lying down, she pulled the comforter over her head, allowing herself to relax under its weight, and cried herself to sleep.

Chapter 7

January 3rd

The next day, I was awake earlier than normal for a Sunday. I didn't want to admit it, but I was excited to see if anyone had contacted me.

What if my soulmate has already reached out? I bounced out of bed. I was almost giddy with anticipation.

Mittens greeted me in the kitchen with a look that said he was obviously starving (even though it was only 7:00 a.m.) and how dare I sleep while his food dish was empty? It turned out it was empty because he'd dumped his dry food all over the floor. I opened a can of his breakfast food and slopped it into the dish, sweeping the dry food into a pile with my foot.

"You know this is going back in the dish when you're done, right?"

He lifted his head and held my eyes as he sauntered into the pile, sat down and whipped his fluffy black-and-white tail across the floor, propelling most of the pellets under the fridge. My cat owned me, and we both knew it.

Ten minutes later, coffee in hand, I smoothed the pledge

napkin onto my thigh like a talisman, opened my laptop and checked my email. Mittens jumped into my lap and I absently ran my fingers through his fur.

I had twenty-five new messages. Twenty-five new messages! Twenty-five messages from twenty-five eligible matches. I couldn't believe it. I thought I'd be lucky to get two or three, but twenty-five? I grabbed my phone to call Julie and then remembered her rule about never again calling her before 11:00 a.m. So I waited.

And waited.

I tried to watch TV. I tried to read a book. I would have tried to go for a walk if it wasn't so unbearably cold outside. And I owned a pair of snowshoes.

After two hours, I couldn't wait anymore. I needed to see who had contacted me and how many of them were matches. Besides, this couldn't be that hard. I could totally do it myself.

I clicked on the first link in the email: Mitch, thirty-five, had kids and didn't want more. Moderately attractive. Despite his profile having several grammatical errors and LOLs, he seemed okay. I read his message:

I don't think we would fit long term, but I could see us exploring an alternative solution. Do you have an open mind, Kate?

What did that mean? Why wouldn't we fit long term? What kind of alternate solution?

I'd wait to talk to Julie about that one.

Next was Joel. He looked all right. I scrolled down to read his profile. "I write rap music and roast coffee. Sometimes I make out." Interesting. Maybe he was really nice. I liked him back.

Next.

Chet. First of all, who named their kid Chet? He looked young. He was young. Twenty-five. I guess he'd missed the part on my profile where I'd said what age range I was looking for. What could a forty-three-year-old woman possibly offer a twenty-five-year-old guy?

Twenty-five was when you started thinking about marriage and kids. Twenty-five was a good ten years before your first divorce. If you didn't have kids already, did you want them, Chet? Because, at this point in my life, I couldn't guarantee that, my friend.

And what would happen when I was fifty and you were thirty-two? Were you going to stick around while I went through menopause when you could hang out with someone who knew what bands you were talking about?

Sorry Chet, hard pass.

I scrolled through the remaining alerts, each one adding to my level of disappointment. The messages were one word, a request to come over, or a very clearly copied and pasted, three-paragraph monologue.

The profiles weren't much better. So many chest shots. So many dudes in sunglasses. So many "adrenaline junkies," whatever that meant.

True to Julie's warning, there was also an alarming number of guys who were "really good at massages," so that was gross.

My phone vibrated.

Have you found your dream man yet?

Obviously, Julie knew me well enough to know I would start without her, but I was already tired of this.

Coffee? I texted back.

I glanced down at the thumbs-up emoji she texted back, closed my laptop and tried not to think about all the shows I could be watching instead of scrolling through messages.

This had better be worth it.

Chapter 8

I instantly felt better when I pulled open the door of Beans 'n' Brews. The smell of espresso and baked goods surrounded me like a comforting hug. I surveyed the cozy, couch-strewn space, a few stray Christmas decorations still hanging on the walls. It was surprisingly empty for a Sunday afternoon. The tables were usually full of trendy moms—their giant strollers containing cute toddlers drinking five-dollar hot chocolates.

Today, there was just a dude with his laptop, bopping along to whatever was flowing through his ear buds, and an older couple drinking their coffees and reading. That was what I wanted—someone to sit and read with, to share interesting things with, or to sit in comfortable silence with.

I smiled as I walked past them to claim our usual spot: two comfy, mismatched armchairs in the corner. I loved this place. The soft lighting and warm colours, random shelves filled with used books. No matter what mood I was in, I always felt better when I was here.

The door opened and I looked up, expecting to see Julie. Two twenty-somethings, a guy and girl, literally hanging off each other, tumbled in with a burst of cold air. His hand proprietarily slid under her coat and into her back pocket. He whispered something in her ear, and she giggled and latched her pink lips onto his face.

I caught the eye of Jesse, my favourite barista, and mimicked a dry heave. He smiled and turned away so they couldn't see him laugh. He didn't have to worry though—they were so desperately in love with each other that they didn't see the world around them. They flopped onto a sofa and continued their love whispers and kisses, never once breaking contact. I rolled my eyes as I took off my puffy blue jacket and hung it on a wooden hook by the window.

Jesse handed me a coffee when I made it up to the counter. Medium-sized dark roast, my usual, ready to go. One of the many reasons he was my favourite.

"I saw some great shots of you on Facebook Saturday morning." He grinned.

My face turned red, heating up like a sunburn. "Oh, crap," I breathed, lowering my head to grab my wallet and pretending it was stuck in my purse. "I thought I'd un-tagged myself."

"Yeah, I must have seen it before you woke up." He laughed and held up his hand. "Nice work. High five."

I looked up and smiled, begrudgingly giving him the high five he was waiting for.

"Where's Julie?" he asked, turning as the bells jingled over the door.

Julie walked in looking stunning as usual in black yoga pants and a fitted grey peacoat, her blonde hair gathered up in a messy ponytail. The guy with the laptop glanced up, not minding the interruption. The two lovebirds in the corner even stopped making out for five seconds as they watched her graceful entrance. She was, as usual, oblivious.

She leaned on the counter, eyes wide. "Is she telling you all about her foray into online dating?!"

"No…" Jesse raised an eyebrow. "No, she isn't."

"It's nothing." I grabbed my coffee and pushed Julie to the table. For some reason, I was more embarrassed about this than I was about Jesse seeing the picture of me lying on the floor with my ass hanging out of my dress.

"But coffee." Julie squirmed out of my grasp. "I'll tell him then."

I watched Jesse as he leaned in and listened to Julie. His face lit up like he'd just heard a piece of juicy gossip, which I guess he had, really. I sipped my coffee, pretending I didn't care one bit that they were discussing my dating life, or non-dating life, as it still appeared to be.

If I was honest, I'd had a bit of a crush on Jesse when we'd met three years ago. I remember him standing behind the counter, all fresh and new. Cute smile, blue eyes and curly blond hair. He'd been so kind and eager to please. I was at the coffee shop all the time, so we became friends right away. After I'd found out he was much younger than me—fourteen years younger to be exact—any flame that had been lit was quickly extinguished.

Ten minutes later, Julie walked over, scone in hand, grinning like she'd just won the lottery. "Jesse thinks you should try speed dating."

"Speed dating?" I almost choked on my coffee. "No.

I'm not ready for speed dating. I've barely broken the surface of online dating. I haven't even talked to anyone. No."

She laughed as she pulled off her coat and stuffed it between the chairs. "You're going to have to interact with men in real life at some point, you know."

"I know," I admitted. "I smiled at one of the cute guys in my building this morning. Well, actually, I smiled at his dog. I'm counting it though."

As Julie sipped her coffee, I told her about the guys who had contacted me so far.

"Yeah, that's normal," she said. "There are a bunch of guys who are on every site, and no offence, but they'll talk to anyone. The normal guys are out there though. You just might have to make the first move. There are weird women out there too, you know. Men have to put up with almost as much crap as we do."

I found it hard to believe that a guy would be put off by a picture of a girl's chest, but what did I know? "One guy said he didn't see us fitting long term but I should have an open mind," I said. "What does that mean?"

"It means he just wants to sleep with you, and he's probably married." She sat back, casually broke off a piece of her scone and popped it delicately into her mouth.

"Right."

"Let me see," she said, and I handed her my phone. "Oh, look." She sat up. "You have a match. Did you like someone already?"

"Yeah, some guy liked me, and I liked him back."

"What did you like about him?" she asked, eyebrows raised. "That he writes rap or that he likes to make out?"

"I know, I know. I just felt bad."

She shook her head.

"What? I'm trying to be nice."

"There is no room for nice in online dating. If you're nice to everyone, you'll end up wasting all your energy and time and quit before you find someone good."

"Well, maybe he's nice. Maybe he's just a little nerdy like me. Did he say anything?" I leaned back in what I thought was a casual pose.

"Kate, ew," she said. "This guy is actually kissing his bicep. Did you even look at his pictures?"

"This is already frustrating." I pouted, breaking off a piece of her scone and shoving it in my mouth as crumbs fell on my shirt.

"It is, but you'll get used to it. What about this guy?" She laid the phone on the table and pointed at a guy in full running gear.

I grabbed it and swiped through five more pictures of him either running or stretching. "He 'loves living life' and his passion is running. He's looking for someone to 'join him in the marathon of life.' His goal is to run a marathon. I wonder if this guy likes running. Should I ask him?"

"If you're not going to take this seriously, you're never going to get anything out of it." She grabbed my phone back.

"How can you possibly take this guy seriously?" I protested. "He says one of his skills is knowing how to find a good pair of running shoes."

"What about this guy?"

"He's wearing a stormtrooper mask in one of his pictures. Pass."

She breathed out heavily and tried again. "This guy looks good. He's forty-three, has a full-time job, no stormtrooper pictures. He doesn't smoke, likes to read."

"He does sound promising." I sat up with interest and scrolled down to the bottom of his profile. And there we go. "I can't wait to see your fine booty in person," I read aloud, probably too loud, as I heard a stifled snort from Jesse.

"On the other hand," she said, "perhaps he isn't the one for you."

"You think?"

"Unless…" she tried.

"No."

"He also 'hates fatties,' so that's delightful." I made a sound of disgust, logged out of the app and slipped my phone into my purse.

We both finished our coffees and decided we'd had enough online dating adventures for today. I had too much stuff to do to waste my time feeling disappointed by strangers.

We put on our coats and waved goodbye to Jesse on our way out.

"Good luck," he said and winked. "I hope you find someone to kiss!"

I glared at Julie as she pushed through the door, laughing.

"Thanks, friend," I called back. Based on past experiences, I would need all the luck he was willing to give.

Chapter 9

Twenty years ago
Kate

I didn't want to be here. The pub was hot and loud, and all I wanted to do was go home and watch the *Gilmore Girls* episode I'd taped last night. There were so many people—bodies pressed together, sweating in their winter coats—that I had started to feel claustrophobic. And, to top it off, for some reason we were discussing my least favourite topic—my dating life.

"You've never had much luck with dating though," Julie said. "No offence."

"You know, saying 'no offence' after saying something offensive doesn't actually help." I shot her an irritated look and continued peeling the label off my beer bottle.

"Yeah, that was pretty dumb. No offence," Ben said, laughing as Julie threw a napkin at him.

She was right though. I'd had tons of crushes, but I'd always been too shy to do anything about them; always a permanent fixture in Julie's glorious shadow.

"Sorry," she said, not sorry at all. "But you know what

I mean. You always fall in love so hard, like 'slipping on the dance floor and falling on your face' hard."

"So?" The fall was always so easy. I didn't even think about it. I would meet someone at a bar or party, we'd make out for a bit and then we'd be dating. I never weighed pros and cons or thought about whether I could see myself with him for the rest of my life. I could see myself with him at that moment, and that was all that mattered.

"When is this band going to start anyway?" Ben looked at his watch. "We've been sitting here for over an hour. I have a job interview tomorrow."

"Just get another beer," I said. "Time will go by faster. And don't worry; you're an IT wizard, you'll totally get the job."

"Do you even know what I do?" He tried to look angry, but his eyes were twinkling.

"Yeah, computer stuff."

"I'm a coder. I write code."

"Exactly, computer stuff."

I turned to Julie. "Seriously though, when is this band going to start?"

And, like they'd read my mind, the band appeared. I watched them walk onto the stage, seemingly oblivious to the cheers and shouts coming from the audience, looking unabashedly apathetic in the way only a group of guys in their twenties could convincingly pull off. Especially one of them. I'd never seen him around before.

"Who's that guy?" I whispered in Julie's ear.

"The nerd in the hat?"

"Well, he is wearing a hat, yes," I said.

"That's Justin. He's nice. Not my type, but nice."

Julie's type was the lead singer, Aaron. The guy she was "casually" dating—blond hair, chiselled features, muscular body. The type of guy that would naturally be with someone as gorgeous as Julie. Justin was plainer; brown hair peeking out of a backwards ball cap, shy smile, eyes down as he sat in the background with his drums. Justin was someone who could naturally be with someone like me.

After the first set, Julie dragged me to go meet the band. We walked into the bong-water-smelling green room and Aaron grabbed her like he owned her, shoving his tongue into her mouth.

"Gross," I whispered, and someone laughed.

I turned and there was Justin, drinking a bottle of water. "I mean, get a room, right?" He took his cap off, smoothed his hands over his hair, and put it back on again.

And that was that. I was smitten.

We dated for six months and were basically inseparable. We talked on the phone almost every night and held hands wherever we went. I met his parents; he met my mom. It was just my mom and me by then—my dad had already left; my mom's constant bullying finally wearing him down. I vowed I would never be like her, and with Justin, I was sure I was doing something right; six months was the longest I'd dated anyone up to that point.

And then the inevitable happened. Inevitable for me, anyway.

The few times I'd dated guys after high school, I seemed to be way more into them than they were into me, trying to be the perfect girlfriend, barreling on ahead with my battering ram of neediness, wondering why they weren't calling and why they didn't say they loved me when they dropped me off. What had I done? How could I make it better?

And so on.

I hated when I got like that, yet I found it so hard to stop. With Justin, it was no different.

After six months of bliss, my insecurities set in and everything took a turn.

"Do you think Justin still loves me?" I asked Ben one night as we were waiting for Julie to get ready for Tequila Tuesday at our favourite club.

Ben looked up, his eyes touching on mine then flickering away. "Why are you asking?"

"I don't know." I sighed in the typical dramatic fashion of someone in their mid-twenties. "It feels like he's pulling away or something. When he calls me, it's like he's doing it out of obligation, not because he wants to."

"Well, you did tell him he had to call you every day, so he kind of is obliged." Ben's lips turned up in a half-grin.

"*I know.*" I pouted. "But shouldn't he also want to? Also, he was supposed to come tonight and he bailed at the last minute. Do you think he's seeing someone else?"

Ben sighed. "No, I don't think he's seeing someone else. Maybe he just wanted some time alone."

"Maybe I shouldn't have said I didn't like the Terminator movies," I mused. "He seemed pretty put off by that."

"But you don't like the Terminator movies."

"Yeah, but *he* does. I should have just pretended." I

sighed again and slouched deeper into Julie's oversized armchair. "Being in a relationship is hard."

Whether Justin had wanted some time alone or not I will never know. One minute, I was dropping Julie off at her apartment after the club, and the next, I was sitting outside his house in my car, hair a mess, fingers curled so tightly my nails punctured the skin on my palms. Why had he *really* not come out tonight? Didn't he want to spend time with me?

And then I was standing at his door, crying, begging for him to let me in.

"Why don't you love me anymore?" I yelled to the closed door. "What did I do? I can change. I'll do anything. Just tell me!" His roommate finally came out, her hand on the door frame, preventing me from entering the house.

"Justin doesn't want to see you anymore," she said, her face a mixture of pity and disgust.

"You're sleeping with him, aren't you?" I said, even though I knew she wasn't.

"I'm choosing to ignore that," she said. "And I also don't agree with him making me do his dirty work. But, just so you know, you are smothering the shit out of him. He can barely breathe when you're around. You need to back off, for both of your sakes."

It wasn't until the door slammed that I finally woke up. How had I gotten to this point? How had I managed to veer from the strong, independent woman I wanted to be to a needy mess who lost control of herself over a man? A man who didn't even have the guts to dump me himself.

This will never happen again, I promised myself. No matter what, I would never humiliate myself—and really all of womankind—by begging a guy not to leave me. Justin just wasn't the one. Besides, there must have been a reason he had fallen out of love with me. Next time I would just need to be better.

Chapter 10

January 4th

On Monday, I woke up before my alarm went off, checked the time on my phone, and groaned inwardly (and outwardly) when I realized I had to get up in ten minutes. I'd been hoping for that glorious feeling of discovering I had a couple of hours left to sleep before facing the day.

I hated my job. And not just in an "I would rather not go to work today" kind of way, but more in a "my stomach started eating itself when I thought about going into the office" kind of way. I worked in public relations and it was every bit not as exciting as it was portrayed on TV. It was not filled with fun parties and celebrity clients. We didn't spend our days solving problems and pitching ideas in dynamic and positive-energy-filled boardrooms with eureka moments, high fives and congratulatory pats on the back.

In reality, it was full of mind-numbing, repetitive bullshit spewed out of the mouths of giant egos who stole your ideas and then sold them as their own. It was backstabbing, missed deadlines, whining, primping and catty behind-your-back exchanges. My boss, Terry Berringer, the VP of client relations, was the worst of them all.

Terry was like no one I'd ever met. He called himself a "disrupter." Before the word had entered our corporate vernacular, people who behaved like he did were just called assholes.

Terry was in your face, all the time, giving the performance of his life. He spoke and reacted to things as if he were starring in a play. His loud, perfectly enunciated, well-projected voice and overemphasized hand gestures dramatically complemented his elongated strides and theatrical turns toward his audience.

During the five years I'd worked as his assistant, I'd learned when to laugh at his jokes (always), when to compliment him on his choice of power suit (also, always) and when to stay away so as to avoid his bad moods. It took every ounce of strength I had to play my role in this Broadway-level theatre production every day.

As I was lying in bed, pondering for perhaps the thousandth time whether or not I should just quit my job and live in my car, my phone dinged. *Check out your Monday matches!* the alert cheerfully proclaimed. I decided I might as well stay in bed for a few more minutes while I checked them out. Terry never came in on time anyway because he was always "putting out fires" from home.

My Monday matches were: a guy who was married but his wife "totally approved" of him meeting women online, a guy who was sixty-five and looked like my dad, a guy whose only picture was of his car, a guy whose only picture was of the contents of his unzipped pants and a guy whose profile promised free breast exams. I sighed and rolled out of bed to find, seconds too late, that Mittens had puked in my slipper. It was a great day to be alive.

I arrived at work ten minutes late and was stunned to find that Terry was actually at his desk. Shit. I just couldn't win. "You're late," he said as I walked past his office.

"I know, sorry," I mumbled. "Is that a new tie? It's amazing."

"It is!" He beamed, looking down at it lovingly. "It's Burberry. I know, I know, I'm supposed to be on a money diet, but I've been so good lately that I deserve a treat. It's been almost two days since I bought anything online."

"Good for you," I said, inwardly rolling my eyes. "I wish I had your willpower."

He looked at my chosen outfit for the day: mom jeans and a sweatshirt with a cat on it.

"Don't be so hard on yourself, it looks like you've got plenty of willpower."

He followed me to my desk and I shrugged off my jacket and sat down, bracing myself for the inevitable Monday "how was your weekend" conversation. Every Monday Terry would ask me how my weekend was so he could tell me about all the fun things he'd done and all the amazing people he'd met, while I said things like "oh wow" and "that sounds amazing" and covertly checked my email.

Today, though, he passed my desk and went straight to the boardroom, which explained why he was here. He was only ever on time when a client was coming in. And, by the looks of his outfit, the client was definitely female.

I reluctantly turned on my computer and started going

through my emails. A Monday motivation email from our CEO, which I immediately deleted. An email about a staff potluck asking if anyone had any allergies, and twenty-five reply-alls, including one from our communications director, ensuring the entire company knew her husband couldn't eat shrimp.

The last email was from Terry. He wanted me to print out five PowerPoints—he refused to print things out himself. I was just about to start, thankful that I had a degree in public relations and a certificate in business writing to assist me with the momentous challenge ahead, when my phone vibrated. I swiped in my password and an alert popped up. *"You have a message from David!"*

Now that I'd been online dating for a few days, I felt like the alerts were mocking me, introducing me to yet another charmer whose profile said he liked "full-figured women who weren't afraid to show their love," which Julie had dryly informed me should be interpreted as "likes big boobs and blow jobs."

I clicked on the message and to my surprise found a nice, well-worded, grammatically correct sentence:

Hi, I laughed at your profile. I also appreciate a good sense of humour. Maybe we can chat?

He'd actually read my profile, which was a check on the plus side. I scanned his; it was pretty well written, and he seemed like an interesting guy. He didn't smoke, he was within my age range, and he had a face. No photos of him on his wedding day and nothing mentioning threesomes. I think we have a winner, folks. This guy deserved a message back. But later—I didn't want to appear too eager.

I took advantage of my mundane printing task to compose a great reply to David in my head. I didn't want to sound too desperate, but I also didn't want to come across as too aloof. I would mention something in his profile that interested me and ask a question about it, pushing the conversation forward. Genius. I finished separating the PowerPoints, slid a paperclip neatly over each corner, laid them in a perfectly aligned row on Terry's desk and went back to compose my message.

Hi David, I'd love to chat. I see you've been to Egypt. I've always wanted to go there. What was that like?

I read it over three more times and pressed send. It was a pretty solid first message. I was so proud of myself.

But then my heart started racing and I had to wipe my palms on my pants twice before I could steady myself. What if he didn't respond? What if he *did* respond? I would just have to keep my mind on work, turn off my phone and try not to think about it.

I tried not to think about it as I went through the rest of my emails and listened in to our weekly divisional staff meeting. I tried not to think about it as I stood in the doorway of Terry's office while he took off my neatly placed paperclips and threw each of them into the air because he "hated paperclips." Most of all, I tried not to think about it as I discreetly looked for job opportunities and updated my LinkedIn profile.

By the time I sat at my desk with my lunch, I was almost shaking with anticipation. I turned on my phone, closed my eyes and waited for the inevitable ding.

Except there wasn't one. And now I was disappointed.

Disappointed about not hearing from a guy I didn't know and had never talked to before. I scrunched my nose in disgust and tossed my phone into my purse.

Wait, was that a ding? Nope. Wait, was *that* a ding? Nope. This was going to be a long day.

Thankfully, Terry picked that afternoon to completely lose his shit over an email I'd sent to one of our clients. At least my mind would be occupied by something else.

I always knew when Terry was pissed because he called me not into his office, which had some element of privacy, but to a not-quite-soundproof conference room with floor-to-ceiling windows. That way everyone could see, and sometimes hear, the ineptitude he had to deal with on a regular basis. Today the room smelled like feet.

"I'm just going to get right to it," he said as I sat down to face him. "While I was working last night, at eleven, I saw that you'd replied to Tammy's email that you'd help her set up a Facebook page. Is that true?"

"Is it true that I emailed her or…"

"You *know* what I mean," he spat.

"I thought I was being helpful."

"It is not *your* job to create a Facebook page. We have a team for that." He gestured wildly around the room like the team was there watching. (They were.)

"I know," I said as I shrank back from his flailing arms. "She doesn't want us to manage it, she just wanted some basic tips on how to set one up. I figured because I'm pretty active on Facebook I'd—"

"It's not your job to develop social media pages for our clients. Only a rookie would make that kind of mistake."

He leaned forward, his eyes flickering to the side to see if he still had an audience.

"I've been here for five years."

"Act like it then," he boomed. "Email her back and let her know you made a mistake. If she wants a Facebook page, she can damn well go through me for it. We don't make money by giving out freebies." He stood abruptly, opened the door with a flourish, and stormed out of the room.

Happy Monday, I thought to myself as I followed, trying not to make eye contact with the design team, who were all staring at me like they'd just witnessed a kitten being eaten by a jackal.

When I got back to my desk, I checked my phone. David had sent me a message back. My stomach flipped involuntarily as I opened it.

Hi Kate, Egypt was great! I really enjoyed learning about the culture and eating the cuisine. Have you travelled anywhere interesting? How is your day going so far?

Now what? Should I send him a message back right away? Would that make me seem desperate? I started typing:

My day is going about as good as you would expect for a Monday.

No, too negative.

My day is going great!

Nope, too perky.

My day is going well, how about yours? I've travelled to Europe a couple of times but would love to travel more. Australia is definitely on my bucket list!

Was Australia still cool? I didn't care. I hit send.

As I put my phone down, another notification popped up on the screen. Another message! *I'm so popular today.* This time from someone named R.J.

Hey

Hey.

If they weren't going to put any effort into it, I wasn't going to either.

How's it goin'?

Good, you?

Good.

I waited for about five minutes and then put my phone down.

Thirty minutes later:

What do you like?

Like, hobbies? Have you read my profile?

No, like, with the sex.

And that was enough for today. I wanted to give everyone a chance, but I didn't want to ignore the obvious red flags. Again.

Chapter 11

Fifteen years ago
Kate

He was three hours late. I checked my watch one more time, even though I'd checked it two minutes ago. What if something had happened? This was the first time he'd driven his new car on the highway. What if he'd been going too fast and had gotten out of control?

I shoved the thoughts of his tragic death out of my mind. He was often late. I always asked him to call so I wouldn't worry, but he never did. "Stop nagging me and let me live my life," he would say.

An engine revved in the parking lot and I ran to the patio window. It was him! He'd made it. He was okay.

I sauntered down the apartment stairs, trying not to look too eager.

As soon as I saw him, I dropped the façade. "Peter, you're home!" I ran into his arms. This was the first time we'd been apart since we'd moved in together. I couldn't wait to hear how his first business trip had been.

After my fallout with Justin, I had been pretty eager to

try again; ready to puzzle together the pieces of a successful relationship. Ready to prove I could get it right. It had taken a few years but, right out of college, I was certain I was well on my way to achieving one.

Peter hugged me tight and handed me his bag to carry back up to our apartment. "Did you miss me?"

"Of course I did." I couldn't stop smiling. "I wish you'd called to let me know you were going to be late though. I was worried…" I trailed off when his face darkened. "It's okay though, you're here now."

I sat on the bed as he unpacked and talked about his weekend. When he got to the bottom of the suitcase, he handed me a hastily wrapped gift.

"Oh!" I exclaimed. "This is unexpected." We'd been together for almost a year and I'd convinced myself that the romantic ship had sailed. Maybe it wasn't too late. He obviously still thought of me, even when we were apart.

"Open it already," he teased.

"It's a book!" The perfect gift. He knew me so well. I excitedly wondered if he'd figured out my reading tastes yet.

I ripped off the rest of the paper and turned it over in my hands. As I looked at the cover, my heart sank. "It's an… um… What is it?"

"A self-help book. It's really great, it's filled with tips on how to be a better person. Go on, look inside." He smiled, eager for me to see the jewels he'd hidden within.

I flipped through the pages and saw that he had thoughtfully made notes in the sections where he figured I needed the most work. Sections like "Think Outside the Box" and "Be More Positive."

He handed me a pen. "Now you can do me."

Right from the beginning of the relationship, he'd dropped hints on how I could be better. It had started subtly, a head tilt and questioning smile when I was too judgmental, a gentle hand on my leg when I swore.

After we'd been dating for a few months, it had become a bit more obvious. When we argued, he would bring up incidents that he'd carefully tucked away and describe, in detail, how I could have handled them better. He would tell me what to wear when we went out because sometimes my clothes embarrassed him. He would correct my grammar and laugh when I didn't understand something. "They don't use that word on *Grey's Anatomy*?"

I so desperately wanted this relationship to work that I just accepted it. I probably *did* need to improve. I did swear a lot. I did drink too much. I definitely was too judgmental. I could probably watch something more mentally stimulating on TV. Everyone could be a bit kinder, more giving. Who *wouldn't* want tips on how to be better in bed?

"We're going to try counselling," I said to Ben and Julie as we waited in line at a Spirit of the West concert. Ben looked away.

"What? Are you mad at me?" I asked, trying to catch his eye.

"Why do you put up with it?" he said, shoulders tensed.

"What do you mean?"

"The way he treats you."

"What do you mean the way he treats me? It's totally normal," I said.

"It's not totally normal," Julie said and Ben visibly relaxed. "You know the frog in boiling water parable?"

"No. What? Why would someone put a frog in boiling water?" I asked.

"Just listen. If you put a frog in water when the water's boiling, the clever sucker jumps right out. But if you put him in water that's cold and gradually turn up the heat, the poor guy doesn't notice and boils to death. That's what's happening to you. You're the frog." She poked me in the arm.

"I don't understand," I said, but I did. I had been thinking about it myself lately, I just didn't want to admit how bad it had gotten.

Julie put her hand on my shoulder, her expression direct but kind. "It's not normal that he makes fun of you in front of his friends. It's not normal that he shows up to things four hours late and never calls. It's not normal that he bought you that book."

If I spoke, I'd start crying, so I just nodded.

"It's not normal that he tells you after sex that you could have been better."

"Oh, Jesus," Ben whispered as he rubbed his forehead with his hand.

We were in counselling one month later, and one month after that we were sitting together on the couch while he clarified why he was moving out.

"You just don't make me happy." He stretched out like it was a lazy Sunday.

I wiped the tears from my eyes and blew my nose for the fifth time.

"Why?" I finally asked. "If I didn't make you happy, if you were so displeased about the way I acted, about the way I was, why did you even bother? Why did we last so long?"

He sat up and took my hand in his, looking at me with his endlessly patient gaze. With all sincerity, he said, "I truly thought I could change you."

I guess I showed him.

Chapter 12

Terry had significantly cheered up by Monday afternoon. He'd received an unexpected delivery of fancy donuts for a random, likely fake, reason and spent the rest of the day alternately calling people into his office to see them and posting pictures of them on Instagram.

His preoccupation gave me plenty of time to obsessively check if David had replied. I was checking for the twentieth time when it occurred to me: I didn't have to wait for some guy to dictate the direction my day was going to go. I was a strong, independent woman. I was going to go ahead and ask him out myself. I would be bold and take charge.

Maybe you'd like to get together for coffee or something and chat further?

I hit send without even thinking. Bam. Just like that, I'd asked a guy on a date.

And then immediately regretted it.

What happened now? What if he said no? Julie said to always wait for the guy to ask, and I totally hadn't, and now I might have ruined this potential relationship forever. What if he thought I was desperate? What if he thought I was too forward? Oh God, what had I done?

I turned my phone to silent and threw it under some files in the bottom drawer of my desk. Not the most adult solution, but at least my heart slowed down.

I spent the rest of the afternoon listening to Terry talk about how grateful he was for all the love people showered on him, and when I couldn't take it anymore, I got ready to leave. I dug my phone out of my drawer and finally allowed myself to check it.

David had sent me a message back! However, the bright sun of victory lasted mere seconds before the cloud of potential rejection scrubbed it away.

Is this what it it's going to be like all the time? Am I going to be riding this second-by-second roller coaster of excitement and fear for the rest of my life?

I clicked on the notification and closed my eyes. Lifting one eye open, I peeked at the message:

Sounds great. How about a week from Friday?

Yes! I'd done it! I was going on a date!

Oh, God, I was going on a date.

This was the first date I'd been on in a decade. What if it was a disaster? But also, more importantly, what if it was great? What if this date turned into another date and then another? Then what happened? I'd been single for so long I wasn't sure I knew how to behave in those kinds of situations anymore.

Did I shake his hand and wish him well? Did I let him kiss me goodnight? Did I ask him up to my apartment for "coffee?" Did people do that anymore? And if I did invite him up for "coffee," then what? What if he got all nervous and weird? What if *I* got all nervous and weird? What if things were going really well and clothes started coming off? Was I ready for that? What if he unhooked my bra and popcorn fell out like it had last night when I was changing for bed?

My heart felt like it was going to beat right out of my chest. I hadn't realized that was actually a thing. I'd always thought it was just a literary device. I was sweating and gasping, trying to catch my breath. I didn't seem to be able to swallow. I picked up my phone, dropped it and picked it up again. My hands shook as I typed.

How do you know if you're having a panic attack?

I texted the only person I knew who would know the answer. Ben called immediately.

"Are you seriously having a panic attack?" His voice was tight with concern.

"I don't know," I gasped. "I can't breathe. Does it feel like a heart attack?"

"Okay. Take a deep breath," he said calmly.

"I'm trying," I wheezed.

"Listen to my voice. It's okay. Yes, you are probably having a panic attack. But it's okay. It will be over soon. Breathe with me. In…"

"I think I'm dying."

"You're not dying. Breathe in."

I did. In short spurts.

"Now, slowly breathe out."

I breathed out the small puff of air I'd managed to get into my lungs.

"Again, in."

I breathed in again. It was easier this time. And still

easier the next. Ben being so calm and kind was starting to relax me. It was possible I wasn't going to die after all. I sipped from my bottle of water.

"Thank you," I said.

"You're welcome." We sat together in silence, listening to the sound of each other breathing. Ben and I hadn't been hanging out that much lately, but I felt oddly close to him right then. Like we'd been through something big and had made it to the other side.

"I've never had a panic attack before," I whispered, not wanting to break the spell.

"Well…" he began, "technically, you didn't have a panic attack; you most likely had an anxiety attack. A panic attack presents with a fear of dying and losing control, and often with a feeling of leaving your body. It doesn't sound like you experienced those symptoms."

And the spell was broken.

"Well, thanks again!" Awkwardness drifted into the conversation like a cloying scent. "I feel a lot better."

"Are you sure you're okay? What triggered the attack?" he asked, then added, "Never mind, it's none of my business."

"Oh, it was nothing." I forced a laugh. "It was stupid, really. I just, well, I have a date next week and I got really nervous all of a sudden."

"Oh," he said, clearly not interested. "Well, good luck with it."

"Thanks. It should be fun. Or not. I don't care." I laughed. *What is wrong with me?* "I should really get going. I know I've said it a hundred times already, but thank you. I'm really grateful for your help."

"Anytime. Well, not anytime." He paused. "I mean I hope it doesn't happen again. But I mean I'll help if it does." Another pause. "But I hope it doesn't."

"Okay then!" I yelled, desperate to end this horribly awkward ordeal. "Bye!"

Well, that was terrible.

Chapter 13

Ben

Well, that was terrible.

Ben put his phone on the nightstand and sat on his bed, lowering his head into his hands. When Kate's name had come up on the screen, he'd felt a small surge of excitement—excitement that had quickly turned to fear.

He was almost relieved to hear it had only been an anxiety attack. Not that he would wish that on anybody, of course.

Technically, you didn't have a panic attack. He cringed.

Why on earth had he corrected her? Who cared what kind of attack it was? She had clearly been struggling. He'd only made it worse with his rigid adherence to semantics. They had been having a moment and he'd ruined it.

The fact that she had called him—not Julie, him—still lingered though, and his face flushed. He had helped. *Helped her prepare for a date,* he reminded himself, his stomach sinking. Maybe he shouldn't feel so proud after all.

He lay on his bed feeling his heartbeat begin to slow. Of course she had called him; he was the panic attack expert.

When he was a kid, he'd had them all the time, sitting at his desk at school, not knowing the answer, hands clenched in his seven-year-old lap, praying to whatever God there was that the teacher wouldn't call on him. Trying to gasp out the words but just shaking his head, tears poking out of his tightly squeezed-shut eyes.

Julie was the only one who'd known. The only one who had understood how hard it had been. She would see him getting picked on and yell at the other kids to leave him alone. She'd stuck up for him at school and at home. She'd known he was having the attacks before their parents did; even before he did.

And for that, he felt terrible. No matter how hard it was for him, it must have been as hard, if not harder, for Julie. He was her big brother; he was supposed to protect her, not the other way around. Julie had always played the role of the older sibling, weighed down by the heaviness of responsibility. It wasn't until the day he'd had to come home from university that he'd been able to be there for her when she'd needed him the most.

When they were kids, though, she was so busy protecting him and taking care of him and looking after all his needs that she didn't look after herself. She didn't have any friends either, and she was the "normal" one.

That was until Kate. He still remembered the day Julie had rescued him, yet again, from a group of boys who had somehow gotten his shoe and were throwing it back and forth like a football. Julie had stepped in, grabbed the shoe, and given it back to him, squeezing his hand in support. As a reward, one of the older boys had shoved her, causing her books to fall to the ground. When Julie turned around, there was Kate, picking them up and handing them to her with a smile. They had been best friends ever since, united against the assholes, helping each other through the trials and tribulations of adolescence.

He'd never forgotten that day. That was the day he felt a little less guilty about what he was putting his sister through. He'd been too young to know what he was feeling for Kate; he'd never had a crush before. It had felt more like gratitude than anything else. Finally, Julie had a friend. Finally, she was allowed to have some fun.

Kate. Just thinking her name made his heart race. She'd been a life raft for Julie. And Julie had provided her with somewhere she could escape. Somewhere she could go when her parents were fighting. They gave each other strength and comfort and support when no one else around them was.

He had been in awe of her patience and her kindness, and all he had wanted to do when she'd come over crying after a particularly bad parental fight was wrap her in a hug and say he would protect her forever. But, of course, he never did. Even when, over the years, the crush had turned into love.

All he could do was be there. Observing. Listening. Making sure she was okay. Making sure her favourite soda water was in the fridge and favourite snacks were in the pantry. Making sure she felt at home and safe.

He'd never thought about telling her how he felt. How could he? He knew she knew a bit about his problems with anxiety, but he also knew she had no idea how much it controlled his life. She had no idea that, even though he could now manage his panic attacks and hide his idiosyncrasies, he was often still that scared little boy. Kate deserved better than him.

He sighed. This would just have to be his life now. Helping Kate with her love life and watching her go on dates. Watching her fall in love with someone who might finally deserve her—wishing that someone was him.

Chapter 14

"Tonight's the night!" I yelled into the phone.

"What the hell, Kate?" Julie moaned. "I just woke up. Take it down a notch."

"Sorry, I'm excited. I don't think this week could have possibly gone any slower."

"What's his name again?"

"David. We've been texting all week. I feel like I've really gotten to know him."

"Tell me about him," she murmured like she was asking me to tell her a bedtime story.

"He's never been married, doesn't have kids, he has a degree in history, loves being outdoors and doesn't smoke or do drugs. His favourite food is Thai, and he likes action movies but also romances if he's in that type of mood."

"You sound like you're reading notes."

"I may have made notes. I'm just so excited to find out what he's like in person. Judging by his texts, he's amazing."

"Just remember what I said..." she started.

"I know, don't get my hopes up." Too late.

"All right, I have to get up now and get ready for work," she said. "Keep me posted."

I sat at my desk at the end of the day, willing the seconds of the last hour to tick by faster than time actually moved. Out of the corner of my eye, I saw Terry coming toward my desk.

"K-D!" he barked, so everyone knew he was there. Not that anyone wouldn't. He was wearing what sounded like tap shoes. K-D is what he called me when he was in a good mood because I'd once brought a box of Kraft Dinner for lunch. He thought it was hilarious.

"Yes, Terry?" I turned my chair and gave him my full attention, grabbing my notebook and pen. I'd learned the hard way that if you were not instantly prepared to write down whatever came out of his mouth at all times, he would call you out in front of your colleagues and make you go back to your desk to get your notebook. Every. Time.

"I just wanted to tell you that I'm going to be leaving early today for an appointment." He waited until I understood that, yes, this was something I needed to write down. I wrote it down.

"Great," I said. I put down my notebook and pen.

"Also..." he said, and I picked both back up again. "If all goes well, I might be late Monday morning, if you know what I mean."

I didn't.

"Okay, sounds good." I looked down at my book for as long as I could, willing him to walk away.

He didn't.

"Okay, okay, I'll tell you!" he said. "I have a date!"

I was never getting out of here.

"Oh, wow, that's great! I hope you have fun."

He still didn't leave.

"Should I be writing this down?" I asked, half-seriously.

"Oh, sweetie, no, I just had to tell someone. Look." He took out his phone and showed me a picture of an extremely attractive woman. "This is her, isn't she amazing?"

"She's very pretty."

"As if I'd date someone who wasn't. She's smart too. She has a degree in physics, or chemistry or something. I don't care; she's hot and I'm going to get la-aid," he sang out. "I'm going to get a glass of wine. Want one?"

"Actually, no, I have to… I mean, funnily enough, I also have a da—"

"Too late! I already poured you one." He stepped back behind the cubicle wall and pulled out two very full glasses of white.

"Oh, thanks, but…"

"Let's go sit in the kitchen. My brain is totally fried from all the fires I had to put out this week."

"I still need to finish this report," I tried.

"You can work on it this weekend. Let's go." He swept the glasses off my desk and took several gulps from one.

"Okay, I'll be right there," I relented.

After about ten more minutes of working and five more minutes of listening to Terry call my name every thirty seconds, I gave up, closed my laptop and joined the group in the kitchen. Cody and Nate each had a beer and were arguing in the most hipster way possible about which craft beer was the best.

The only good thing about our job was that booze was readily available. The fridge was always stocked with beer, wine, coolers and ciders, no matter what day or time. Fancy a cocktail? Well, look no further than the giant liquor cupboard filled with any type of alcohol you could possibly imagine. It was an alcoholic's dream. Or nightmare. I guess leadership figured if they couldn't treat their employees like real people, at least they could ensure they were too drunk to notice.

I sat beside Nate as Terry finished the same story he'd just told me, with an exuberant rendition of "I'm going to get la-aid!" at the end. It looked like he'd almost finished his wine, so maybe this wouldn't be as bad as I'd thought. Maybe he would actually leave early. I mean he was usually gone before 4:00 p.m. so he was using the word "early" a bit loosely. I looked at my watch, knowing I was supposed to meet David at 6:00 p.m. I sipped my wine slowly, hoping Terry didn't decide to have another.

"When's your date?" I asked.

"Oh, shoot, five thirty. I guess I should get going."

Thank God.

He pushed the rolling chair away from the table, spun around twice, got up, and wobbled to the dishwasher, placing his glass on the counter just above it. "Later losers! Don't wait up!"

"What does that even mean?" I said to Cody.

"I think it means he's going to get la-aid," Cody sang.

I got up and dumped the rest of my wine in the sink,

knowing it would take more than one glass to calm my nerves. I needed to do something to keep my mind off the date, so I went back to my desk to work on my report.

The last actual date I'd gone on was the reason I had decided to just enjoy being single. In hindsight, I wasn't even sure it was meant to be a date. Maybe he'd seen it as just friends hanging out; that certainly would have explained his behaviour. Tonight couldn't possibly be worse than that. I hoped.

Chapter 15

Ten years ago
Kate

"Do you think that guy looks like Brad Pitt in *Legends of the Fall*?" I leaned over and whispered loudly in Julie's ear.

"Seriously?" Ben said under his breath.

"That movie came out twenty years ago. You need to update your fantasies," Julie said and burst into laughter.

"Well, I think he does," I huffed. His blond hair was pulled back into a ponytail and he had the beginnings of a scruffy beard. Normally, I was attracted to short-haired and clean-shaven men, but the long hair and ruggedness was appealing on him. Our eyes met a couple of times, and smiles were shared over passed appetizers. Eventually, he made his way down to our end of the table and sat across from me.

"I'm Will," he said. "I work with Ben."

"I'm Kate," I said. "Julie's best friend. She's…" I looked around.

Ben nodded in the direction of the booths where she was sitting on a random guy's lap.

"Never mind."

As Will and I chatted, I caught Ben's eye and subtly motioned for him to meet me by the bar.

Even though it was his birthday, Ben still managed to be on the periphery of the action, watching everyone in comfortable silence.

He obediently walked over. His brown eyes met mine while he attempted a casual lean on the bar, thought better of it, and stood, sliding his hands into his jean pockets.

"So, what's Will's story?" I asked in what I hoped was a nonchalant tone.

"Will? Oh. Well, he works with me, I guess, um…" His hand automatically went to the back of his neck, where it rested when he was uncomfortable. Which was most of the time we were in public.

"No," I said with a patient smile. "I mean his story; like is he dating anyone or…"

"I don't think so." He glanced in Will's direction. "He's never mentioned a girlfriend."

"And what's he like?" I probed further. "Nice? An asshole?"

"He's okay." Ben looked like he was going to say something more, a flicker of emotion I couldn't quite place, and then his lips curved into his trademark half-smile. "Honestly, I don't really know him that well, but he seems… fine."

We stood in silence for a couple of seconds longer, Ben playing with a thread on his pale blue T-shirt. "Thanks, friend," I finally said. I gave him a quick half-hug and turned to grab a glass of water from the side of the bar. "Do you want one?" I asked, glancing over my shoulder. But he was already gone.

After texting back and forth for a week or so, Will and I agreed we should meet for dinner. Neither of us actually said the word "date" so I was determined to play it cool, but the butterflies in my stomach had other ideas. I spent hours getting ready, making sure I picked the perfect outfit. I wanted to look good but in the kind of way that confidently said I didn't care if I did.

We decided on a nice Greek restaurant, so I didn't want to wear jeans, but I also didn't want to wear a ballgown. After going through my entire closet (twice) and bursting into tears (once), I finally settled on a pair of grey palazzo pants and a slim-fitting rose-coloured top that hugged my hips. I have a pretty basic style. Most of the things I wear are either bought right off the mannequin or they're neutral because I don't know how to match.

We planned to meet at the restaurant at 7:00 p.m. so, at 6:30 p.m., after checking my make-up in the mirror for the twentieth time, I called a taxi and was on my way.

I'd never been to this place before. Will had chosen it because it was close to where he lived, and as we pulled up, my stomach fluttered a bit more. It was perfect; he somehow knew exactly what I liked. As I got out of the cab, I admired the beautiful marble columns and ornate lettering on the front of the pale stucco building. I walked through the door and breathed in the tangy smells, anxious to have a peek at the menu.

The evening was still warm so I asked if we could be seated on the patio. Surprisingly, there were still seats available.

Due to our painfully long winters, Saskatchewanians will often try to pack in as much patio-sitting as possible in the summer. It's like winning the lottery if you can actually find a place to sit.

I sat at a tucked-away table for two and smoothed my hand over the red-and-white checked tablecloth, admiring the white twinkle lights strung around the rustic wooden beams.

This is going to be so romantic when it gets dark. I smiled to myself as I looked over the wine list. I couldn't wait.

But I did wait. Until 7:05 p.m. and then 7:10 p.m. and then, after checking my phone multiple times, at 7:20 p.m., I saw someone running up the street toward the restaurant, clearly out of breath. Everyone on the patio turned and watched the show: a young, sweaty man, running for his life, flip-flops slapping on the pavement, stopping once to re-tie the drawstring of what appeared to be swimming trunks.

Of course it was Will.

"Hey!" he yelled when he saw me and then doubled over to catch his breath. "I'll be right in."

I wasn't sure what to think. Was he okay? Was there some sort of swimming emergency? I waited patiently, hands in my lap, certain it would all be explained.

There wasn't a swimming emergency. He had apparently just run the entire way because he didn't want to be late.

"Yeah, because I know it bothers you so, you know, I ran so I wouldn't be," he said, wiping sweat off his forehead.

"But you are late."

"No, it's seven twenty."

"Oh." I must have misunderstood the time. "Sorry, I thought we said we were going to meet at seven."

"Yeah. Seven. We did." He grabbed the menu.

"It's seven twenty."

"Yeah."

Okay. The fact that he didn't understand how time worked definitely concerned me, but not wanting to ruin the evening, and, more so, wanting to know the story behind what he was wearing, I let it go and waited for him to explain.

He didn't.

"Have you been here before?" I asked, trying to encourage him.

"Yeah, fancy hey?" He winced and reached under the table.

"Are you okay?"

"My feet hurt from running in these flip-flops."

"Right. And why are you wearing flip-flops again?"

He shrugged and chugged an entire glass of water. "Could I get some more water?" he called to the server as she walked by.

So, we were off to a great start. I mean running to make sure he wasn't late—even though he was—was a nice thought, but he was literally dripping with sweat. And I don't use the word "literally" lightly. There were actual drops of sweat on the pavement.

Determined not to let this ruin our meal, I grabbed a menu and pretended I hadn't already decided what I wanted.

"The souvlaki looks good," I pondered aloud as the server refilled our waters.

"We're ready to order." Will grabbed his glass and gulped down three quarters of it.

I looked up.

"Right? You're getting the souvlaki?"

"Sure, yes, that sounds good." I was going to suggest we get some appies, but I wasn't going to be picky.

"I'll get the pita bread and hummus," he said.

So, we were getting appies, okay. "I'll get the shrimp scampi to start and then the souvlaki, please," I put my menu down.

"Thanks." He pushed the menu into the server's hand.

"You're not getting a main?"

"No, I'm not super hungry."

What the hell? "Maybe because you just pounded two entire glasses of water," I said under my breath.

"What?"

"Nothing." I looked up at the server. "Can I change my order, please? I'll just have scampi."

"Aren't you hungry?" he asked.

I was starving.

"Oh, no, I'm good. Something small is fine for me." I'd decided at this point I would just spend my money on wine.

"Anything to drink?" the server asked.

"Just water for me," he said.

She looked at me, pen hovering over her pad. "Water for me as we—" *No, you know what? Fuck it.* "Actually, I'll have a glass of the riesling. And I'll have the souvlaki instead of the scampi. Thanks." I handed her my menu.

The night went downhill from there. Will talked the

entire time and ate about five bites of his bread, which gave me five brief seconds to get a word in. Not that he asked me anything about myself, so it was just me commenting on whatever he happened to have an opinion on.

"Sorry I wasn't chattier. I wasn't feeling well," Will said at the end of the night as we stood on the curb.

Are you serious?

"It's okay," I said instead.

"Yeah? Text me then, let's plan something else." He moved in and gave me a sticky hug before limping off, his flip-flops rubbing on what I assumed were newly formed blisters.

I pulled my phone from my purse and immediately texted Ben.

Your friend Will has problems.

He's not really my friend... Want to come over for a drink? Julie's here.

As I pulled into the parking lot of Ben's apartment building, I felt my phone vibrate in my pocket. It was a Facebook message from Will. An unsurprisingly very long Facebook message. A very long Facebook message outlining why he thought I was having a hard time finding someone (I never told him that) and did I know what would help? Sex with him.

"Because he's been told he is 'really good at it,'" I said, out of breath after running up the stairs to show Ben and Julie.

Ben started laughing.

"What a douche," Julie said.

"He said I was too needy!" I breathed. "And that guys

don't like girls who talk too much. I said five fucking words the whole time!"

"Sorry," Ben said, trying to hide his half-grin. "I didn't know he was such a jerk."

I sighed. "It's not your fault. I'm just bad at this. I can't figure out how to make anything work."

"It's not you," Ben said gently, the laughter gone. "Maybe... maybe you just haven't met the right guy yet."

"I can't do this anymore," I said. "I don't want to try again. I'm too tired. I think I'm just one of those women who was meant to be single. And maybe that's okay, right?" I looked at them both, my eyes pleading with them to agree with me.

"Sure," Julie said slowly. And then with more enthusiasm, "Of course it is! You don't need a man to be happy. You are doing perfectly fine on your own."

I looked at Ben.

"Yeah!" he said and half-heartedly pumped his fist in the air. "Men suck!"

"Not all men suck," I said and gave him a hug.

At least there was someone I could count on.

Chapter 16

Ten dateless years had passed since Will. I couldn't believe it had been that long. Despite my dating drought and the precedent Will had set, my hopes were high for David. At least it was too cold for swimming trunks.

I arrived fifteen minutes early for the date so I could scope the place out and hopefully find a place to sit that was a bit private. I had chosen my second favourite coffee shop located in the trendy district on 13th Avenue. I loved the vibe of the cozy old house, and, most importantly, the coffee was great. I'd also chosen it because I didn't want to run into anyone I knew; namely Jesse from Beans 'n' Brews. I kind of felt like I was coffee shop cheating, but I also felt it was worth it not to have to put up with being observed like I was an unwilling reality TV participant.

Apparently, David also liked to arrive early. As I walked through the door and took off my gloves, he waved at me from a table right in the center of the room. Surrounded by people. Great.

Now, I was obviously not against internet dating. However, that was not to say I wanted everyone there to know I was on a date with someone I'd met online.

A small piece of me still found the whole thing slightly embarrassing. So, you can imagine my mortification when, as I approached the table, he stood and yelled out, "Tinder delivery!"

I stopped momentarily but, true to form, pretended it didn't bother me and kept walking. I laughed and looked around, smiling like I couldn't believe how hilarious he was.

He walked over and pulled back my chair. *Well*, I thought, *what a gentleman, how nice.* Maybe he'd just yelled because he was as nervous as I was. Maybe it would be just a blip on an otherwise amazing night.

It wasn't.

I'd forgotten how much a text could hide someone's real personality; how much they could edit themselves into being the person they wanted to portray. David's texts told me he was smart and clever. That he was kind and had an amazing sense of humour. He was complimentary, but not so much that he was disingenuous. He was attentive, but not so much that he seemed like a stalker. We shared the same interests and we enjoyed the same things. I could totally see us finishing each other's sentences one day.

The real David was nothing like his texts. He was also nothing like his pictures. I didn't want to be superficial, but looks did matter to me, at least a little. If I wasn't physically attracted to someone, I couldn't see how anything could move forward. Real-life David looked about twenty years older than his picture and 150 pounds heavier. He was also desperately grasping on to the last few scraggly hairs on his head in the form of a terrible comb-over, which was disappointing. I'd always found a guy who confidently owned his baldness very sexy.

"You look a bit different from your picture," I said after sitting down.

"Yeah." He grinned. "I learned that people are too superficial to see the real me when I post a current picture of myself, so I use one from a few years ago. Keeps the bitches on their toes." I winced.

"Isn't that kind of dishonest?"

"Maybe. But isn't it kind of cunty to judge a book by its cover?" He laughed.

My eyes widened and I held in a gasp. What kind of guy said that on the first date? On any date for that matter. *Okay,* I said to myself. I'd give him one more chance. Everyone deserves a chance. I could be cool. I thought about the pledge napkin I had tucked inside my purse.

"Sure, bitches be crazy," I said and immediately hated myself.

The date got worse from there. Real-life David turned out to be loud, brash and called his ex-girlfriend "the slut show." Despite the fact that he was "totally over her," she was the main topic of our conversation. The rest of the time, he talked about himself. Loudly. If people hadn't known I was on an online date before, they certainly did now. And from the sympathetic glances being thrown my way, they definitely felt sorry for me.

He didn't ask me one question about myself, and the few times I got a word in edgewise, he nodded absently, without the slightest flicker of interest. I don't think I'd drunk a cup of coffee so quickly in my life.

Once I'd finished, burning my throat in the process, he called the barista over (by snapping his fingers) and motioned for another round.

"Actually, I'm not feeling well," I said quickly and reached for my coat. "I think we should call it a night."

We walked down the wooden stairs together, and when we got to the door, he held it open for me. It was now clear that his gentlemanliness was purely for show.

"Well, thanks for meeting me." I turned to walk toward my car, dodging a man pulling two kids on a sled.

"Did you want to grab dinner somewhere? We can go back to my place for dessert." He winked.

Was he serious? And also, gross. "No, I need to get home. Thanks though."

He leaned in for what could have been just a hug but ended up being nothing because I reflexively stepped back.

"It's because I'm fat, isn't it?" he sneered.

"No, what? No," I stammered. "I, um, I just don't think we're a match."

"You're just like everyone else," he snapped. "You're only after looks, never thinking about personality. You really need to take a good hard look at reality. You're not so hot yourself, you know."

I opened my mouth to speak, but nothing could save this. So I just turned around and walked away.

Chapter 17

I slid into my frozen car, started it, and turned on my heated seat. Now what? I looked at my phone, hoping it would tell me what to do. Julie had texted five times:

How was it?

Or IS it?

Hopefully it's still going strong!

I want to hear everything!!

Are you in love yet?

I started to text her back, but I couldn't face it. Despite Julie's warnings, I hadn't been prepared for the date to be *this* awful. I waited for my car to warm up and slumped back into the seat. I'd actually thought this was it. I'd thought I would be one of the lucky ones. Against all odds, I thought I'd dodged the bullets every other woman my age had to face—scrolling through endless dudes, going on terrible dates for months and months. I had foolishly thought David would be my someone to kiss. And the fact that he wasn't even close… how could I have been so naïve?

My eyes filled with bitter tears. *Don't you dare cry over this,* I thought. *That jerk is not worth your disappointment.*

I knew what I needed. Coffee and a treat. Maybe a

ginger cookie, maybe an entire cake. I deserved it after this disaster.

I parked across the street from Beans 'n' Brews, and when I saw Jesse through the glass door, my eyes stung with fresh tears. I was so happy to see a friendly face. Thankfully, I managed to rein in the tears as I pushed the door open.

The bells rang over the door and he looked up and smiled. I instantly knew I'd made the right decision. "Kate!" he greeted me cheerfully. "What a nice surprise!"

I barely squeaked out a "hello." I guess I hadn't managed to rein the tears in after all.

He dropped the cloth he'd been using to wipe down the counter and hurried over.

"Oh no, Kate, what's wrong? Are you okay? Are you hurt?" He guided me to a table in the corner and we sat down.

"I'm fine," I said. "Sorry, I'm really fine." I breathed deeply and tried to contain myself. "It's just…" Nope. This was happening. Crying in a coffee shop in front of a friend I used to have a crush on and what appeared to be a homeless person. This was not my finest hour.

Jesse jumped up from the table, presumably to escape whatever sweet hell I'd brought in, but then returned with a handful of napkins. "Sorry, this is all I've got," he said, moving in closer and giving my hand a quick squeeze.

"No, I'm sorry," I said, my cheeks flushing. "This is so embarrassing. I'm not usually like this. I mean the only time I let myself cry is when I'm watching *Grey's Anatomy.*"

He burst into laughter, which made me laugh too. I

laughed so hard my stomach hurt. This was good. This was how I'd wanted my night to be.

In between Jesse jumping up to serve customers and then coming back to my table, I told him all about my awful date and he actually listened to me. Attentively. He asked questions and shook his head, and not once did he tell me about a similar experience he'd had that was way worse. The conversation was all about me, and it was exactly what I needed.

"What a jerk!" he said when I was done, putting his hand on top of mine. "You can do better; you know that, right?"

I glanced down at his hand and tried to ignore the jolt of electricity that shivered down my spine.

Why couldn't the date have been more like this? I asked myself when he went back up to the counter. If only I were fourteen years younger, maybe Jesse and I would be dating and I wouldn't have to go through any of this. I stopped that train of thought abruptly. I hadn't thought about Jesse in that way since I'd found out how old he was. I'd thought I'd firmly fastened the spigot on that emotional faucet. I mean I still thought he was adorable, but I'd never seriously entertained the fantasy that we could be more than friends.

Jesse came back with coffee and cake "on the house."

"There's just one thing I don't understand," he said as he set them down.

"Why I'm such a hot mess?"

He chuckled. "No, why… Sorry, I'm trying to put this delicately…"

"Just say it," I said. "I think we're past that point."

"Why didn't you just tell him off? I mean even I can tell he was an asshole right from the start and I'm a dude. Why didn't you just walk out when you saw he didn't look like his picture?"

I paused. Why hadn't I just walked out when I'd seen he didn't look like his picture? Or when he'd said people were cunty? I'd had plenty of opportunities to leave, plenty of opportunities to tell him what I thought.

"I don't know," I said. But I did. Telling him off was something my mom would have done.

"You're going to keep trying though, right?" he said, holding my eyes. "I mean you still have almost a year to reach your goal."

I shrugged. "Maybe. I should, probably. I guess this was a good lesson to learn. I'll need to be more realistic and not get my hopes up. I mean Julie did warn me. I feel like a kid who just found out Santa Claus isn't real, even though her parents told her several times they were the ones who bought presents and wrapped them up every year. Oh, you mean he's *really* not real. Okay. I get it now."

"Don't give up." He patted my hand. "You'll find your Santa Claus." That set us off again and I laughed until I started to choke, and he had to get me a glass of water.

While he was gone, my thoughts went once again to his hand on mine and I blushed as I imagined his hand visiting other places. *What am I doing?* I abruptly pulled myself back to reality. No good could come of that way of thinking. I had to nip this in the bud before it got out of control. He couldn't possibly think of me in any way other than a friend.

I grabbed my purse and got up to leave, waving at Jesse as I walked by the counter.

"You don't want your water?"

"No, I'm good," I said as I rushed to the door, bumping into a table in my haste. "Thanks for tonight. It really helped."

"Anytime." He touched two fingers to his forehead in a clumsy salute. "Don't give up. Any guy would be lucky to have you. You're a great catch."

"Thanks." I ducked my head and smiled in an "aw shucks" kind of way. "See you later."

I pushed open the door and, despite the cold, the flush from his unexpected compliment warmed my face. What a nice thing to say.

And then I stopped. What if he'd meant it as more than a compliment? He'd never said anything like that to me before. I thought again about the way he had taken my hand earlier. Was I wrong? Did he want something more?

I stood outside, watching him through the window as he cleaned a table. He looked up at me and lifted his lips into a shy, crooked grin. A shy, super cute, crooked grin.

Shit.

Chapter 18

January 16th

On Saturday, I decided to give my dating plan a break for a couple of weeks. I was both discouraged about the one date I'd managed to go on and slightly confused about Jesse. The obvious solution, and the one I chose to move forward with, was to ignore both things and keep myself so busy that I didn't have time to think about either of them.

I also ignored Julie's hourly texts requesting an update. This was one update I didn't want to give. I finally gave in and called her while I was making supper.

"Finally," she said when she answered.

"Hello to you too," I said as I dumped a box of Kraft Dinner in some boiling water.

"Don't be an asshole. You know very well I've been waiting all day for this."

I laughed. "Okay, you asked for it." I told her the whole story. Well, not the whole story. I left out the part where I'd cried in front of Jesse. And the part where he'd held my hand. And the cute, crooked grin he'd given me afterward.

"I'm sorry, Kate," she said when I was done. "Sometimes

it takes a lot of shitty dates before you find a good one. Don't let it discourage you from trying again."

"I won't," I said. "I just want to take a break."

"Last weekend," she said, "I hooked up with a guy and all he talked about after was how much he loved banana bread and did I know how to make banana bread? I don't know if that was his 'thing' or what, but I certainly wasn't going to get up and make him any."

I sighed. "Do you think there are actually any good guys on these things? I know there are people out there who have found amazing partners online, but in the back of my mind, I still think that might be a myth."

"I don't know," she said. "I've never met anyone I would want to be in a relationship with, but I've also never really thought about it that way. We're both online for very different reasons."

"True," I said. "It just seems like there are a lot more oddballs out there than good ones." There was a long pause while I watched the pasta boil; then I added, "Speaking of weird, did Ben mention anything about me?"

"No, why?"

"Oh, nothing." I tried to sound casual. "I just spoke to him the other day and thought maybe he'd mention it." I took the pot off the burner and dumped the pasta in a strainer.

"Nope, nothing. Although you know what he's like; Ben isn't one to just volunteer information like that. If I asked him directly whether he'd spoken to you, he'd say he did, but he's not the greatest at starting conversations."

"Fair enough," I said, relieved that Ben hadn't told Julie

about my panic attack. "Well, I'm going to go." I stirred in the powdered cheese. "I have a gourmet meal waiting for me."

"All right." She laughed. "Enjoy your Kraft Dinner. And don't lose hope. I'm sure your dream man is out there just waiting for you to answer his message."

"Unlikely. Have a good night."

I spent the rest of the evening lying on the couch, watching TV and eating chips. Ben texted to see if I was okay, which was really nice. That was why I loved having him as a friend; I knew he always had my back. I had meant it when I'd told him I'd missed him when he'd gone away. Whatever the reason for it, I was really glad he'd come home.

Chapter 19

January 30th

After two weeks of avoiding the dating app, I charged into the weekend with a brand-new attitude. Jesse hadn't texted or called, so I determined I had just been imagining things. And so what if my first date had sucked? All first dates were terrible. But I'd gotten mine out of the way. I was going to get right back out there and keep trying. I refused to let one douchebag bring me down. I had plenty of time to find someone better.

As my coffee brewed, I pulled out a kitchen chair, sat down and opened my laptop. Mittens took this opportunity to jump on the table and place a single paw neatly into the centre of my peanut butter toast.

Asshole.

I gently lifted him off the table and pointlessly blew on my toast before I took a bite. He jumped back up and walked across the keyboard. This was a fun game we played from time to time.

I placed Mittens in my lap, logged into my online dating account and started sifting through notifications. There were a lot.

Well, that's fine with me, I thought, in a glass-half-full kind of way. More alerts meant more options. And the more options I had the more likely one would be a keeper.

The first message was from a guy who lived across the country and worked in nanotechnology. He sometimes had nanotechnology conferences where I lived so, if I wanted, he could give me a shout one night when he was in my area. No, thanks.

Next was one from a self-described "bad boy with an edge" who only had two pictures, both of his chest. In one, he was wearing what looked like a denim jumper zipped down to his navel. What in the actual hell? How did he zip up that thing with all that chest hair? I kept scrolling.

A profile picture of a tiger.

Another tiger.

A poster of Homer Simpson.

"Not looking for anything serious."

"Just checking this out."

"Just checking this out."

I saw a lot of acronyms and had no sweet clue what they meant. I was honestly too scared to google them.

By the time I was done, my great mood had turned pretty sour. I'd just spent an hour going through multiple messages and comments and not one was from someone I wanted to pursue. They were either too young, too creepy, too married or clearly hadn't read my profile.

If they weren't going to read my profile, why had I bothered putting so much effort into it in the first place? I'd tried so hard to come across as a normal, fun woman— someone who a normal, fun man would want to date—but what was the point if no one was going to read it? I might as well write what I really thought.

I spent the rest of the morning rewriting my profile but couldn't quite work up the nerve to post it. This was the real me and if people didn't like it, on the one hand too bad, but on the other, I'd be alone forever. I took a deep breath, closed my eyes and hit save.

> **My self-summary:**
> *I have a very dry sense of humour. I like travelling, as evidenced by my photos, and eating, also evidenced by the less-than-flattering (but true-to-life) photo of me eating a donut. I do not enjoy camping. I figure I'd let you know now before you read too far. I know you're probably shocked because everyone on here loves camping, but I do not. At all. To be physically attracted to someone is important to me (it's the reality), but equally important is a sense of humour and an open mind. I promise that in return.*
>
> *PS: To me, an open mind does not mean I'm interested in hooking up with married men. I guess I have to clarify that now.*
>
> **Favourite movies, books, shows, food:**
> *I'm not entirely convinced that this information would make a difference to anyone.*
>
> **The five things I could never do without:**
> *Family, friends, coffee, Netflix, coffee.*

You should message me if:

Please don't message me if you're twenty-one. I'm forty-three. You could literally be my son. Smoking is a deal breaker. That means you should not contact me if you smoke. Or if you want to have an affair. Also, I will not give you my phone number or come over tonight.

PS: Even if you're trying to quit, that still means you smoke.

Let's see how this works.

Chapter 20

February 1st

Monday hit me like a punch in the face. When my alarm went off, I almost started crying. I hated my job so much. I automatically looked at my phone to see if I had any messages and, unsurprisingly, I didn't.

Maybe keeping it real wasn't the best plan after all.

I was honestly a bit torn. Was not having to talk to idiots better than the fact that none of the idiots wanted to talk to me anymore? I really didn't know.

I spent the entire morning at work checking my phone, wrapped in an emotional fusion of relief and indignation.

Finally, just before lunch, I heard my phone vibrate in my purse. Terry was busy telling yet another person about the amazing weekend he'd had with all his "lady friends" so I slipped it out to take a look.

Your profile is great. Looks like you're really enjoying that donut. LOL. I also like to watch Netflix. What are you binging?

Well, this has potential. A full sentence AND he'd obviously read my new and improved profile. I also liked how he asked something original and not, "How was your weekend?" or, "Do you like great massages?"

I just caught up to the rest of the world and I'm watching You.
Should I have admitted that?

That show freaks me out. That guy could totally exist. I'm Darren, by the way.

Another full sentence. With punctuation! So much promise. Time to dive in and see what he looked like.

I clicked on the little icon of his face, or what appeared to be his face—the picture was small and really blurry. Except, it turned out, it wasn't blurry. He was wearing a motorcycle helmet. And that was his only picture. I mean it was bad enough when a guy wore a hat and sunglasses in all his pictures, but a motorcycle helmet? Come on.

I was just about to tell him I wasn't interested when I had a change of heart. *You know what? Maybe I shouldn't let looks guide me.* Maybe this guy was great and a perfect match. Who knew? I would be the bigger person here and not base my decision on what he looked like. After all, I wished guys would show me that same courtesy. No more being shallow. I was going to give this guy a chance.

I'm Kate. Nice to meet you, Darren. Did you maybe want to meet for a coffee and chat more in person?

I was so proud of myself. What a humanitarian.

That would be great!

He sounded so thrilled! I wondered how many women actually asked him out. Probably not many. I bet I'd made his day.

We made plans to meet for sushi, and not to toot my own horn, but I felt pretty good about myself. If I'd learned anything about online dating so far it was that it was so superficial, and that could be really defeating. If more people were brave like me and took a chance on someone who looked a bit different to what they were expecting, maybe we would all find love just that much quicker.

I picked up my phone, ready to drop it back in my purse, when it vibrated with another alert. I smiled, certain it was Darren, thanking me again for giving him a chance.

A message popped up:

A bit of homework before our date ☺. *If you could be any animal, which one would you be?*

"If you could be any animal, which one would you be?" I asked Cody and Nate like it was a perfectly normal lunchtime question.

Cody looked up from his Thai takeout. "What kind of question is that?"

"Just a question. Trying to make small talk."

"A tiger, for sure," Nate said, like he was asked this question every day.

Cody shoved a forkful of food in his mouth as he often did right before speaking. "Why a tiger?"

"Dude, gross, swallow your food. I can't understand what you're saying," Nate said.

Cody made a big deal out of swallowing and loudly overenunciated, *"Why. A. Tiger?"*

Nate sat back. "Because they're cool. And tough. And powerful. King of the jungle, you know? That's me. I basically run this place."

Terry chose this point to walk into the lunchroom and

we all looked like we'd been caught red-handed. He liked to stand outside and listen to see if people were talking about him and we sometimes forgot and talked freely like normal people did at their place of work. Not that we were talking about him, but in his mind, everyone was always talking about him so, either way, we were guilty.

"First off," Terry said, "the lion is the king of the jungle. And two, you don't run this place, ass-wipe."

"I was joking," Nate said as he rolled his eyes. (He wasn't.)

Terry sat down and very deliberately set a small bottle of what appeared to be prescription pills on the table. We glanced at them and then at one another, knowing he wanted us to ask what they were for. I seriously considered picking up my half-eaten lunch and walking out; I really didn't feel like playing this game today. Cody and Nate were eating the rest of their lunches as fast as they could, clearly thinking the same thing.

Terry sat back in his chair and pretended to watch whatever game show was on TV, sneaking glances at his pill bottle, no doubt wondering if it was placed in the perfect spot for us to see. He picked it up, seemingly absently, and looked at the label. Then he put it down again and sighed. The fact that we were not asking him what they were for was clearly killing him, which actually made this much more entertaining than I'd thought it would be.

Nate slowly looked down at the pill bottle and then up at Terry. "Anything exciting planned for tonight, Kate?" he asked.

Terry picked up the pill bottle and stormed out.

"That was so worth the interruption," I said as we all laughed.

Cody shook his head. "What a tool, why bring them in here? He didn't even take one."

"Now I kind of want to know what they're for," I said in mock frustration.

"Syphilis. For sure," Nate said. He took his dishes to the sink and walked out.

Cody leaned in. "Speaking of syphilis, how's the online dating going?"

"How did you know I was online dating?" I asked, my face reddening.

He sat back and crossed his arms. "I'm not giving up my sources."

"I'm sure you saw my profile," I said, trying to sound like I didn't care. "It's not a secret that you're on all of them."

"Maybe. So, how's it going?"

"Please don't tell anyone. I don't want people to know yet."

"I won't. If you tell me how it's going. And, by the way, online dating is very socially accepted now."

I winced. "I know, and no offence, I just haven't fully accepted that it's what I should be doing." I paused, wondering how much I should tell him or, in other words, how much I wanted the rest of the office to know. "It's not going great," I said finally.

"Like not great in the quality of bangs or not great in the quantity?"

"What?" I said, genuinely confused.

"How many dudes have you banged so far?"

"Zero."

"Well, you're doing it wrong then." He laughed.

"You sound like Julie," I said and then added, "No, I'm not giving you her number. I'm not online dating to 'bang dudes,' I'm doing it to find a relationship. I know that's probably difficult for you to understand."

"I understand the concept—" he grinned "—I just don't understand the practice."

I got up to leave but stopped and sat back down again. "Can I ask you something?"

"Sure."

"For real. Like seriously?"

"Sure. For real. Like seriously," he mocked.

"What did you think of my profile?"

He leaned back, hands behind his head, biceps flexed beneath his dress shirt. He really was quite attractive if you could get past the fact that he was kind of a pig. "I never read the profiles."

Why didn't that surprise me? "Well, can you read mine and tell me what you think?"

"I thought you didn't want to attract a guy like me."

"I don't. But you're still a guy. I wouldn't mind getting a guy's opinion."

He snorted. "Awwwkwarrrd."

"For the love of… Just pretend you're looking for a relationship and you don't know it's me."

He took out his phone. "Which one are you on again?"

"Here, use mine." I handed him my phone.

As he read, I watched his face but, as always, I couldn't

tell what he was thinking. One of Cody's superpowers was keeping his face devoid of emotion whenever he wanted. It served him well at work and in his personal life. He could turn his feelings on and off like a faucet.

After what seemed like forever, he slid the phone back to me across the table.

"It's good."

"What do you mean, 'good'? Like 'well-written' good? 'I'd like to meet her' good? What kind of good?"

"It's good. It's funny. If I were looking for a long-term relationship, and I didn't know it was you, I might send you a message."

"But?"

"No buts."

I looked at him skeptically. I knew him. I knew there was a but.

"Fine." He gave in. "It's just that I know your sense of humour because I know you. It's very dry, which is cool, *but* for those who don't know you, it can come off a bit abrupt, or even cold sometimes—"

I opened my mouth to object.

"Just wait, I know it's your humour. But it took me a while to get it."

"So, you're trying to say…"

"I'm trying to say your profile, to me, is funny because I know you, but to someone who doesn't…"

"What the hell? Shouldn't I be myself?" My embarrassment came out as anger. "And if someone doesn't like that, doesn't that mean I shouldn't be with them anyway?"

He shrugged. "I guess. Maybe try to be a bit nicer.

You'll get more likes that way. You know, attract more bees with honey or whatever? It's like you'll attract more dudes with sweetness."

"Fake sweetness. And it's flies. You attract more flies with honey."

"Whatever," he said. "The point is, once you attract the *flies*, then you can be more like… you. Also, guys don't like girls who are funnier than they are. They like to be the funny ones. So maybe tone down the humour just a bit."

"You're kidding me. Your advice is to pretend I'm a generic, girly, sweet young thing who doesn't want to show up her man by being too opinionated and funny. And then, once I've tricked him into meeting me, I'm allowed to start showing him who I really am?"

"Basically, yes. Or, you know, don't." He started to get up, likely regretting agreeing to participate in this unfortunate conversation.

"Don't what? Show him who I really am?"

"Yeah," he said and sighed, sitting back down. "Just be agreeable. Men like a woman who agrees with them. I mean did you ever wonder why you and I never hooked up?"

"Not really."

"I think you're great," he continued anyway, "fun to work with, fun to party with, good looking in a 'not hot' sort of way."

"Thanks?"

"But you'd be more my type in the dateable sense if you didn't argue so much."

"This is total bullshit!" I crossed my arms and sat back in a huff.

"And you swear *a lot*."

"Well." I pushed away from the table, scraping the chair against the floor aggressively. "Thank you *so* much for your insight."

He held up his hands in protest. "You asked."

"Yes, yes, I did. That was clearly my mistake."

"Hey, don't be mad." He looked at me with sad puppy eyes. "I was just being honest. Aren't you chicks always saying we should be more honest?"

"That we are," I said. "I guess us 'chicks' need to think that through."

I took my dishes off the table, shoved them into the dishwasher and slammed the dishwasher door closed. I knew I was being childish, but I couldn't stop. I wanted to be myself, but a small part of me couldn't help but think that Cody was right. Maybe men didn't like it when a woman was too opinionated and argumentative. My dad had left my mom for those very reasons. My mind instantly went to Peter. Maybe he had been right all those years ago. I probably still did need to work on myself more.

"Drinks after work?" Cody said as I left the lunchroom.

"No," I said loudly as I stomped out of the kitchen. The last thing I wanted was for him to think he was right.

After that, work didn't get much better. Terry, I guess because the prescription bottle game hadn't gotten him the attention he'd wanted, spent the rest of the day being a total asshole to anyone who deigned to speak to him about anything.

As soon as 5:00 p.m. hit, my computer was off, my

phone was in my purse, and I was sneaking out the back door so I didn't have to walk past Terry's office. On the odd occasions when he was still working at the end of the day, if he noticed anyone leaving, he liked to call them in and talk about absolutely nothing, just to prove he was still at his desk.

I looked out the window; it was snowing—light, fluffy flakes that would have been welcome in December but that I had really had enough of now that it was February. *Two more months of winter,* I told myself, even though I knew it would be closer to four.

Where would I be in June? Would I have found someone to kiss? Or would I be in panic mode, scraping the bottom of the barrel? I traced the drop of a melted snowflake with my finger, lost in thought, not wanting to go outside because I'd forgotten a hat. Again.

"I hope that prescription is for Terry's personality," Cody said, and I jumped.

"If only we were so lucky."

"Are we cool?" He gave me a playful punch on the arm, his version of "sorry."

I looked down so he couldn't see my reddening cheeks. "I overreacted. I did ask for your honest opinion, and that's what I got."

His smile widened. "Drinks then?"

"Thanks, but no. I just want to go home. It's been a day. All I want to do is put my pyjamas on and settle in with a good book." Except, instead of book, I meant phone. He didn't have to know I was looking forward to seeing what kind of messages I'd gotten on the dating site. I hadn't had a chance to check and I was actually kind of excited again to see what was going on.

"Well, I'm not going without you," he said, pouting. "Next time then." He turned back to walk down the hall.

"For sure," I said. "See ya."

"See ya."

As he turned the corner, I heard him calling down the hall, "Hey, Nate, want to go for a drink?"

Chapter 21

I arrived home, dropped my purse on the floor, and removed my pants, shoes, shirt and bra as I walked down the hall. Fifteen seconds later, I was in my pyjamas. My clothes marked a trail down the hallway that, in a movie, would have been an intro to a steamy sex scene but, in my life, was just an intro to me sitting on the couch, eating cereal for supper and watching TV.

I slipped on my fuzzy socks, gathered my hair up into a messy bun and settled in, ready to binge while I scrolled through potential matches.

Mittens joined me on the couch and started pawing my leg. "What do you need, buddy?" I said, scratching his head. "Are you hungry?" I set him on the ground and went into the kitchen to fill his dish, hearing the happy jingle of the bell on his collar as he pranced behind me.

I was just about to settle back onto the couch when the door buzzer screeched, scaring a happily eating Mittens (and me) half to death.

"Who on earth is that?" I grumbled. Everyone knew my evenings were for TV time.

I pushed the intercom button. "Yes?"

"It's Ben."

What was Ben doing here?

"Come on up."

I opened the door and peeked down the hall, waiting for him to come up the stairs.

The stairwell door opened and there he was, breathing heavily, nose red from the cold.

"Hey," I said. "Whatcha got there?"

"I brought you something." He handed me a cloth bag from the farmers' market.

"Vegetables?"

He laughed. "No, books. Can I come in?"

"Oh, sure. Sorry, I'm being rude. I don't have guests that often." I stepped aside and let him through the door.

He walked in and took his hat off, balling it up and stuffing it in his jacket pocket.

"So," he said.

"So…"

What was happening?

"So… these books are for…" I opened the bag and pulled one out, putting both the bag and the book on the table.

"Oh!" he said, suddenly animated. "They're about anxiety. I found they really helped me when I was trying to figure out my own stuff. I thought they might help you, you know, if you ever feel like you're having a panic attack again."

"That's so kind," I said. "How thoughtful, thank you so much."

We both reached into the bag at the same time and our fingers brushed.

Ben jerked his hand back like it had been burned.

"You're welcome. I've been thinking about you, I mean your panic attack, and I just wanted to make sure you had all the tools available to you." He rubbed the back of his neck. "These books are really good. They helped me a lot."

"This is so nice of you," I said, genuinely touched.

"Yeah. Thanks. That's what I'm here for." He looked up and the side of his mouth rose in a half-grin. "If you need anything, I'm always here for you. And everyone, you know, I'm here for everyone. To help."

"Did you want to stay for a coffee or a drink or something? I know you're a beer guy, but I have some pretty decent wine."

"Thanks, but no," he said, pulling his hat out of his pocket and tugging on his gloves. "I have an early start tomorrow. I just wanted to drop these off."

"Okay." I walked with him toward the door. "Well, thanks again. I really appreciate it. When did you want them back?"

"Oh, whenever." He opened the door and stepped into the hall, where the temperature was much cooler than inside my cozy apartment. "Whenever you're done with them."

"Okay, thanks."

"You're welcome." He paused. "How's the dating going?"

"It's going okay." I shrugged. "I haven't found someone to kiss yet."

"There's still time." He smiled and turned to leave. I watched him walk toward the stairwell door.

"Ben?" I called when he was halfway down the hall.

He turned. "Yeah?"

"You're a really great friend."

He smiled and turned away. "Yeah. I know."

Chapter 22

Valentine's Day

Hi Kate,
Happy Valentine's Day! I liked your profile. Maybe we could chat?
Joe.

Hi Kate,
Just wanted to check to see if you got my message.
I'm a great guy once you get to know me.
What's the harm in giving me a chance?
Joe.

Sorry, Joe, I was busy. Happy Valentine's Day to you too. How's your night going?

Hi Kate,
Thanks for the message! My night is going great. How is your night going?
Joe.

Your profile says you're married, Joe. Are you married?

Yes. I'm very honest about that on my profile.

Thanks for being honest, but I'm not interested in married men. I'm very honest about that on my profile.

May I ask why not?

Because I don't want to be part of an affair.

It's not an affair.

Does your wife know you're trying to hook up with women online?

No.

Then it's an affair.

My wife doesn't live in this country, so it's okay.

That doesn't actually mean it's okay.

I have needs, like every man, and I need to have those needs met.

Sorry, I'm not interested.

I think you're being a prude.

I think you should stop contacting me.

Bitch.

Chapter 23

Julie slouched in an old, faded lounger with her feet up on her coffee table and scrolled through the phone numbers she'd saved. She had a folder for Tinder matches. And one for OkCupid. One for Bumble. One for every dating site. The folders said things like "Work" and "Family." No one else needed to know how many men she'd slept with.

Her latest text had been from a charming twenty-two-year-old who'd told her that age didn't matter when you were looking for some "quick fun." She liked them young, but that was going a bit far. And if she was going to have "fun" with a younger guy, it had better not be quick.

She put her phone down on the table and took a sip of wine. She didn't need anyone tonight. Tonight, she could just be alone. Even if it was Friday.

She hadn't admitted this to anyone yet, not even fully to herself, but there was a slight possibility she might be a bit out of control. What had started as something fun had turned into a full-time job. She was finding it challenging to keep all the men straight. This had become painfully obvious a week ago when her pick of the night had arrived and she'd realized they'd actually already met (and slept together) a couple of months previous. He hadn't seemed to remember her though or, if he had, he hadn't cared. Why would he? It wasn't like guys were that picky about who they fucked.

She'd opened the door in a white button-down shirt, a short plaid skirt and white knee-high socks (a fan favourite) and stepped back a bit when she'd recognized his face. He hadn't been looking at her face, though, so that might have been where the disconnect had happened. He'd also been very high. He'd shoved a bottle of wine into her hands and waited to be invited in, swaying back and forth on unsteady feet.

Despite having a one-time-only rule, she'd gone along with it. She had shaved her legs after all and had already drunk half a bottle of wine. She didn't want to waste smooth legs and a good buzz. And if he was too high to recognize her, it didn't really count as a second time, right? She couldn't for the life of her remember if he was any good or not. Turned out he wasn't. She really was going to have to start taking better notes.

After a couple more glasses of wine and listening to a rambling treatise on why action movies were windows into a person's soul, she told him to shut up and took off her top. He was happy to oblige but was so dazed and sloppy she ended up faking a climax just so he'd stop licking her face.

And, to make things worse, he then fell asleep. In her bed. The worst possible outcome. She didn't know what to do. This guy would not wake up. She shoved him and poked him and called his name, or what she thought was his name. But nothing. He just lay there snoring and drooling on one of her pillows. She dragged her comforter to the couch to try to sleep unencumbered by sweaty, hairy arms.

She gave him a couple of hours while she stewed in her own rage and resentment; then that was it. She couldn't wait any longer. Being kind was for other people. Turned out a glass of water could do wonders when thrown on a sleeping man.

She smiled in spite of herself at the memory. At least she hadn't had to ghost him like all the other guys who wanted to see her again. Maybe pissing them off when it was over was the way to go. It sure was less messy. Except for the cleaning up the water part.

Her smile faded and she shifted her tired bones so her face was on her oversized pillow, her feet tucked in behind her. *When did this become my life?* she wondered. Endless, meaningless sex with men, none of whom she knew anything about. Not that sex had to mean something; she was fine with just enjoying it for what it was, but at some point it had crossed the line from an enjoyable pastime to thoughtless desperation. Desperate to find something. Desperate to feel something different. Desperate not to feel so empty.

Her hand automatically reached towards her glass. She tipped it back without even thinking, the warm liquid filling all the empty spaces. *Sleep will come easier now,* she thought. At least there was that.

Chapter 24

March 17th

I was sitting at my desk on a Wednesday morning when Terry called me into the glass room.

"Sit," he said and closed the sliding door.

I sat in one of the uncomfortable wooden chairs, well aware that everyone who walked by was wondering what I'd done to deserve being asked into the fishbowl of failure. I shifted slightly before opening my notebook.

"So," he started. "I won't take up too much of your time."

He smiled. I smiled, pen at the ready.

"What's up?" I asked, scanning my brain frantically, trying to figure out what I'd done so I could prepare for the fallout.

He leaned in like he was going to share a secret. "You used to have a personal trainer, right?"

"Um… what?" Was I not in trouble?

"A couple of years ago, didn't you go to a personal trainer?"

"I guess so, I mean, yes. I did, yes."

"I'm trying to get back into shape, for my new lady friend," he said.

Gross.

"So, I'd like you to put together a program for me."

"I'm not a personal trainer though," I said. "I went to one. Two years ago. For, like, a month. I don't think I'm qualified to put together a program for you."

"Sure, you are," he said. "How hard can it be? Just whip something up and email it to me." He sat back in his chair. "No squats though, I have bad knees, and—" he looked at my notebook "—are you going to write this down?"

I sighed inwardly, trying desperately not to roll my eyes. Of course I was going to write it down.

I picked up my pen as if in a trance and wrote down all the exercises he "couldn't do" and all the ones he "wouldn't do" and tried to figure out how I was going to make up a program for him if all he liked to do was stretch. How was it suddenly my job to create a workout program for him? And more importantly, why wasn't I saying no?

As I frantically hate-wrote, I couldn't help but be slightly in awe of his cleverness. He knew that by taking me into this room that I would a) be so relieved I wasn't getting in trouble that I would do anything he asked, and b) feel like I had to do it because he was asking me in what appeared to be a professional capacity.

And he was right. I was so stunned at what he was asking, and so confused about how to proceed, that I immediately started obeying. And now, as I was writing down that he didn't need to do lunges because he already had an "ass you could bounce a quarter off of," I knew I was too far in to go back and say no. He had known that was exactly what would happen. What a jerk.

By the time we were done, I had to clasp my hands together to keep them from shaking. I knew I'd been taken advantage of and I knew he knew it too. And yet, I still didn't say anything. I would still do it. I would create an exercise program for him on my own time, where I basically would have him doing nothing, and he would fail, and it would somehow be my fault.

"Neither of you would ever do something like this," I said to Julie and Ben at lunch. "Julie, you'd tell him to fuck right off and you would still have a job after."

"Dude, I've been fired four times." She unfolded her napkin and placed it on her lap as Ben snort-laughed with a mouth full of water.

"Why can't I stick up for myself?" I said, ignoring her and handing Ben a napkin.

"I think the question you need to be asking is why do you need to in this circumstance?" Ben said after he recovered. "You shouldn't have to tell your boss you can't make him an exercise program because he shouldn't be asking you in the first place. I've said it before, but something is seriously wrong with that guy. You need to leave."

"I know," I said and hung my head. "But what if I can't find anything? What if no one will hire me? What if I hate the new place more than I hate this place?"

"Your new place couldn't possibly be worse. You deserve better than this. They're lucky to have you," he said, emphasizing his point by poking me gently with his fork.

We'd had this conversation many times. Every time we met for lunch, in fact. I was surprised they put up with it. I would have told myself to stop whining a long time ago. I knew I needed to leave, but I just couldn't find the energy, or, more accurately, I couldn't find the courage to end something I had put so much time and effort into. I don't like to leave things. I don't like to feel like a quitter.

I wanted to ask Julie how she'd had the courage to quit all the jobs she'd quit when she wasn't happy. How she didn't allow herself to be pushed around by bosses who were jerks. How she started over again and again with new jobs, new people and new places without even batting an eye. Our jobs were perfect metaphors for our relationships.

Instead, I asked her: "If you were an animal, what kind of animal would you be?"

"What," she looked up, "are you talking about?"

"I'm finally going out on Friday with that guy I was telling you about. He asked me that question."

"What did you tell him?" Ben asked, his attention consumed with examining the old record covers on the wall.

"I said a bird. He said it meant something spiritual and he would tell me what that was tonight."

"He'd better be hot," Julie said, rolling her eyes.

"Well, I'm not sure what he looks like exactly."

"Meaning?"

"So… the thing is the only picture I have of him is one where he's wearing a motorcycle helmet."

Julie dropped her fork onto the table with a clatter. "Jesus, Kate," she said. "I've warned you about this. The men who don't show pictures of themselves are already being deceptive. If he can't be honest at the beginning and show what he really looks like, how can you know if he's ever being honest with you?"

"But maybe he's a really nice guy," I said. "I don't like to be judged by my looks alone. I want to give everyone a chance."

"That's your problem." She shook her head. "It's a nice idea in theory, but if you give everyone a chance, you're going to waste so much time that you'll get frustrated. What if he's repulsive?"

"What if he's not?"

"Fine," she said, giving up. "I just hope he shows up for your date in a motorcycle helmet or you're not going to know who you're meeting."

Luckily, the server came over to take our order and I didn't have to admit that I hadn't considered that possibility.

"What are you both getting?" I asked as the server waited with her hand on her hip.

"The usual," Ben said and then looked up at the server. "Hamburger and fries, please."

Julie closed her menu and handed it to the server. "Quinoa salad, please." Everyone stared expectantly at me. "Kate, we come here every month, how do you not know what you want?"

"I know, I know. I just can't decide today. Veggie flatbread," I said and slid my menu across the table. "No, wait. Cheeseburger. No, flatbread." I looked up at the server sheepishly. "What would you recommend?"

The server hated me.

"You've had both on multiple occasions," she said.

"Yes, but what would *you* recommend?"

She sighed. "Flatbread, I guess."

I paused to consider this. "Cheeseburger, please," I said sweetly. "With yam fries."

"That was kind of bitchy," Julie said after the server walked away.

"Yeah, I feel kind of bitchy today."

As we waited, I looked around the crowded tavern. We said we came here because we liked the food, but Julie and I both knew we came here because it was almost always full of men. And we both loved a man in a business suit. Ben came because it had the best selection of craft beer in the city. He also liked it because the building was old and cool and used to be a bank in the twenties. I knew this because he said, "Did you know Vic's Tavern used to be a bank in the twenties?" almost every time we came here.

It was also always very loud. The thing about men in business suits was that they often worked in a profession that involved actual business, which meant they were high achievers, or wanted to be, and so they were always trying to impress. Talking over each other, interrupting, laughing loudly. Usually I didn't mind this; in fact, it often energized me in a weird way. But today I couldn't take it.

"Could I please get a glass of the Shiraz? Just the five-ounce," I asked the server as she walked by.

She looked at Julie. "Anything for—"

"Cab sauv, nine ounces," she interrupted without thinking about it. "Please." She looked at me with a large grin. "Yes! Lunch drinks. I love lunch drinks. You never drink at lunch."

"You love drinks no matter what time it is."

"Pile O'Bones White IPA, please," Ben said with a grin. "What's the occasion?"

"I'm just irritable," I said irritably.

"You're always irritable," Julie said. "That's not an occasion."

I tilted my head and gave her a look. "Fine. I'm nervous about my date on Friday."

"Right, with motorcycle guy." Our wine came and she grabbed her glass and took a sip.

"His *name* is Darren."

"I'm actually really curious to hear about what he looks like," she said, swirling her wine in her glass. "Can you sneak in a short video when you get there? Facebook Live?"

"Absolutely not."

"I was kidding. Mostly." She grinned. "Just remember, don't get your hopes up. I don't want you to get weepy every time a guy turns out to be a dud. There are a lot of duds out there."

"Thanks, you're making me feel a lot better," I said dryly. "Who knows, if it doesn't work out, maybe we'll just become friends. I could always use more guy friends."

She laughed. "Right."

"Here we go." Ben rolled his eyes.

"What?"

"Men and women can't be friends." Julie sipped her wine.

"What do you mean?" I said. "I have guy friends. You have guy friends."

"I don't have guy friends."

"Well, I do."

"No, you don't."

She was starting to piss me off. "If you plan on being deliberately vague for the rest of lunch, I'm leaving."

She paused while our food arrived, waited until the server left and took another sip of wine. "What's my favourite movie?"

"*Toy Story*?" I said and Ben laughed.

"*When Harry Met Sally*," she said, ignoring me. "I love it because the question the movie dissects, or, I guess, dissected over two decades ago was: can men and women be friends? Like, really friends. Without the sex and stuff. And, just to be clear, when I say friends, I mean close friends who hang out all the time. Not just friends you chat with at the office or hang out with sometimes in a group setting."

I nodded and shoved a fry in my mouth. "Got it."

"I used to think it was a misconception that when girls and guys are friends, at least one of them wants to have sex and the sexual tension just hangs around and gets in the way of things. Or they actually do have sex and completely mess up the relationship. I would always scoff and shake my head because I had plenty of friendships with guys where there wasn't any sex or sexual feelings at all." She took a bite of salad and then pointed at me with her fork.

"But when I actually thought about it and went through my list of 'close guy friends,' I realized that, for all of them, at least one of the following criteria applied: I wanted to fuck them—"

I winced and looked around self-consciously while Ben

rubbed the back of his neck. Julie got louder when she drank and the room had gotten noticeably quieter.

"Oh, God," she said to both of us. "Don't be so sensitive." She leaned in closer and, thankfully, also brought her voice down. "Either I wanted to *sleep with* them or they wanted to *sleep with* me. *Or* we actually did sleep together and were a) no longer friends, b) not as good friends as we were before, or c) still friends but we both just pretended it didn't happen. Every. Single. One."

"So, that's you," I said, not wanting to buy into her cynicism.

"No, that's everyone. I honestly don't believe that any heterosexual man and woman can be close friends without some sort of sex or sexual tension on one or both sides."

"But I have guy friends."

"Cody and Nate don't count. You only hang out with them at work. And, honestly, I bet both of them would sleep with you in a second if you wanted to."

"Disagree. What about Ben?"

Ben held up his hands as if to say please don't bring me into this.

"Ben's my brother, he doesn't count."

"How so?"

"Because that means he's like your brother and you obviously can't have sex with your brother."

Ben put his head in his hands and emitted a low groan. "Please wake up from this nightmare," he whispered.

"Jesse," I said. "We're friends."

She gave me a skeptical look.

"What?" I lowered my eyes.

"You totally want to f— *sleep with* Jesse."

I tried to look shocked. "What? I do not! What?"

She looked at me knowingly.

"Shut up!" I sat back and crossed my arms. "This just makes me sad. I think you're wrong."

"Hey, don't shoot the messenger." She drained her wine and plunked the glass on the table.

"What about friends with benefits?" I asked.

"Do you really think you can do that again? Remember when you tried and thought it was fun and then, of course, you wanted more but then found out he'd started dating someone and it was 'pretty serious' and you cried for a literal month?"

"This lunch is depressing," I sulked.

"And uncomfortable?" Ben offered.

"Sorry, I'm just preparing you for the real world of dating," Julie said. "It's not pretty."

We finished our meals in silence and motioned to the server for our bill.

"I only want to protect you, you know," Julie said as we got up to leave. "You're my best friend and I love you. I don't want you to get hurt."

"I know," I said as I put on my coat and then gave her a hug. "I just don't think it's the same for everyone. I still have hope that I'm going to find someone. And I still have hope for friendship as a consolation prize. I have to. Or else I'm doing this all for nothing."

"I get that," she said. "Oh, I forgot to mention something." She dug into her purse and pulled out her phone. "Some group on Facebook is trying to set the world record for speed dating next month. We should totally go."

"Seriously?" I said. "You want to do something like that?"

"Well, I wouldn't be going to find my soul mate, I'd be going for you. And also to laugh at people. If anything, it's sure to be entertaining."

"It's probably just going to be a bunch of half-naked twenty-year-old girls," I said.

"No, it says right here: 'all ages,' and when you sign up, you have to select your age range so there's no chance of you getting put with the twenty-year-olds. Unless you want to be—wink, wink," she said, leering at me.

I smiled, my mood slightly improving. If I was going to do this, I might as well try everything. "Sure, why not? You're right, it'll definitely be an experience. What better way to try speed dating for the first time than to attempt a world record?"

"It'll probably be a train wreck," she said. "But it might be fun." A spark flickered in her eyes.

"I can sign us up tonight," I said. "And I'm signing us both up. You're not ditching me for the twenty-year-old group." I grabbed my emergency umbrella and moved toward the door. The snow had finally disappeared (for now), which meant we were moving into the season of surprise rain showers. The possibility of an early spring this year, and now something new to try, had turned my nervousness into hope.

"Sign Ben up as well," she said with a wicked grin.

"That would be a hard no." Ben held the door open for us as we walked out.

"Come on," I begged. "It'll be fun. Do it for me? I'll need the support."

Ben's eyes softened as they met mine. "Fine." He sighed. "For you. And for the half-naked twenty-year-olds," he added with a grin.

We hugged and went our opposite ways and I briefly wondered what I'd gotten myself into. Then, smiling in anticipation, I tucked my umbrella into my purse, breathed in the almost-spring air and, with a skip in my step, made my way back to work.

Chapter 25

March 19th

Friday night, I was late getting home from work as usual and had to rush around to get ready for my date with Darren. I ran into my bedroom, gave Mittens a quick pet (and apology), tore off my work clothes and threw on a pair of jeans I found on my floor. I grabbed the only nice-ish shirt that wasn't wrinkled and put it on as I walked into the bathroom. I didn't have time to do my make-up, so I just blotted my face, ran my fingers through my curly hair and was ready to go. Mittens howled with displeasure as I left, slamming the door behind me.

While I didn't find shoving a giant piece of food in my mouth with utensils I could barely operate the best choice for a first date, I had agreed to sushi immediately. Mostly because I didn't have a better idea, nor did I want to think of one.

The smell of rice and soy sauce made my stomach growl as I walked into the restaurant. The walls were painted a deep red, with Japanese characters stenciled in gold. It was warm and cozy and I started to relax. This seemed like a great little place.

The host led me to where Darren was sitting in a booth, facing the window. At least I assumed it was Darren; he wasn't wearing a motorcycle helmet. He smiled when I walked in and stood like a gentleman.

I tried to think of how to describe him so I could accurately report back to Julie, but the only word that came to mind was "average." He had short, sandy-blond hair and small, closely set blue eyes. He was of medium build and height. Average. That was it. I could do average though. I allowed a tiny bubble of hope to float to the surface.

"Hey there!" he said enthusiastically and then, oh God, gave me a big hug.

"Hey there, yourself," I said, my voice muffled because my face was pressed into his chest. I tried to pull away and failed.

"I'm Darren," he said, finally releasing me.

"I hope so." I smiled wide, hoping it made me look less embarrassed. "I'm Kate." I stuck out my hand out of habit and then slowly dropped it down by my side.

He barked out a laugh. "Oh, I think that ship has sailed!"

Indeed.

I felt like everyone was looking at us. Mostly because everyone was. A couple of twenty-somethings whispered to each other behind their hands and giggled. *Stupid kids,* I thought and then forced a smile and looked up.

"This is a nice place," I said. "I've never been here before."

He slid a menu across the table. "It's one of my favourites. Do you like green tea? I ordered us a pot."

"I do." (I don't.) "That sounds lovely." *Lovely?*

While he was standing, he'd taken off his jacket to reveal a white T-shirt with a Molson Canadian logo and the "I am Canadian" branding from the early 2000s on it. And not in an "ironic hipster" way, more in an "I only wear clothes I get for free in a case of beer" way. I mean I wasn't dressed up, but at least I'd tried a bit. A forty-five-year-old man was not really pulling this look off. Whatever this look was.

I silently sighed and told myself to stop judging. He seemed nice. I needed to get out of my head, let go of my expectations and relax. Who knew where this would go? Nowhere if I kept being a jerk about everything.

The green tea came and I took a sip, trying to pretend it was delicious and I hadn't just burnt my tongue. He went through the menu and told me what was good and what was *really* good and he ordered for me when I couldn't decide.

After the server left, I looked down at my tea, suddenly shy. I could feel him staring and it was making me uncomfortable. I forced myself to look up and smile, waiting for him to say something. He didn't though. He just stared and smiled. He wasn't even drinking his tea, which was making me even more uncomfortable.

"So," I began because he clearly wasn't going to. "What does your animal mean?" I was kind of looking forward to finding out what wanting to be a bird meant, so maybe if I brought up his animal, he would tell me.

Instead, he talked for twenty minutes about how he was a cheetah and how that meant he was strong, independent and adventurous. He even did a bit of a meow-snarl combo thing, which was probably supposed to be sexy but came off more like he had something stuck in his throat.

While he talked about himself, he fitted in no less than three stories about the many times in his life when birds had been inexplicably attracted to him, including once when an owl had landed on his head.

"But aren't owls really big?" I asked.

"This one wasn't," he said and seamlessly segued into a story about the time a bird flew into his car. "It got stuck under the dash and was there for days until it just flew out and sat on my shoulder while I was driving to work."

"It just sat on your shoulder?"

"Yeah, just sat there, quiet as could be." He tipped his head and smiled.

"It was still alive after being under your dashboard for days?"

"Sure was."

"Interesting."

"I've always attracted birds; I guess they just really like me." He winked.

Even though I now understood that he'd clearly just wanted to know what kind of animal I'd be so he could fit it into his stories somehow, I thought there was a small chance that he actually did know what it meant. So, despite my better judgement, I asked.

"Oh, I don't know," he said. "You, like, want to be free or something."

And there you had it.

The rest of the date was more of the same. More bird

stories. More innocuously odd behaviours that I couldn't quite reconcile. At one point, he told me that honesty was the quality he valued most, and seconds later he took a call and told the person on the other end he was at a doctor's appointment.

By the time an hour rolled around, I just wanted to leave. Despite Julie's cynicism, I was kind of hoping we could have been friends if the date didn't work out, but I didn't think I could put up with this on a regular basis.

Not only did he not ask me any questions about my life, but whenever I tried to contribute to the conversation, he just smiled and nodded and looked over my head like he was waiting for me to finish so he could tell me another bird story.

"Well," I finally said, clearing my throat. "I have a lot to do tomorrow so I guess I should call it a night."

"Oh, that's too bad," he said. "I was hoping we could go somewhere for drinks."

No way.

I smiled and shrugged noncommittally.

We both got up and the date officially ended with another suffocating hug and a promise to text me soon because he thought the date went really well and would love to see me again.

"Me too," I lied before I knew it was coming out.

What the hell is wrong with me?

He walked me out, and in front of the window, in full view of everyone at the restaurant, performed some sort of low, sweeping bow.

"Goodnight, my sweet," he said and reached for my hand.

Not wanting him to kiss it, I pretended I didn't see him reach and, instead, managed to execute a flippy kind of wave.

Don't say, "See you," don't say, "See you," don't say, "See you."

"See you!" I said and hung my head. I was having a *really* hard time with this saying "no" thing.

I walked to the parking lot and prayed he would never text me again. Unfortunately, when I got in my car and took my phone out of my purse, I found he already had.

I had a great time tonight. When can I see you again?

Never? I honestly didn't know what to do. I didn't want to not answer, but I certainly didn't want to see him again. But what would I say if he asked why? I thought you were weird? It was true but not very kind.

I hadn't realized how much harder a "no" would be once I'd actually met the person. Clearly it was way too hard for me to say it to his face.

Did I tell the truth and risk being called a bitch (or worse)? Or did I not say anything? I wanted to call Julie, but I knew what she'd say. I needed a guy's perspective, so I called Ben.

He answered after the fifth ring.

"Sorry," I said, "were you sleeping?" And then I added, "It's Kate."

"No, it's fine," he said, his voice gruff. He had been sleeping.

"I can call back."

"It's okay. Are you okay? Is something wrong?" he asked, like he was trying to temper his concern.

"No… it's… um…" I could feel my face start to flush. "I just wanted your opinion on something. As a guy. And a friend. But mostly as a guy."

"This is about online dating, isn't it?" he said.

"Maybe."

Silence. I'd irritated him. I'd woken him up to ask a silly question about online dating and now he was mad. I instantly regretted my decision.

"Well?" he said, not unkindly.

"Are you mad? Sorry, this is a dumb reason to call."

"Not at all," he said after a brief pause. "Go ahead, I'm happy to help. Seriously. Are you on the date right now?"

"No, I'm driving."

"You shouldn't be talking on your phone while you're driving."

"Thanks, Dad. I'm on hands-free, it's fine."

He laughed and I relaxed.

"You know how at lunch on Wednesday you and Julie were saying how I shouldn't be so nice to people and stop giving everyone a chance?"

"*We* weren't saying that; Julie was saying that. Just to clarify," he said.

I told Ben about the date and how Darren was nice but also how he lied and talked about himself all the time, plus the real reason for the animal question, which Ben found highly amusing, and finally, that I just didn't want to see him again.

"But he thinks the date went great and he's asked to meet up again. What should I do? Should I say I'm sick?"

He laughed. "Well, I'm not an expert at online dating by any means, but I don't know how long you would be able to keep that up before he got suspicious."

"If you were him, what would you want?"

"I'd want to go on another date," he said. "Obviously."

"But if I didn't want to. Would you want me to tell you?"

"Maybe he was nervous and that's why he was weird and talked about himself all the time," he tried. Ben was the kindest person I knew. I should have known he'd give Darren the benefit of the doubt.

"I don't think so," I said. "I think that's probably just the way he is. I'm sure he would be a great catch for someone else, just not for me. Plus... I wasn't attracted to him. At all."

Ben cleared his throat. "Some people don't feel a romantic connection right away, but it can grow over time. Also, if you hadn't noticed, I don't subscribe to Julie's idea that men and women can't be friends. Sometimes they can—" he paused "—and sometimes that friendship develops into something more."

"I get what you're saying, and I love that you always see the best in everyone, but I'm pretty positive there's nothing there. And if I go on another date with him, wouldn't I be leading him on? I know he's interested, and if I'm not and we go out again, I feel like that makes me a jerk."

"I don't think it makes you a jerk; you would never deliberately hurt someone," Ben said, his voice soft. "Why don't you just tell him you're not interested?"

"Because I don't want to be called a bitch again."

"What?" The softness was gone, a hint of anger in its place.

"Never mind."

And then I tried to explain what I couldn't even figure out myself. "I want to reply to everyone who tries because I'd feel terrible if I sent a message to someone and he didn't respond. I want to be kind. The only time I don't reply is if it's some sort of perv message—"

"Wait, what?"

"You have to let me finish this," I said. "Or I'll never figure out what I mean."

"That was confusing, but okay."

"I guess what I'm trying to determine is: do I stop replying if I feel it isn't going anywhere, and feel guilty, or do I keep replying to everyone, give everyone a chance, and end up wanting to shoot myself?"

"That's a bit extreme," he said.

"I know." I sighed dramatically. "Sorry, I'm frustrated. What would you want if you were him?" I tried again.

Silence. One thing I loved about Ben was that he thought things through before he said anything. He didn't automatically say what he thought you wanted to hear. I admired that. But I was also impatient so, at this particular time, it was annoying.

"Well?"

I heard him take a deep breath.

"Sorry, I just want to say the right thing," he said, after what seemed like forever. "I think, because you actually went out with him, you owe him at least a text telling him you're not interested. You don't have to go into detail. Just keep it simple." He cleared his throat. "If I were him, and I went out with you, or someone, and I really liked you, I mean her, and wanted to go out again, I would want to know if she wasn't interested. Otherwise, I would just be waiting to hear back and hoping she felt the same way. And even though it would hurt to hear that she wasn't interested in me, at least I could move on and not keep wondering for the rest of my life what would have happened if I'd just said something—you know, *something*—just so she knew."

"That's oddly specific."

"Well, you asked," he said and cleared his throat again.

"Okay, would you help me with the message?" Silence. "You don't have to," I said. "You've already been a lot of help."

"Of course I will," he said softly. "Of course I'll help."

Chapter 26

Ben

Ben put down his phone, laid back on his pillow and closed his eyes. Of all the things he thought he would be doing tonight, helping Kate with her online dating problems wasn't one of them.

Sleeping was what he wanted to be doing the most—he hadn't slept in weeks. Every time he felt himself slipping into slumber, he unconsciously jolted awake, never wanting to leave the land of the watchful. Waiting for something, afraid he would miss it, not quite knowing what he was waiting for.

He'd been lying in bed, wide awake, when Kate had called and he'd welcomed the distraction from his scattered thoughts. He knew he shouldn't have given away so much when he had advised her what to do, but he also knew she wouldn't have figured out what he was really saying. Never in a million years would she guess he had feelings for her. That he'd had them for years.

His heart sped up just thinking about it, anxiety tightening his chest. This was just one more secret he would have to keep. A part of him he would never let her see. It was safer that way. Kate deserved someone fun and exciting, someone she could share adventures with, not someone who considered it an adventure just leaving the house. Besides, Julie was right; it was clear she didn't see him in a romantic way, he was more like a brother to her than anything else.

He tried to stay in the moment, inhaling deep, diaphragmatic breaths, but his stubborn head wouldn't empty itself of random thoughts. He could be yawning all day, but as soon as he would get to bed, his brain would automatically go back in time and start replaying all the things he wanted to forget. All the things he felt guilty about, all the things he was ashamed of, all the chances he hadn't taken. It was like every night his brain needed to remind him, so he didn't forget how hard his life used to be.

His psychologist had told him he needed to think about his childhood and try to remember good things, remember what they felt like, and focus on those feelings. He didn't remember being a particularly happy child, but he did miss how free he had been, how little responsibility he'd had, how little he'd cared. He'd known he was different then; he just hadn't understood how much.

University had been a godsend. It had taken him a while to get there—three years of working to save up and two more years to get his software development certificate—but, despite going way beyond his comfort zone, he'd known he had to do it. Julie had begged him not to go, her worry for him consistently breaking his heart. That was why he was going. He'd been planning his escape since high school. He was going to go away and he wasn't going to come back. Not because he didn't want to come back, but because he knew it would be better for everyone else. He was finally going to take responsibility for himself and let Julie have a life of her own.

He knew going in that it wasn't going to be easy. He had only applied to universities at the opposite end of the country. Ones in larger city centres—University of British Columbia, University of Toronto—ones where, once he got his computer science degree, he would have a better chance of getting a job.

Having come from a smaller city, he knew moving to a large one would be an adjustment. All of it would. Living somewhere new—living alone, new school, new people, but, more importantly, new Ben. He wanted to do everything new all at once, no matter how anxious he got. Starting over was the only way to do it.

What he didn't admit to himself was the other reason he was leaving. No more Kate in the background, always there but out of reach. No more parties, hanging out until all hours of the morning to make sure she was okay. No more pining over someone who would be shocked if he told her how he really felt.

So, he left, expecting it to be hard, expecting it to be unbearable. Secretly expecting to fail and quit and start working at an electronics store advising people which laptop would be best for their grandson's graduation.

But he was wrong. After a bit of a bumpy start, he really started to enjoy university. He actually thrived. He'd been able to successfully start over at a place where people didn't know him. A place where people didn't know how different he felt.

He was pleasantly surprised to find that, at university, being smart and doing well didn't mean he'd be teased. People actually liked and respected him. People didn't laugh when he was called on in class; they listened. And then they asked questions and they all had a conversation. The other students were impressed by his viewpoints and what he could bring to the table. People stopped him after class and invited him out for coffee and drinks so they could discuss his ideas further. After a couple of months, he realized that these people were actually his friends. He'd finally found friends.

And, best of all, he had found people who were just like him. People who were smart and quiet and different. Some who suffered from anxiety and depression and talked about their experiences. He began to understand what was going on in his brain. And he realized he wasn't alone, and he wasn't broken.

He found a support group and started seeing a psychiatrist and psychologist, meditating and exercising, and things started to change. He started feeling better. He started feeling like his version of normal and he learned how to better manage it when he didn't.

And then one day Julie called, completely destroyed, and he knew it was over. He knew he had to go home. It was his turn to make a sacrifice. It was his turn to take care of her. And he knew he finally could.

Chapter 27

March 22nd

Surprisingly, Darren took the brush-off quite well. Likely thanks to Ben's help with the message I sent. He asked if we could still be friends, and I said of course, knowing I would never hear from him again.

I arrived at work on Monday to find a group of people crowded around Terry's desk and automatically turned around and went the long way. I heard him say something about being an "empath" and I knew, once again, he had taken on someone else's tragedy, hijacking their emotions and selling them as his own. He "feels the feelings of others so strongly," he would say. "It's a curse." I rolled my eyes in disgust. *Not today, Terry.*

My phone dinged as I sat down and I reflexively winced. Oh, the good ol' days when a phone ding meant something exciting like getting a text from a friend or maybe an email saying that a delivery was on its way. Now a ding meant a message from someone in the online dating world. A message that, lately, I could do without.

I clicked on the alert and my wariness was validated:

Hey, sexy, what's your address?

I turned off my phone, put it in my drawer, and got to work.

The next month was more of the same. Julie and I finally found time to go for coffee a couple of weeks before the big speed dating event, though I could barely find the energy to agree to meet up.

So, are we going or what? she texted late that afternoon.

Sure, I guess.

Well, don't sound too excited. I can always make other plans.

Sorry. I'm just tired. And frustrated. And defeated. It's already the end of March and I'm no closer to finding someone than when I started. I do want to meet you for coffee. Let's meet for coffee! Yay, coffee!

She texted that we were meeting at Beans 'n' Brews, and she didn't care how I felt about it, so I guessed it was time to get over the little episode that had happened the last time I was there. I was actually looking forward to seeing Jesse. Even though I still felt a few butterflies in my stomach, I quickly pushed the feeling away. He was just my friend, nothing more.

When I arrived, I was greeted by the comfort of all the familiar smells. Coffee, baking, and just a hint of cinnamon. It had been way too long.

The place was virtually empty. Julie was leaning over the counter and talking to Jesse, completely unaware that the only two men in the shop were both staring at her ass. The rest of the patrons, all women, were doing their best to pretend she wasn't there. She saw me come in, straightened and waved me over.

"Hey girl," she said in a sassy drawl. "What can I get you?"

"Just a mint tea, please," I said.

"What, are you eighty?"

"Last time I had coffee this late it took me three hours to fall asleep."

"So, you *are* eighty." Jesse grinned. "Long time no see, stranger. How's it going? How's the napkin pledge?"

I started to blush, so I quickly turned and looked out the window, pretending I'd heard something. Smooth.

"It's going great!" I said a bit too enthusiastically.

I turned back and looked up. I kept forgetting how cute he was. *And young,* I reminded myself. "How's life with the coffee… and… things?" I stammered like a teenager.

He laughed. "Life with the coffee is good. Speaking of which, here is yours. Well, here's your tea."

"Thanks," I smiled, eyes down.

"What in the hell was that all about?" Julie asked as we headed to our table. "You look like you just came face-to-face with your boyband crush."

I sat down. "Nothing. I was just slightly out of sorts last time I came here. It's a little embarrassing."

That was all it was, right? Embarrassment? That made the most sense.

"And speaking of embarrassment"—I lowered my voice—"let's just keep the whole speed dating thing to ourselves. I don't really want everyone in the world to know."

"Sure," Julie said. "You know no one will care though, right?"

I shrugged.

After we'd been there for about an hour, Jesse walked over and sat down, something he normally did when he didn't have any other customers.

"Any fun plans for the weekend?" He sat back and perched one foot on top of his knee.

"Well—" Julie started.

"We're going speed dating next month!" I interrupted loudly. "A world record breaker."

"WTF?" Julie mouthed.

"Right, I read about that one on Facebook," Jesse said. "Something about the most speed dates at once?"

"Something like that," Julie said. "We're not really going for the record-breaking stuff though. We're going to find Kate's soulmate."

I blushed. Again. And kicked her under the table.

"What?" she said, oblivious. "That's why we're going. Well, that's why you're going. I'm going for the entertainment." She looked at Jesse. "You should come."

"I think it's sold out," I blurted, not knowing at all if it was sold out.

Julie looked at me, her eyes questioning. "I don't think it's sold out."

"I probably can't go anyway," Jesse said. "I'm pretty sure I'll have to work."

"Oh bummer," I said quickly. "It's probably going to be lame." (Lame?)

A customer walked in and Jesse got up. "Good luck." He winked.

"You're weird," Julie said as he walked away. "And I'm tired. Let's roll."

We waved goodbye to Jesse, and as I turned towards the door, I tripped over the throw rug and slammed into a bookshelf.

"I'm fine," I yelled.

Julie looked at me like one would look at someone doing a snow angel in their bathing suit. "You're weird," she said and walked out the door.

Chapter 28

April 16th

It was Friday night and I was a nervous wreck. I didn't know what to expect at this speed dating extravaganza and I got stressed when I didn't know what to expect. Why had I thought this would be a good idea? Thinking of all the people who might be there made me claustrophobic and I hadn't even left my apartment yet.

Work had been a shit show, of course. I had barely been able to focus on anything, so the day had been a cascade of stupid mistakes. Except where I worked, you weren't allowed to make mistakes. You weren't allowed to fail. And if you did, everyone knew about it.

By the end of the day, Terry was so frustrated by my "ineptness" that he told me in front of a boardroom full of people that I was "walking on thin ice" and that there was a lineup of people who would "give up their firstborn" to work for him so I'd better "shape up or ship out." Terry liked clichés, especially when he was angry. He thought the prose and familiarity made for a better performance.

I ended up staying late because if I'd left before Terry,

he would have been even angrier, and he knew that I knew this, so he stayed late as well. The only thing that made me feel better was that I knew it was killing him to stay after 5:00 p.m. on a Friday. But it was more important for him to make a point so, you know, priorities.

I finally won when, at 5:30 p.m., he got up in a huff and barked out something about work taking over his life and now he was going to be late for a super important party. He left without saying goodbye.

I waited an extra fifteen minutes because I knew he would be having a cigarette out front to see if he could catch me leaving. At 5:45 p.m., I slipped out the back door, ran down the stairs, jumped in my car and sped home, mentally preparing what I was going to wear. Julie and Ben would be at my place to pick me up in just over thirty minutes.

Mittens met me at the door with an angry yowl that clearly indicated he was not a fan of me barely having been home over the last few months.

I scooped him up and nuzzled my face in his fur. "I know, buddy, but it's not like I'm actually enjoying myself." It was true. I had been on a handful of dates over the last few weeks and none of them had had even a small chance of developing into anything further. "Maybe tonight will be it," I murmured into his furry neck. "If tonight's the night I find someone to kiss, we will hang out here for the rest of the year, I promise."

I kissed him on the head, set him down and filled his bowl with food. Then I ran into the bathroom to quickly wash my face, reapply my make-up and swipe on some extra deodorant (no time for a shower—thanks, Terry).

I now had exactly ten minutes to find something to wear. But almost everything I owned was in a pile on my floor and was either dirty or needed ironing so, really, my choices were limited. I settled on an old pair of jeans that were a bit too tight around the middle and a slim-fitting, button-up, jersey-style navy top with a toothpaste stain on the cuff. I finished the look off with black strappy heels I could barely walk in and a black clutch that was secured shut with a butterfly clip. I was ready for a night on the town.

Julie and Ben arrived right on time. I buzzed them up and they let themselves in as I was spritzing some rarely used, stale-smelling perfume behind my ears. "Almost ready," I called. "There's beer in the fridge if you want one."

"I brought wine," Julie said as I mouthed her exact words to myself in the mirror. I knew her well.

I heard the fridge open and close and hoped Ben was pleased with my selection. I had picked up some craft beer on my lunch break.

"Nice," I heard him say, and I smiled. He deserved it for all the help he had been lately.

Julie handed me a glass of red as I walked into the living room. "You look great," she said.

"I don't, but thanks for lying. You, on the other hand, look stunning as usual." She was wearing a black-and-white tartan tweed mini-skirt that fit perfectly, a low-cut pale grey blousy top that slid off one shoulder, chunky black heels and a simple gold chain. Her long blonde hair hung in perfect waves, framing a face of such natural beauty she barely had to wear any make-up. She had it so easy. I hated her and loved her all at once.

"You look nice too," I said to Ben. Surprisingly, he was dressed really well in beige khakis and a light blue button-down shirt. I didn't think I'd ever seen him in anything but jeans and a hoodie.

"Thanks." He looked at his feet.

"So," I said to Julie, "do you know anything about this at all? Like what to expect? I've never done one of these things."

"About this one specifically, no. All I know is that they're trying to break a world record for the number of people speed dating at one time. I haven't put a lot of thought into how they're going to do that. The only thing I've thought about is whether or not there'll be a bar."

"What about speed dating in general? How does it work? How many people am I going to have to talk to?" I put the glass of wine on the table, too nervous to drink any.

"I've only been to a couple," she started, "but they've been more or less the same. You sit at a table with a guy, talk for ten minutes, and when the buzzer dings, the guy moves to the next table and you stay seated."

"Why do the men move?"

"I haven't the faintest idea." She seemed to be in a delightful mood.

"Awesome. Shall we?" I said, about to dump my wine down the sink.

"Don't you dare," Julie said and threw it back in a couple of gulps.

"What?" she said as I stared. "Ben's driving."

"Oh, wait." I looked around in a panic. "I need my napkin." I ran back to my room and found it stuffed in the pocket of another pair of jeans. I spread it out, folded it up neatly, shoved it in my purse and ran back to the door. "Okay, ready," I said, out of breath.

"Cool," Julie said. "That wasn't weird at all."

Chapter 29

We arrived at the venue just after doors opened at 7:00 p.m. for what I had assumed would be some sort of relaxed mix and mingle. I was wrong. It was absolute chaos.

The room was packed with about six hundred men and women of all ages—and by "all ages" I mean ninety-five percent were in their twenties, four percent were our age, and about five people were over fifty.

I felt the sorriest for the people over fifty because their speed dating experience was going to be remarkably short. But I also felt sorry for me because, out of the four percent of people who looked to be in their forties, two thirds of them were women.

The room was packed, hot and sweaty and was starting to smell. People were supposed to be mixing, but it looked like most people were just talking to the friend or friends they'd come with. Or they were sitting by themselves, staring at their phone, not making eye contact with anyone around them. Because you wouldn't want to step across the boundaries and actually try to meet someone outside the structure of the speed dating activity. That would have been bananas.

However, what unified everyone was that no one was paying attention to the announcements that were calmly being presented, and not amplified at all, because the host was using a microphone connected to a speaker she was carrying over her arm like a purse.

There was one bar for six hundred people so it was, of course, lined up beyond belief. Except that everyone was in a large, sweaty clump because there wasn't room for an actual line due to the fact that six hundred chairs had been crammed into a room that was not meant for six hundred sit-down guests.

"This is my literal nightmare," Ben said, his face pale and sweaty, as he desperately searched for a place to stand where he wouldn't be touching someone. I steered us over to a corner of the room that was somewhat less packed.

"I guess we're not getting a drink," I said.

"Let's go back outside. I stashed a bottle in the car," Julie said and Ben almost ran to the door.

"What about the line to get in?" I said. "And it's supposed to start soon." I kind of wanted a drink, but I had a really hard time breaking the rules.

"There is no line to get in." Julie grabbed my arm. "Everyone on the planet is in this room. Put it this way, if I don't get a drink soon, I'm going to stab someone. Do you want that on your conscience?"

I didn't.

Julie and Ben started running to the car as soon as we were outside, but I could barely walk in my shoes, let alone run; plus, it had started raining. So, I settled for a slow slide.

"Come on," Julie yelled, "we need to move fast."

"I can't. Just forget me. Save yourselves," I yelled and started to giggle.

Ben jogged back and, to my incredible surprise, scooped me up like I weighed nothing and carried me in the direction of the car. "Why did you wear those shoes anyway?" he said. "You can't even walk."

"I thought we'd be sitting for most of the night." I looked up. Despite not even breathing hard, his face was flushed and he couldn't look me in the eyes. I settled into the warmth of his strong arms. He smelled like Ben; spicy and clean, familiar and comforting. "It's like you're my knight in shining armour," I joked, trying to get him to look at me. He wouldn't.

"Aren't high heels only effective when you stand?" he asked logically.

"Well, clearly I didn't think this through," I said and lifted my head up. "You can put me down, we're almost there."

He put me down and my hand rested on his shoulder as I steadied myself. He met my eyes and smiled.

"Thanks," I said, not wanting to look away. Why couldn't I look away? "You really didn't need to do that. You could have just had a drink on your own while I waited inside."

"You're the one who's going to meet your soulmate." He brushed away a large raindrop that had fallen on my face. "You can't be expected to do that without one drink."

We slid into the backseat with Julie, who had already started on the bottle of cinnamon schnapps she'd stashed.

"Wow, this really brings me back to our bar-hopping

days." I took a small sip and felt the warm liquid both burn my throat and boost my resolve.

I handed the bottle to Ben and he sniffed the opening. "Nope, still disgusting," he said as he screwed the top back on.

"Okay, let's go," I said, already anxious that we might be late.

"Here." Julie threw me a pair of black flats. "I brought these in case my feet started to hurt, but it looks like you already need them."

I thanked her and gratefully put them on after easing my poor feet out of my stupid heels. "I hate you," I whispered to them.

We ran back and arrived just as people had started to sit down. It seemed that the organizer had given up on her crappy speaker purse as her voice now boomed over a sound system.

From what I could gather, we were being asked to go to certain areas based on the age groups we'd selected. However, there was no signage anywhere, so this was proving pretty challenging for everyone.

Volunteers were guiding people to their sections like dogs herding sheep and we stopped and asked one where the thirty-five-to-forty-five-year-old section was. She yelled (she had to yell because it was so incredibly loud) that, because of a lack of males in that age group, we were being merged with the twenty-five-to-thirty-five-year-olds and waved us in the general direction of the southwest corner.

"Fantastic," I said with a grim look. At least Julie was

pleased. She pulled her top down so her boobs almost fell out and we made our way over.

On the other hand, Ben looked like he was about to be sick. I didn't blame him. It had now been an hour since the event was supposed to have started. I had begun to accept the fact that we were never going home.

As I tried to figure out where to go and why I'd come, I heard—somehow, because it was *so loud*—cries of "No way" and "This sucks." The people in the exceptionally long line at the bar had started to disperse. Angrily.

"Looks like they closed it so people will start sitting down," Julie yelled. Because what made being in a crowd of people waiting an hour for an event to start feel better? Being sober. And mad. And by people, I meant me.

Ben looked like he was going to have a nervous breakdown, but we pushed on and eventually figured out where we were supposed to sit. We took our seats, not at tables like Julie had experienced, but on single chairs in rows of twenty. Those chairs faced a row of twenty other chairs, one side for men and one side for women.

As we sat, a volunteer passed out sheets of paper that explained the rules. The idea, in a perfect world, was to face your "date" for ten minutes, ask questions, and then, after a bell rang, the men would stand up and move one seat to their right. At the very end, everyone would have had twenty dates. Easy, right?

No.

In reality, it was absolute bedlam. I'm sure whoever had organized it had had every intention of bringing joy to all involved in this potentially fun night, but as I looked around at what was actually happening, I began to feel a bit panicky. And if I was starting to feel panicky, I knew Ben must have truly been living a nightmare. I tried to catch his eye, but he was looking around with the same stunned expression on his face as me.

We were currently two of six hundred people stuffed into a giant concrete room that was not giant enough because there was so little remaining space that we were not only back to back with the row behind us but we were also uncomfortably touching knees with our "dates" in front of us. And what made it even more uncomfortable was, because the event hadn't actually started yet, we were all trying not to talk to each other, lest we should cheat somehow. I knew this because when I tried to talk to the guy in front of me, he held up his finger as if to say, "Hold your horses, I'm sure it will start any second."

It did not.

After *one hour* of basically sitting in a stranger's lap and trying to make small talk with the ladies beside me, both of whom appeared to be my age and about as impressed as I was at the lack of men who were also our age, it finally, *finally* started.

The organizer opened with a short apology about how chaotic it was and also about the bar situation, which, in hindsight, didn't really matter because there was nowhere to put drinks anyway. Then she read the entire page of rules, just in case we hadn't been able to read them in the hour we had been waiting for everyone to get their shit together.

She explained that, in order to beat the world record,

all six hundred of us would have to speed date consistently for three hours. That meant no one could leave. For three hours. And, if someone had to get up, even if it was to go to the bathroom (although I found it hard to believe that would happen, what with no liquid being available), they had to raise their hand and then the *entire event* had to stop while they went. So, if I had to go to the bathroom, I not only had to climb over ten people to get out, but everyone else had to stop what they were doing and wait while I peed. Excellent.

I leaned toward my date as the organizer continued to drone on. "I feel like I'm in a jail—"

"Shhh!" He held a finger to his lips. He was definitely not getting a check mark.

After the host had finished reading the rules, and we waited for all the people who were terrified of peeing their pants in the middle of the event (me) to come back from the bathroom, the first bell went off and we started.

Now, when we had all been milling around not really talking to one another, it had been loud and I had naïvely thought that was about as loud as it could be. I was wrong. Because there were so many of us packed into the room, and the room was made of concrete, the sound of six hundred people all talking at once had nowhere to go. It was not absorbed by anything. So, my first conversation with the dude who kept shushing me went something like this:

"HI, I'M KATE."

"WHAT? I CAN'T HEAR YOU. IT'S TOO LOUD. I'M BRAD." (Or something, I honestly had no idea.)

"WHAT? OKAY, I'LL TALK LOUDER. WHAT DID YOU SAY YOUR NAME WAS? BRAD?"

"NO, I SAID (something that wasn't Brad)."

"OH, SORRY, OKAY."

"WHAT KINDS OF THINGS DO YOU LIKE TO DO?"

"OH, YOU KNOW, I LIKE…"

"CAMPING?"

"NO, I DON'T LIKE CAMPING."

"AWESOME. I LIKE CAMPING TOO."

"NO, I SAID… *Fuck it…* GREAT." I gave him the thumbs-up.

And it wasn't just me. That was how everyone's conversation was going. A lot of yelling, a lot of WHAT?ing and a lot of frustration. (I could only assume the frustration part. I was certainly frustrated.)

So, of course, with all the noise, no one could hear the bell, and when it went off, no one moved. Actually, some people did hear the bell, so they got up, but the majority of us continued to sit and yell or wonder why there were a few people standing and looking cranky.

Eventually, we all realized the bell had rung, so, after another twenty minutes of getting settled, we got ready to start again. It was about this time that I started to sweat like I was having a hot flash. It was so hot and stuffy and we were pressed up so close together that I was turning into a disgusting mess. Other people were starting to sweat too. I know this because I could see them but also because I could smell them. And none of us had anything to drink, not even water.

Before we began the second round of dates, the host grabbed the microphone. She was starting to look frazzled herself. "Hope you're having fun," she tried unconvincingly before she was unceremoniously interrupted by someone who "needed some fucking water." She then looked like she was about to cry.

And then someone had to go to the bathroom. And now that that person had gotten up, about a hundred other people decided they also had to go and the rest of the room started getting antsy.

While we waited, my second date yelled to a couple of volunteers that the LCD display in front of him was way too bright while shielding his face like the sun itself was setting fire to his retinas. Perfect.

When everyone was back in their seats, which took a while because, it turned out, there weren't a hundred toilets in the building, the host gave us a "gentle reminder" that we should all talk at a lower volume so we could better hear each other. And failing that, just move closer. I raised my hand to "gently remind" her that there was no possible way we could get any closer, but Julie gave me a look, so I put my hand down.

Round two began and speaking at a lower volume did not seem to be working, so my date and I leaned in close and yelled in each other's ears. I found out his name was Roger; he worked at a radio station as an overnight DJ and he liked dogs. He didn't like camping, which was a clear win, but I'd already decided I didn't like him due to his alarming light sensitivity, so I marked an "X" next to his name.

Realizing that the bell idea wasn't a great one, this time when the round was over the host yelled "DING" into the microphone, which scared the crap out of everyone but also made us laugh, so that was a step in the right direction.

We all abruptly stopped talking, moved seats and paused, once again, while volunteers handed out plastic cups of water (finally). This presented another conundrum as I really wanted a glass of water but drinking something would mean more trips to the bathroom for me and, consequently, everyone else.

At the last minute, I decided to take a cup because thirst won over logic. I wasn't sweating as much as I had been before though, probably because I was dehydrated. At least I was lucky enough to be a woman so I could slip my cup of water under my chair and leave it there. I felt bad for the guys who had to move and pick up their cups each time.

The next guy seemed like he actually could be an option. He looked to be around my age, was fairly attractive, and didn't open the conversation with a complaint. We were about three minutes in when he told me he was actually the host's boyfriend. He was there because there weren't enough men. He laughed. "You wouldn't believe how many dudes here aren't single."

"Should you be telling me this?" I asked. "I mean that seems like cheating."

"Nah. I don't know. I got twenty bucks, you know? Plus, I'm not even sure what's happening. Does the dude who gets the most points win money or something? Do you have any snacks?"

"Where on earth would I put snacks?"

"Oh man, I'm so high." He giggled.

Perhaps the woman who had landed herself this gem shouldn't have been hosting any activities related to dating. I felt a bit ripped off.

We both sat there, not talking to each other for the rest of our "date." Me drinking water. Him alternating between swaying in his seat and mumbling something about ordering a pizza. The host walked by and I met her eye with a stern stare. She pretended she didn't see me.

That was pretty much how the next two hours went. About halfway through, people started taking off their clothes because they were so hot. A large group left during the next bathroom break and didn't return. The event was a failure. I would almost have felt bad for the host if I hadn't known she'd paid guys to be there.

My sixth date was with a dude with a man bun and it ended with a four-minute soliloquy about why he thought the bottles that turned ordinary water into soda water were the best invention ever.

My seventh date lived with his parents.

My next date opened with: "Hey, Baby Cakes."

With an hour left to go, the host tearfully let us know that too many people had left, so we weren't going to break the world record, but because she truly believed that for some of us our one forever love was here in the building, she welcomed us to finish our dates.

I met Julie's eye and she nodded that she wanted to continue. And far be it from me to break a rule of any sort, so I nodded back. "Where's Ben?" I mouthed.

She shrugged. I hadn't seen him since we'd first sat

down, but I'd also been otherwise engaged. He could very well have been moved to another group to fill an empty seat, so I didn't really think about it, desperate to push through and end this terrible experience. At least with so many people leaving, I could breathe again.

My second last date was with a guy who had been kissing all the women's hands. Some of them blushed and giggled, others quickly pulled their hands away. He was really invested in the whole gentleman routine.

When the bell rang, he leaned close (too close) and wetly whispered in my ear that his name was Toby and he thought I was the most beautiful woman he'd met so far.

I'd had enough by this point so, as he reached for my hand, I said, "What about her?" and gestured at the cute redhead beside me. "I just heard you say she was the most beautiful woman you've met so far." I was taking a chance on this; I hadn't heard him say that, but I was ninety-five percent sure he had.

He looked flustered for about half a second but quickly contained himself, looked deep into my eyes and smiled. "She was until I met you."

Barf.

He then put his hand on my knee and squeezed.

"I'm done," I announced and stood, pushing my chair so forcefully into the guy behind me that he had to stand up along with me so he didn't face plant onto his date's lap. "Sorry," I said to both of them as I pushed my way through the line of knees.

I caught the eye of the last guy I was supposed to meet, who looked like he was about eighteen, and said, "I'm sure you're great, but I've had enough." I showed him my sheet of paper littered with Xs and made an oversized checkmark next to his number. "See? This is how great I'm sure you are."

I folded up the paper and looked around. At the beginning, we'd been told that if someone we picked also picked us, they would send us each other's emails and we could plan a real date. I was sure they had also told us where to put our paper when we were done, but I was so hot and so tired and so frustrated I couldn't for the life of me remember where.

"Where do I put this fucking thing?" I yelled before I could stop myself.

The room went quiet. Out of nowhere, the host was behind me, pushing me towards the door.

"But I need to register my votes," I protested. "What if I miss out on a date with the guy who kept adjusting himself? You know"—my voice rose as I looked around the room wildly—"just because I'm looking at your face doesn't mean I can't see what you're doing down there. It's called peripheral vision," I yelled.

The host grabbed the paper from my hand and put it in a box. "Don't worry," I yelled to her as I walked out the door. "I didn't vote for your boyfriend." I turned back and added, "Also, he might have a drug problem."

And then I was outside, with blessed air that was cool and fresh and didn't smell like six hundred hot, sweaty bodies. I inhaled deeply a few times and calmed myself down. It was only then that I realized what I'd done.

Chapter 30

I got to the car and found Ben sitting in the front seat with his headphones on. The tight ball of frustration I had been holding in my stomach disappeared. I relaxed for the first time that night.

I startled him, despite my gentle knock, but his eyes brightened and he grinned when he saw it was me. He unlocked the door and slid over to the driver's seat.

"That was a nightmare." I collapsed into the seat and immediately settled into the comfort of just being myself. Being around Ben was so easy. I didn't have to pretend to be someone I wasn't, someone who enjoyed meeting and talking to other people.

He handed me the half-empty bottle of cinnamon schnapps from the backseat. "Any luck?"

I took a sip from the bottle and laughed, relieved he hadn't been there to see my temper tantrum. "Nope. You?"

"That was literally my own personal hell."

"It was stupid anyways," I said and passed the bottle over. He shook his head, responsible as always.

We both leaned our heads back in the seats, sitting

together in comfortable silence, listening to the rain patter against the windshield.

Eventually, Ben shifted in his seat and turned to face me. "Kate, I—"

"Julie seemed—" I said at the same time. We both laughed.

"Go ahead." He smiled. "Julie seemed what?"

"To be having fun," I finished. "She always does. She always seems to make the best out of a bad situation. She always comes out on top, you know?"

"I guess," he said.

I turned to look at him. "You don't think so? I mean, not only is she blessed with physical perfection, but nothing ever goes wrong for her. Everything always happens exactly how she wants it to. She has it so easy."

"How so?" Ben asked quietly, his eyes questioning.

"I don't know," I said. "I don't have any specific examples, I guess. She's just never had to work that hard for anything, and when she does have something, she's never really that tied to it—jobs, relationships—it's like easy come, easy go. She just gets what she wants and doesn't really have to think about it." I turned my head. "Sorry, was that too harsh?"

"Maybe a bit," Ben said.

I sighed. "You know I love her more than anything. Ever since we've been kids, she's been my person. My most favorite person in the world. I want her to have everything, I do, and I want it to be easy. I guess… I guess I just get jealous sometimes."

Ben shifted and picked at a small hole on the dashboard.

"That's normal," he said. "But have you ever considered that maybe she hasn't always had it as easy as you think? That maybe she makes things look effortless on purpose?" He rubbed the back of his neck.

"No, not really. I mean I know she had a hard time when we were younger, we talked about it a lot, but," I said, just realizing it myself, "over the last few years, we haven't really talked about anything that was bothering her, so I just assumed. We haven't really talked about much, really."

I stopped talking. Not knowing what to think. It was true—we didn't talk like we used to. We hadn't for a while. How had I missed that?

We sat again in stillness as I tried to remember the last time we'd had one of our really good talks. I couldn't.

I looked down, tears in my eyes. "I miss her. I miss our talks."

"Maybe it will have to be up to you to start them again," he said, brushing a stray tear from my face with his thumb.

I smiled weakly and rested the side of my face on the headrest. *Being with Ben is so simple,* I thought.

"I'm sorry we dragged you to this thing tonight," I said. "I know it's not your jam. When did you leave?"

He laughed. "I snuck out pretty close to the beginning— when the first wave of people went to the bathroom. I'm really sorry; I thought I could handle it, but sitting knee to knee with all those women, I started to feel the walls closing in. I feel bad about ruining the world record."

"Oh, you didn't." I put my hand on his knee. "The world record was ruined several times over after you left."

He looked down at my hand and then raised his head so our eyes met.

I shivered. Why was I suddenly finding it hard to breathe?

"Are you cold?" he asked, moving closer. "I could turn on the heat."

"I'm good," I said. In fact, I was actually quite warm.

"Kate," he almost whispered. "I need to tell—"

We both jumped, interrupted by a pounding on the window and Julie on the other side. I snatched my hand away from Ben's knee and unlocked the door.

"What the hell happened to you in there?" She slid into the backseat.

"I guess I went a little crazy," I said. Ben looked at me with his eyebrows raised.

"You think?" Julie said. "I guess this means we're not staying for the afterparty."

I jumped out of the car, went around to the backseat, and wrapped my arms around her, tears filling my eyes again.

"What the hell?" she said as she hugged me back. "What's going on?"

"Nothing," I said, stepping back. "I just wanted to hug my best friend. Why don't we go somewhere for a dri—"

"*Yes!*" Julie yelled before I could finish. "I know the perfect place."

Chapter 31

The outside of the pub looked like it had seen better days. Chipped green paint outlined cracked windows that settled in the crumbling red brick. Some of the windows were boarded up and covered in inexplicable graffiti.

How did anyone get up there to paint that? I thought.

We walked up the broken sidewalk, stepping over weeds and rocks, and were greeted by a heavy, rusted metal door. I looked up and squinted, trying to see what this place could have been. The April rain had turned to snow, which was, sadly, typical for Saskatchewan, and the soft white flakes made me feel like I was stuck inside a snow globe.

"It's supposed to be spring," I mumbled under my breath. I wrapped my arms around myself, trying to keep warm.

"This looks interesting," Ben said.

"We can leave after I have a glass of wine." Julie pulled open the door.

The inside wasn't in much better shape than the outside. The smell of twenty-year-old stale smoke and spilled beer was suffocating. Considering our non-smoking laws in public buildings had been in effect for decades, I tried to calculate how long ago they must have last cleaned the carpets. The light was dim, I could barely see. I squinted to see if there were any empty seats.

"Well," I said. "This place is… different. Why do your friends come here again?"

"It's cool," Julie said, as if that were obvious.

"Well, it sure is busy," Ben said. And he was right; it was completely packed. Brown plastic booths overflowed with people. The ones who weren't in booths either sat at wooden tables with mismatched seats or were just standing on any piece of floor that was left uncovered.

"Did someone say my name?" I looked around, trying to determine where it was coming from.

"Over there." Julie pointed and I saw Cody waving his arms.

As we pushed through the crowd, I glanced back at Ben. He smiled weakly and gave me a thumbs-up. I knew he didn't want to be here and I knew we should leave. But Julie was already well ahead on her way to the table, so I resigned myself to staying for a while.

"Hey." I smiled at Cody and said as a joke, "Do you come here often?"

"I do, actually," he said and gestured to three chairs. "That's how I have seats. A few friends just left, why don't you join us?" He looked past Ben and me and right at Julie.

"Oh, thank God." Julie hung her purse on a chair and sat down heavily. "If I'd had to stand in these shoes for one more second, I think I would have collapsed." She slid her chair out, crossed her legs and lifted one perfectly manicured foot strapped into an extremely high heel.

This earned her a look of distaste from one woman, a nod of respect from another, and pure lust from all the men, including Cody. Ben looked at me and rolled his eyes.

I guess this could be worse, I thought. Maybe I could use this time wisely. Maybe I could take Ben's advice and settle in for a good talk with Julie. I smiled as I thought about it. A glass of wine, a cozy heart-to-heart, just like old times.

I slipped into the chair beside her. "Feel like some Kate and Julie time?" I said and put my hand on her arm.

"Here?" she said.

"Yeah, we could get some wine."

"Right now?"

"That's where I was going with this, yes," I said.

"Aw." She tipped her head to the side. "Rain check?" Then she whispered loudly, "I'm pretty sure this dude is about to buy me a drink."

All right then.

Change of plans. Just because the speed dating event had been a disaster didn't mean I still couldn't try to meet a guy in real life tonight. The year was almost a quarter of the way through, and I hadn't even come close to finding someone to kiss, so I should probably do something. I was starting to wish I'd kept my little napkin goal to myself. Stupid accountability.

I moved down the table to one of the other empty chairs and got ready to meet a random man. I was sure it wouldn't be too difficult; this place was full of them.

I wasn't entirely certain what to do though. I tried to catch the eye of one of the other guys at the table, but he was deep in conversation with one of the other women. Why wasn't anyone ever interested in having a deep conversation with me? I turned my head slightly and watched Julie out of the corner of my eye. She was so smooth and natural she made it look easy. All she had to do was be herself.

I, on the other hand, had been sitting by myself for fifteen minutes and no one was even looking in my direction. I briefly toyed with the idea of pretending to choke on something but settled on subtly mimicking Julie. Obviously, she knew what she was doing.

I watched her sitting back casually, legs crossed so her gorgeous heels were in full view. When she rested her hand on her thigh, she subtly slid her skirt up, just a bit. I wasn't wearing a skirt, nor did I have sexy heels, but I did have legs. I leaned back in what I determined to be a casual fashion and crossed them.

I remembered, too late, that I was sitting on a stool. With no back. Thankfully, even though my legs were tied up, my hand—which seemed to be the only smart part of my body at that moment—grabbed the chair beside me and I righted myself. But not before I inadvertently yelled, "Whoopsie Daisy!" like someone's grandmother. This ensured that if anyone hadn't been looking after hearing the loud scrape from the stool, they were definitely looking now.

"Kate!" Ben jumped up. I wobbled a bit more on the stool and he helped me straighten myself. "Are you okay?"

"Oh, I'm fine." I brushed it off. "I just forgot... Nothing... I'm fine." I flashed everyone at the table what I hoped was a dazzling smile and willed my face to go back to its normal colour. Ben sat down beside me.

I looked at Cody. He raised his eyebrows and mouthed, "Whoopsie Daisy?" and laughed.

"So." Ben turned to me. "I meant to say earlier you look ni—"

"Looks like you could use a shot," Cody yelled at me from across the table.

I smiled, thinking how great it would be if he just shut up so everyone would stop looking at me. "I don't really do shots."

"You sure did at the wedding." He grinned.

"And that's why I don't really do shots. Anymore." *Please don't talk about the wedding.*

"Come on," he said. "We're all doing them. It's a shot party!" He looked at me slyly. "I mean I understand if you don't want to end up under the table with your—"

"Fine," I interrupted so he would stop talking. "I'll do *one* shot. Something fruity." Something that would hopefully mix well with the couple of sips of schnapps I'd had in the car. I was normally fine having a couple of drinks, but I was still dehydrated from the speed dating event and the last time I'd had anything to eat was a salad at lunch.

Maybe this was a good idea, actually. If anything, it would make people forget I'd almost fallen on the floor. Maybe if I did a shot, I would feel more comfortable talking to people.

The shots came and I tipped one back, expecting something fun and manageable like Sour Puss or Crème de Menthe. What I got, however, was a toxic liquid that burned my throat, exploded in my stomach and made my eyes water.

"This wasn't fruity at all," I gasped and wiped my eyes with a napkin.

I looked at Julie, an alcohol-fueled smile of contentment on her face. She was in her element. Julie could drink all women and most men right under the table. Ben looked uncomfortable and ordered an herbal tea.

Then it hit me. The soft punch of warmth and comfort that only hard alcohol can provide.

Then came the confidence. "That wasn't that bad actually." I smiled.

And then—the reason why I didn't do shots—came the extremely poor judgement. "I think I could probably do one more."

By the third one, I was feeling pretty great. Who said I couldn't talk to guys? I was just as good as any woman here.

"At what?" the guy sitting across from me said.

"At what what?" I said, not knowing what he was talking about. He was pretty cute though. Maybe. I couldn't really focus.

He laughed. "You said you were just as good as any woman here. Just as good at what?"

Whoops, I must have said that out loud.

"At being cool." I leaned forward on my elbow in a way I was certain was sexy and flirtatious, even after my elbow slipped and I came close to face-planting the table.

"Yeah, you seem pretty cool."

He is totally flirting with me! I knew it would work. All I had to do was be like Julie. She was a master and I was happy to be her student.

I crossed my legs again, this time making sure I didn't

lean too far back, and tossed my hair off my shoulder, grinning seductively. Out of the corner of my eye I saw Ben watching warily, but I waved my hand at him to let him know he had nothing to worry about. I had it all under control.

Now, what would Julie do next? She would throw him a well-placed compliment; he deserved it. It might have been the booze talking (it was), but he had clearly been waiting patiently to talk to me all night.

"I like your… pants," I said and tipped my chin down to look through my eyelashes.

"My pants? Like, my jeans?"

"Yes," I whispered. "They're so… in style."

"What?" he said (obviously a signal that he wanted me to get closer).

I leaned forward on both my elbows. "Wanna buy me a shot?" I whispered loudly.

"I think you may have had too many shots."

"No way, man. I'm just getting started. It's a shots party! Shots! Shots! Shots!"

He pushed one towards me.

"Yeah!" I yelled. "Hey, wait, where's yours?"

"That is mine. From before. I don't want it, but you're welcome to it."

He totally wanted me.

"Cheers!" I yelled, tipped back the shot and threw up a bit in my mouth.

"Ugh, are you okay?" He grimaced.

"That was a rough one, hey?" I mumbled, leaning forward to seduce him with a sultry, throaty laugh but ending up settling on a hiccup. I turned the shot glass over and the remnants of whatever it was spilled onto the table. He picked up his wallet and put a napkin down on the spill.

"You're supposed to do that," I slurred. "You're supposed to put down the shot glass down upside down because then... you're done. For real. Then all the people know you did it."

"All the people?"

"You're cute."

He opened his mouth to speak, but I cut him off by waving my hand in front of his face.

"I'm not going to sleep with you though, even though you bought me a shot. That's not how this is going to be working here."

"I didn't buy you a shot."

"Not that I don't appreciate it, but I mean, I'm a lady."

He seemed confused. How could I be clearer? I was basically offering myself up on a plate. I leaned even closer.

"I am a pretty good kisser though."

He leaned back and looked around. What was his problem? We both knew where this was headed. Let's just get 'er done. I got up to move over to his side of the table.

"Uh oh," I said as my head started spinning. And then, all of a sudden, Ben had my arm.

"I think it's time we go," he said.

"But I'm totally picking up this cute guy," I thought I whispered but actually yelled. The guy, whatever his name was, lifted his hands and shook his head.

"I think it's time we go," Ben said again.

"Fine." I stumbled over the stool, holding on to Ben to steady myself.

"Let's go," he said gently as he grabbed my jacket and gave it to Julie.

"You smell good," I said.

As Ben guided me out, I turned and pointed in the general direction of the guy I'd been talking to. "It's your loss," I said. "I'm a catch."

That was the last thing I remembered.

Chapter 32

Julie

"What was that all about?" Julie said to Ben as she slid into the passenger seat and closed the door. "Since when does Kate drink that much? This is the second time in three months and she rarely ever drinks."

"No idea." Ben started the car.

She looked at Kate lying on the backseat, gently snoring, drool running down the side of her face. "And how did it happen so quickly? One second she was fine, and the next she was totally shit-faced, hitting on some rando. I mean what the fuck?"

"I said I don't know," Ben said, shoulders tensed.

"'What the fuck' is generally a rhetorical question; I wasn't really expecting you to know."

"Let's not talk about it," Ben said. "Let's just focus on getting her home safely."

"Fine," Julie sniped. "Someone's in a bad mood."

"Well, someone didn't want to go to this in the first place and now someone is really tired and just wants to go to bed and not think about sitting at that table alone while

184

Kate… while both of you ignored me and tried to pick up guys."

"Hey, he was trying to pick up *me*. And anyway—"

"Please just stop talking."

Julie crossed her arms and faced the window. Fine. She didn't want to talk anyway. And Ben was wrong. She hadn't been trying to pick up anyone. Cory, or whatever his name was, had been trying to pick her up.

She felt a twinge of guilt. She knew they had been there for Kate; Kate was the one who had wanted to find someone and she should have been helping her. But he had hit on her, so what was she supposed to have done, tell him to go sit somewhere else because she wasn't interested? That would have been a bit presumptuous.

Sure, she could have left and gone to sit beside Kate and be her wing woman, but she'd seemed to be having fun all on her own and Julie hadn't wanted to interrupt. Plus, Cody (that was his name!) had been buying her drinks.

She shoved the guilt away and tried to focus on the lights streaking past as they drove through the city, roads wet with melted snow. The thing was, though, deep down she knew Kate had really needed her help. She knew her friend; she could tell. And she knew the fact that no one had come to talk to her all night was very likely the reason she'd started drinking. Julie had seen it happen before when they were in their twenties. When all the guys tried to pick up only her. When she got all the attention and Kate got none.

The car stopped, jolting her from her thoughts. Ben got out and opened the back door. "Are you going to help me or not?"

She got out of the car, opened the opposite door and slid in, lifting Kate up into a half-sitting position. Kate blinked and groaned.

"Don't you dare puke on me," Julie said as she pushed her out the door towards Ben.

"Easy," Ben whisper-yelled. "She's not a bag of potatoes."

"Sorry, jeez. I'm just trying to help."

"Well, try to help like you don't want to push her out of the car onto her face."

She watched as Ben gently pulled Kate's arms until she was in a standing position, guarding the top of her head so she didn't bump it on her way out.

She'd never seen Ben take care of anyone before. He had always been the one being taken care of. By her. Shame overwhelmed her. She honestly hadn't thought he had the capability. She'd thought she would be the one taking care of him forever. She hadn't noticed that he hadn't needed her much lately. He hadn't been needing her at all.

"Can you get her keys out of her purse?" he asked.

Julie looked up, interrupted from her train of thought, and reached into the backseat to grab Kate's purse. She took the keys, unlocked the door and stepped back as Ben lifted Kate up and carried her in his arms like a child. She felt like an intruder, almost embarrassed to be interrupting a moment between the two people she loved the most.

"You'll be okay," he whispered as he walked in the door.

Julie silently followed him down the hall and into Kate's apartment. She watched as he laid her on the couch, took off her shoes, and covered her with a fuzzy blanket.

"I'll get her some water," she said, feeling uncomfortable seeing this side of her brother. She walked into the kitchen and crouched down to pet the cat, taking her time, not wanting to go back.

"Where's the water?" Ben walked in and she jumped up to grab it, startling the cat.

"Sorry, I was petting Mittens."

"Hey, buddy." Ben smiled and scratched Mittens' head. "I've always loved that name. He looks hungry. Do you know where she keeps the food? She might not be up in time to feed him."

Julie pointed to the pantry door and then took the water into the living room and placed it on the coffee table. She knew Kate was going to feel terrible when she got up. That girl got the worst hangovers. At least she'd kept her clothes on this time.

"Should we stay?" she asked, not knowing how to handle this new Ben. Not wanting to make the decision. It was his moment, his time to decide.

"No, let's just leave her. She should be okay." He left her phone beside her on the couch and wrote out a note telling her to text them when she woke up.

"Good idea," Julie said, wondering why she hadn't thought of it.

She watched him turn back to look at Kate with tender eyes and a sad smile as they left.

What is happening? she thought as they walked out the door.

A lump formed in her throat and she tried to swallow it, not liking it there, not knowing where it had come from.

Once outside, she turned back to the apartment building and glanced up at Kate's window, as if the darkened square of glass could help explain this subtle shift in energy. Not finding any answers, she quietly slipped the bottle of cinnamon schnapps out of her purse and drained it as she walked to the car.

Chapter 33

Ben

Ben couldn't speak. He was tired. He was sad. He was frustrated. And, for the first time in a long time, he was angry. Angry at the way he kept putting himself in these positions. Angry that he couldn't stop hoping. Angry that he couldn't let things go. He was angry at himself, mostly. But, this time, just a little bit, he was angry at her.

Why would she embarrass herself like that, getting drunk, hitting on a stranger? Why, when he had been sitting right there, waiting for her to talk to him? Waiting to tell her that she looked nice and that no one at that stupid speed dating thing had been good enough for her.

But he hadn't said anything. He now knew he had to make a decision: either tell her how he felt or stop hanging out with her completely. Neither option seemed easier than the other. But if therapy had taught him anything, it was to consciously make the choices that were best for his mental health.

A few months after he'd come home from university to take care of Julie, he'd finally found a good psychiatrist and psychologist, both of whom he'd started seeing fairly regularly. His psychiatrist had changed his life.

The biggest and greatest thing his psychiatrist had done was to talk to him about trying medication. Ben had always thought medication was for people who were weak. For people who weren't strong enough to fix things themselves. He'd told himself he just had to try harder; work at it more, and then he'd fix himself and things would get better.

Each time he'd find something new—a new book or a new tool—and he'd start to feel better, he would think, *This is it. I've finally found what's wrong. I've finally fixed it.* But then time would pass and he'd start to feel bad again. And things would go back to how they always had been.

"It isn't a weakness," his psychiatrist would tell him. "Or a lack of will. It's an illness—a mental illness—and, like anyone suffering from an illness, you might need more than meditation and exercise."

He'd nodded noncommittally, not ready to believe.

"Think of it this way: if you had cancer, would you keep telling yourself to man up and try to overpower it with your mind? Or would you take the medication your doctor prescribed?"

"But you can't help cancer," he'd said. "It's not your fault you get it."

"Exactly. And it's the same with mental illness. It's an illness that doesn't discriminate. You can't help it. You could be living your dream life and still have depression. You could have no stress at all and still suffer from anxiety. Depression is not just being sad. Anxiety is not just being stressed. It's an illness in your brain. And it's not your fault. The only thing that *is* your fault is not accepting that you need help. But you did. And you took the first step. You're here. Now let me help you take the next one."

So, he had. But not right away. He'd waited until he'd had a panic attack in the bathroom at work. After a week of stress leave, and his boss emailing him to come back to the office because "everyone got stressed," he thought he would take his psychiatrist's advice.

It had taken him a while to get used to everything: accepting the term "mental illness" and adjusting his dose from time to time. He hadn't told anyone, not even Julie. He had planned on telling people when the time was right. Or maybe when they asked. Although it had been twenty years and no one had asked yet. Maybe no one had noticed a difference.

He still got anxious, still had good days and bad days. But as the years went on, the good days became more frequent and the bad days didn't last as long as they'd used to. Now, most days he felt good, he could breathe, he was calm. But then something like this happened.

He pulled into his allotted parking spot, turned off the car and rested his head in his hands. He knew he had to do this. It was something he'd known for a long time, but he'd never had the strength. He hadn't had the strength until now. He finally believed he deserved more than following around a woman who would never feel the same. He wanted to tell her, but even when he thought he'd mustered up the courage, he would either chicken out or be rudely interrupted. To keep this up, he would need a lot more therapy. At least now he could commit to the other option, as difficult and as painful as it would be.

In the interest of self-care, if he couldn't get over her, he needed to stop seeing her.

He gave himself a small nod of confirmation as he got out of the car. He walked up the stairs, wiped the tears from his face and closed the door behind him.

Chapter 34

I woke up late Saturday morning on my couch and in my clothes. My face was resting in a patch of dried drool. I had one of the most painful headaches I'd ever had in my life. I must have smelled like death because Mittens wouldn't even come near me. He was softly mewing in the corner, a safe distance away. When I groaned, he tentatively padded towards me but quickly dodged as I jumped off the couch to go puke in the kitchen sink.

Shame tightened my chest as I stood at the sink, my head under the tap, alternately drinking water and soaking my face. I'd done it again. For someone who barely drank, getting this trashed twice in the last few months was pretty excessive.

Mittens already had some dried food in his dish—*thank goodness for thoughtful friends*. I refreshed his water, grabbed some painkillers and went back to the couch. I stank. There was probably puke in my hair, but I couldn't be bothered to shower or change my clothes.

With a wave of nausea, I remembered the shots. I remembered the guy I had been talking to. I remembered my attempts at flirting. His looks of disinterest. Of revulsion. I remembered ignoring Ben all night, despite his multiple attempts to talk to me.

An image of Ben carrying me into my apartment emerged through the fog and my face flushed with what I assumed was embarrassment. I couldn't feel much of anything else right now. I was hot, shaky, smelly and sick. I wanted to sleep forever and not wake up until this hangover from hell was over. But I couldn't sleep. I just kept reliving the night over and over in my head. The look of disappointment in Ben's eyes. The pity in Julie's. I'd disappointed my friends. I'd disappointed myself. I didn't deserve to feel better.

Sunday morning felt a lot like Saturday morning but with less vomiting and increased mobility. I checked my phone and was not surprised to see a text from Julie asking what I was doing that day and if I wanted to meet for coffee. She'd texted me all Saturday and, other than texting a quick, *"I'm fine, thanks for getting me home,"* I hadn't texted anything back. I hadn't had the ability or the brainpower to do anything but lie on my couch and watch TV; today, I just didn't have the will.

Also, why hadn't Ben texted me? He always checked in to see if I was okay. I looked at my phone again.

I guessed I probably deserved the radio silence. I certainly had not been on my best behaviour on Friday. I'd been so wrapped up in trying to get a stranger to like me that I'd treated him the exact same way I was treated whenever a guy tried to pick up Julie.

I checked my phone again, just in case I'd missed the alert. Nothing. I guessed the depression part of my hangover was settling in because since when did not hearing from Ben make me want to cry?

Chapter 35

April 19th

Monday morning was not my friend. Even though I felt physically better, my mental state was less than stellar. The last thing I wanted to do was go to work and face Cody and the merciless taunting that I totally deserved.

On top of that, I'd gotten an email on Sunday with my results from the overwhelmingly unsuccessful speed dating event. The only guy I'd chosen, the guy who looked like he was eighteen, had also chosen me. Both unexpected and unwanted. He'd contacted me and asked if I wanted to go for supper. I'd said yes. I told myself it was because I didn't want him to contact me anymore, so we might as well just get it over with. But maybe, just maybe, a small voice in the back of my mind kept saying, he would turn out to be great and we'd really hit it off. Still, the thought of it was not that big of a motivator to get me out of bed.

All right, I thought. *Enough moping.*

I pushed myself into a sitting position, stretched for about five minutes, and tried to pump myself up to face a day of actually being an adult. I had to do it at some point.

I stood in front of the closet for way too long, trying to decide what to wear. I never really cared what I looked like, but today seemed important somehow. I almost felt like I was going to a job interview. I wanted to wear something that said, "I'm not really trying, but also I'm not a train-wreck; please forget what you saw this weekend."

I decided on a plaid pencil skirt, a dressy grey T-shirt and a black cardigan. Then I decided on slim-fitting black capris, a dressy grey T-shirt and a navy cardigan. Then I decided on dark jeans, a dressy grey T-shirt and a black cardigan. *I might, very possibly, never leave the house.*

Finally, after I settled on my last choice, I ran to the bathroom and quickly showered while the coffee brewed. I blow-dried my hair straight, put on more make-up than I ever wore, washed my face, put on less make-up, left the bathroom, returned to the bathroom, put on a touch more mascara, sprayed on some perfume, washed off the perfume, ran into the kitchen to grab my coffee and a banana and sprinted out the door. I hated myself.

I got to work twelve minutes late and had just sat down, thinking I had arrived undetected, when I heard, "Hey!" from behind me, making me jump. "How was your weekend?" Terry asked.

"Sorry, I'm late," I began, trying to think of a believable lie I hadn't told before. "I was—"

"Don't worry about it," he interrupted as he grabbed my arm and guided me into the boardroom. "You're just in time for the big reveal!"

He was in an oddly good mood—especially for a Monday—which, of course, made me nervous. Was the big reveal that I was going to be fired in front of everyone? I honestly wouldn't have been surprised.

I caught Cody's eye as I walked into the boardroom and my face reddened. He laughed and gave me a thumbs-up and I shrugged, pretending making a fool out of myself was all part of my master plan.

"Well," Terry started and clapped his hands together in excitement. "It looks like you're all here." He waited for a response and we all looked around awkwardly and nodded.

"We sure are, Terry!" Nate yelled in mock excitement and I stifled a snort.

"I love your enthusiasm, Nate." Terry grinned, oblivious. He sat down at the head of the large boardroom table, took off his glasses, and touched them to his lips in a pose he must have thought made him look like a scholar. He'd recently started wearing them and no one knew why. He always bragged about having 20/20 vision and never showing signs of aging.

"I guess you're probably wondering why I called you all here today," he said, raising an eyebrow. He turned to the large TV on the wall, put his glasses on, turned back to us, tore the glasses off with a flourish and held them up, looking at them intently. "Oh, these things?" he answered, even though no one had asked, "they're just readers I bought at the drug store so I can see things better up close. I don't need actual glasses because my eyes are really great. It's *so* frustrating though. I have to put them on to read"—he turned to the TV and put them on—"and then take them off to talk to people"—he snapped his head back and tore them off—"it's *such* a nuisance. I sometimes wish my eyes would age like a normal person's so I could get normal glasses and wouldn't have this cross to bear. If only someone would invent glasses where you could see far and close at the same time."

"They have been invented," Nate said. "They're called progressives."

"I don't *need* progressives." Terry's head snapped up. "My eyesight is virtually 20/20, I just need these to read."

"Right," Nate said. "So, did you call us all here to talk about your glasses? Because I have stuff to do."

Terry turned to give Nate one of his looks of abject loathing but then seemed to remember what exciting news he had in store for us and, instead, broke into an unnaturally wide grin.

"No, silly," he said.

(Silly?)

"I called you here for the big reveal," he continued. "As you all know, I've been struggling a bit trying to get my creative juices flowing."

I hadn't known. I looked around the room and everyone else looked like they hadn't known either. Cody looked at me and shrugged.

"Now, let me stop you right there." He held up his hand. "I know you're thinking that I'm being too hard on myself because most of the creativity that has come out of this brain"—he pointed to his head—"has been pure genius, but I know in my heart that I can do better. I feel things other people don't feel, you know? I don't know if I've told everyone, but I'm what some might call an empath."

"Jesus Christ," Nate whispered loudly.

Terry briefly hesitated, his face flickering with irritation. "So I asked myself," he continued, deciding not to launch into his "empath" monologue after all, "what can I do that will both satisfy my need to get my creative juices flowing and also give back to the people in our community? Give back to you." He opened his arms like he was welcoming us into his congregation. "My people." He paused. "And what I've come up with—" he spun dramatically and pointed the remote control at the TV "—is this."

Nothing.

"Is this." He pushed the button on the remote harder.

"Say 'is this' again," Nate said. "Maybe it will work this time."

Terry looked like he was going to punch him in the face but surprisingly composed himself. "Can someone please help me with this?" he said through gritted teeth.

Three people ran up to try to get the TV to work, plugging in and unplugging cables, restarting his laptop, switching remotes. Everyone was getting restless.

"Why doesn't anything ever fucking work in this place?" he said under his breath. "I'll just email you all the link." Everyone started to leave.

And just like that, the TV turned on, and there was Terry, posing in front of a mirror, shirt off, biceps flexed, phone half-hiding his face, the quintessential male online dating photo, distorted across the wide screen.

There were a few "what the fucks" and some snickers, and those who had started to leave turned around to come back, definitely wanting to see what was going on now. I, for one, couldn't wait to see what kind of holy mess this was. Cody scooted in beside me. "This is going to be amazing," he whispered. I snuck a look his way and breathed a sigh of relief, glad Terry's performance was seemingly overshadowing anything I may or may not have done on Friday.

"Ah, finally," Terry said. "This, my friends, is my new website: *Terry Says.*" He scrolled down and we all moved closer. It looked like screen shots of dating profiles and images of Terry in a variety of poses, none of them flattering. "I'm going to create online dating profiles for people." He beamed. "I've been so successful with online dating that I figured why not share that success with others? And why not get paid for it, right? It's true, a lot of my success obviously comes from this"—he gestured to his face like a game show model—"but some of it comes from my great ability to know what other people are thinking and feeling and knowing how to present other people in their best light."

"Because you're an empath?" Nate asked.

"Exactly. So, make sure you tell your friends and send them the link. This is going to be huge so they'll want to contact me right away. I will, as a gesture of goodwill, be offering a friends-and-family discount to anyone here who would like to up their online dating game. How about you, Kate?" He turned to me and I went bright red. "I saw your profile the other day and it looks like you could use some help."

I was mortified.

"God, no. I mean, no, that's okay," I stuttered. "I'm starting to reconsider the online dating thing anyway," I lied.

"Yeah, I don't blame you," Terry said. "It's hard out there for someone like you."

Someone like me? My head snapped up. What the hell did that mean?

Cody saw my look and gently guided me out of the room.

"Just ignore him," he said. "He has no idea what he's talking about."

As we walked out, I was very aware of the pressure of his hand on the small of my back. I knew I was starting to turn red again and dropped my head so he didn't notice. "He's such an asshole," I said.

"Want to go for a coffee?" he asked. "My treat."

What on earth? Cody never treated. Maybe it was because I had online dating on my mind, but I couldn't help but wonder if I'd been missing something here. What if Cody was supposed to be my someone to kiss? What if it was someone who had been right in front of my face this whole time?

"Sure," I said. I couldn't quite catch my breath. "Let me grab my purse."

I needed to steady myself. I quickly thought back over the last few months to see if there was anything I hadn't noticed. Any behaviour I might have misconstrued. He had been nicer to me lately. And he'd seemed really happy to see me at the pub. Was this going to be one of those "friends to lovers" things I read about in my Christmas romance novels? Did I want it to be? I felt his eyes on me and realized he had said something.

"What?"

"I said I'd treat; you don't need money."

"Oh, right, my phone then. I need my phone."

"It's in your hand," he said, laughing. "What's wrong with you?"

"Nothing." I forced a laugh. "Still stunned by the 'big reveal,' I guess."

We continued down the hall and towards the back door.

"After you," he said as he held the door open.

"Thanks." I flushed. I really needed to stop blushing.

We walked to the coffee shop in silence, stopping only once so I could give a man playing his guitar on the corner some change. The sun was finally shining and people had ventured out of their offices like bears emerging from hibernation, sunning themselves on the concrete benches and eating hotdogs, giddy with the promise of warmer weather.

We walked into the coffee shop and Cody motioned to the table. "Want to sit for a bit?"

"Sure," I said as he went up to the counter. "Small coffee, please. Black."

As I waited, I thought of the pledge napkin I had tucked in my pocket that morning. Could this be it? I mean Cody wasn't my dream man by any means, but time was running out, the year was almost half over. He was very attractive. And he was pretty nice. Sort of. When he wanted to be. He was certainly immature, but that was probably something I would get used to. His childlike qualities could be kind of charming in their own little ways. Sometimes fart jokes were funny.

"Did you fall asleep?" I jumped as he put the coffees on the table, startled out of my thoughts.

"No, just thinking."

"Great, so, speaking of thinking, I wanted to talk to you about something." He sat down.

Was this it? Was he going to ask me out? My stomach rolled and I ignored it. *Let's just get this done.* I mean I had to say yes, right? This was what I'd been waiting for. I really didn't have any other options. Besides, he'd bought me a coffee, I didn't want to make him mad. *Might as well see where it goes.*

I took a deep breath and steadied myself. "What would you like to talk about?"

He leaned in like he was going to tell me a secret and I reflexively sat back.

"What?" he said. "Too close?"

"No." I forced a laugh. "I was just…" I leaned back in reluctantly. I would have to get used to this. "Go ahead," I continued, an eager smile plastered on my face.

The crease between his eyebrows deepened, a flash of momentary confusion, but then he composed himself with a smile. "Your friend Julie is smoking hot."

The relief was so instantaneous that I physically deflated, laying my forehead on the table.

"I mean I've always thought she was hot," Cody continued, not noticing my overly dramatic reaction, "but, after we hung out, I realized she's also pretty cool and probably, you know, down to party. I'm pretty sure we had a good vibe going the other night so, you know, I thought I'd check with you first to see if it was okay if I called her.

And, like, did she say anything about me? I know she's not really into dating, but I'm pretty open to whatever."

As he talked, my head was pulled up with the lightness of a helium balloon. He didn't want to ask me out. He liked Julie. Thank God that was all that it was.

He looked at me expectantly and I smiled. Thankfully, he was too self-involved to realize what had just happened.

"Well?" he asked.

"She didn't say anything," I breathed.

"Oh. Really? Nothing?"

"Nothing. Sorry."

"Oh." He seemed genuinely shocked. "But we had such a great time."

"She has a great time with a lot of people. Don't take it personally," I said as I grabbed my coffee and stood up.

"Oh." He stayed sitting. "Well, her loss." He sipped his coffee. "I could have shown her the time of her life." He leaned back in his chair with his hands behind his head, flexing his biceps.

Gross.

"Let's go," I said, motioning for him to stand up. "I've got a lot of work to do."

"Totally. Hey, are you all right? Why was your head on the table?"

I turned back. "I'm just not feeling great. Residual hangover, I guess."

He actually doubled over laughing. "Oh man, you were *so* wasted," he breathed. "How many times did you puke when you got home?"

"I didn't," I lied.

"You actually scared my friend Dean. He thought you were some sort of psycho cougar."

Awesome. "Did you tell him I wasn't?"

"Nah. It was too hilarious. My favourite part was when you tried to get everyone to read a balled-up napkin you had in your purse."

Great.

"Which reminds me," he said. "If you're still looking for 'someone to kiss,' I have a friend on Facebook you might like. He's newly single and wants to be fixed up. You into it?"

"Sure, what the hell?" I shrugged, happy to date anyone who wasn't Cody.

"Cool. It's kind of a weird situation, but I'll tell you more back at the office. I have a meeting…" He checked his watch. "Five minutes ago."

He exited first, letting the door slam back in my face so I had to throw my arm out to catch it. I guess there was no longer a need to impress if there wasn't any chance of him sleeping with my friend.

Chapter 36

Cody and I walked back to the office and went our separate ways to our desks. I sat down and let my purse drop to the floor. What on earth had just happened? I'd never thought that way about Cody before. Was I so desperate to find someone that I'd just pushed all his moral failings aside? How could I have even considered going out with him? Just because I thought he might have liked me? Because I didn't want to make him mad after he bought me a shitty coffee? What would have happened if he'd actually asked me out? I shuddered just thinking about it. I was sure I would have come to my senses at some point. I hoped.

For the rest of the day, I alternated between wanting desperately to go home and dreading going back to my empty apartment. While I was gone, Kevin—the one who looked about eighteen from the speed dating event—had sent me a message asking if next week worked for supper. I accepted reluctantly.

I had a ton of work to do, but my heart wasn't in it. My heart wasn't into anything at the moment. I knew most of it was just the normal "being depressed" phase of my residual hangover, but I also felt a sliver of doubt creeping in. Was striving to reach this goal doing more damage than good?

I heard a shuffle beside me and turned to see Cody watching me with a smirk.

"How long have you been there?" I asked.

He laughed. "I just wanted to see how long it would take for you to notice me. Man, you were totally zoned out. I've been standing here for, like, five minutes."

I forced a smile. "Well, how can I help you then? It must be important if you stood there watching me for five minutes like a creep."

He sat on the edge of my desk, making himself comfortable. "So, the Facebook guy I was talking about setting you up with."

"What Facebook guy?" Nate poked his head around the corner.

Great. The gang's all here.

"This has nothing to do with work," I said, hoping he would take the hint. He didn't.

"I'm setting Kate up with a guy I know on Facebook." Cody took out his phone.

"Wow." Nate looked at me and raised an eyebrow. "Brave."

"I haven't a hundred percent agreed to this yet." I reached for Cody's phone. "I don't even know what he looks like. Can I at least see a picture before I get my medal of valour?"

"Not really," Cody said.

"What do you mean not really?" Nate laughed. "Can't you just show us his profile picture?"

"Well, no. He said he used to have a stalker, so his profile picture is of his cat and he doesn't use his real name."

"So, he might be a murderer then, great," I said. "Can't he send you a picture?"

"No."

"I'm not doing this." I turned back to my desk and started checking my email.

"Come on," Cody whined. "He hates online dating and people choosing who they like based on looks. He wants to get to know someone like in the olden days. You know, when you just talked to someone in person instead of analyzing their pictures."

Nate scoffed. "What do you mean 'talked to someone in person'? Who does that?"

"Besides, pictures always lie," Cody continued. "He wants to meet someone and get to know them with a clean slate, no preconceptions."

I had to admit I felt the same way. This guy seemed to have really thought it through. Maybe he was genuine.

"Hundred bucks he's super fat," Nate said and laughed like the high school jock he never was.

"I can vouch for him that he's not." Cody nodded emphatically. "I have actually met him in person." He slipped his phone into his pocket.

"Either way," I said, frowning at Nate, "that's mean. I honestly don't care how much someone weighs as long as they're not an asshole." I looked pointedly at each of them.

"Well, he has a great personality as well," Cody said, surprisingly abashed. "He's funny. Smart. Hell, I'd date him if I was into dudes. I'm not," he added.

"Thanks for clarifying." I rolled my eyes.

"So, can I tell him you'll meet him for a drink or something?"

"Sure, what the hell. I have a date next week, but maybe sometime the week after?"

"Cool, I'll let him know. You'll have fun!" he said, possibly with a bit too much enthusiasm.

They both went back to their desks and I was left to continue regretting every choice I'd ever made. Maybe this choice would be the start of things turning around.

Chapter 37

April 30th

Julie: How's the date going?

Kate: He hasn't arrived yet.

Julie: What's his name again?

Kate: Kevin.

Julie: And this is the guy we met at the speed dating event who looked like an 18-year-old?

Kate: Sure is.

Julie: Let me know how it goes.

Kate: Will do.

Kate: How long is too long to wait for someone to show up for a date?

Julie: 5 minutes. How long have you been waiting?

Kate: 30.

Julie: 30 minutes?! Leave!

Kate: What if he's stuck in traffic though? Or something. Plus, I ordered a coffee.

Julie: Did he text you that he was stuck in traffic?

Kate: No.

Julie: Then he's not stuck in traffic.

Kate: Did I just get stood up by an 18-year-old boy who I met at a speed dating event?

Julie: Sorry, babe.

Kate: This goal is stupid.

Chapter 38

May 12th

Downtown was busy for a Wednesday due to it being unseasonably hot for May. The patios were packed for lunch and everyone else in the city seemed to have taken over any green space they could find, blankets spread out, kids running around, teenagers smoking pot by the cenotaph. I hadn't gotten used to the fact that you could smoke pot in public now, the smell still tied to illicit activity at Tragically Hip concerts.

I walked into Vic's Tavern for our monthly lunch, sighing in relief at the fact that they had air conditioning.

I gave Julie a huge, sticky hug when I got to the table. "Where's Ben?" I said as I slid into the booth, scrunching up my face as my skin stuck to the plastic.

"He couldn't make it," she said and picked up the menu. "He said he was busy."

"But he always comes," I said. "He's never missed one.

"Well, he's not here now, are you going to be able to manage?" She tipped her menu down and smiled, eyes sparkling.

"Of course." I picked up my own menu. "It's fine. Of course it's fine."

The server came over.

"Could I please get some fries?" I didn't have to look at the menu this time.

"Wow," Julie said. "You must have had a challenging couple of weeks. I haven't seen you eat fries in months." She turned to the server. "I'll have the clubhouse sandwich, please."

"I have." I watched as a couple of bearded gentlemen walked in the door and sat at one of the high-topped tables. This place was filling up fast.

"Could we get some ice water too, please?" I said as the server walked away. I fanned myself with a cardboard beer coaster.

"Sure thing, hon," she said and I grimaced. I really liked this server, but I hated when people called me hon. I especially hated it when those people were twenty years younger than I was.

"So," Julie said. "Lay it on me, hon."

I waited until the server brought us our water and then did, indeed, lay it on her.

I sighed. "How have you been doing this for so long? I don't know how much more I can take. Online dating is slowly sucking the life out of me. It makes me tired. So tired."

"You just need to be patient." She sat back and sipped her water through a cardboard straw.

"I'm trying to be patient. I'm trying to keep an open mind and give people chances, but I'm having a hard time seeing a light at the end of this tunnel of tragedy."

Julie laughed.

"It's not funny."

"It is funny."

"Listen to what I've had to deal with for the last couple of weeks," I said. "I had to tell a guy that writing 'no fat chicks' on his profile was offensive."

"Ugh."

"Last week, I got a message from a guy who 'wanted to get to know me better' and I had to remind him that we'd actually met *in person* a month earlier. He was like, 'Oh, yeah, I totally knew that. You were just really interesting.'"

She held her hand up to her mouth so I couldn't see her smiling.

I kept going. "Two nights ago, I told a guy who wanted to get together for coffee that eight p.m. was too late for me to meet up on a weeknight. I never heard back."

"Eight p.m. on a weeknight isn't that late," she said unhelpfully.

"It is for me," I said, getting louder. "I get that eight p.m. on a weeknight shouldn't be too late for a couple of twenty-five-year-olds to meet up, but if we met at eight p.m., I'd have to stay at least an hour to make it worthwhile, probably more than that, so let's say I stayed for an hour and a half, that would mean I would get home at around ten p.m. and maybe get to bed at eleven p.m. It usually takes me about an hour to fall asleep so I wouldn't fall asleep until around midnight. I get up at six thirty a.m. so, on a good night, that's only six and a half hours of sleep. And experts recommend at least seven, so when you think about it, this guy, who I really didn't want to meet in the first place, is basically asking me to risk my health to go for coffee. And I refuse to do that." I realized how crazy I was starting to sound.

"Do you realize how crazy you're starting to sound?" Julie laughed.

I sighed. "Maybe I'm just not up for this." I reached for a fry as the server put our food down and shoved it in my mouth.

"What about your napkin pledge?" Julie said as she peeled the tomatoes off her sandwich and put them on my plate.

"What about it?" I shrugged.

She put her sandwich down and looked at me. "Kate, how long have we been best friends?"

"I don't want to age myself so I'm just going to say since elementary school."

"Fine. My point is it's been long enough that I know you very well. You and Ben are my favourite people, both equally important to me."

I smiled, even though my stomach sank a bit when she mentioned Ben. I missed him.

"I know you're kind and loyal, you love animals and hate camping. I know you'll always eat my tomatoes, no matter what." She slopped another one on my plate. "And I also know that your parents' divorce was really hard on you."

I winced and held up my hand, not wanting to talk about it.

"Just hear me out," she said and gently pulled my hand down to rest on the table. "I know you don't want to turn into your mom. But you are nothing like your mom. You're the exact opposite of a bully, sometimes too much."

"What do you mean 'sometimes too much'?"

Her eyes softened. "Sometimes you go along with things just so you don't rock the boat."

I looked down, knowing it was true.

"This is the last time I'm going to say this, I promise," she said. "If you don't like a guy, or if he does something shitty, don't go out with him. I guarantee you he will get over it. And if he doesn't, you weren't meant to be together anyways." She took a large bite out of her sandwich and sighed with contentment. "This is delicious."

I laughed. Only Julie could look beautiful while talking with her mouth packed with food.

"Promise me," she said after she'd swallowed her mouthful.

"I promise."

Chapter 39

May 13th

Kate: Hey Ben, just wanted to check in. You weren't at lunch yesterday, is everything OK? Don't work too hard!

Chapter 40

May 21st

Julie: How was the date last night?

Kate: I spent the whole date watching him talk with food in his mouth. Like, seriously, he talked the whole time with his mouth packed with food. Pieces of half-chewed pizza kept dropping onto his lap. I nearly puked.

Julie: LOL. Gross.

Kate: Have you heard anything from Ben?

Julie: Not lately, why?

Kate: Just wondering.

Chapter 41

May 26th

Kate: Hey Ben, me again! Did you get my last text? I hadn't heard anything back so I thought maybe it got lost somewhere in SMS land. Did you want to maybe meet for coffee sometime soon? Hope you're well!

Chapter 42

June 3rd

Julie: Want to hang?

Kate: I'd love to, but I'm going on another date.

Julie: Good luck!

Kate: Do you think five kids is too many?

Julie: You promised!

*Kate: I know. *sigh**

Chapter 43

June 19th

"I can't believe we're finally hanging out," Julie said as we sat on a park bench, taking a break from our intense five-minute walk.

"I know, sorry." I sipped from my water bottle and looked out onto Wascana Lake, smiling at a family of ducks paddling down the bank. "I've just been busy. I'm very popular, you know." I smirked.

Julie leaned over to pet a giant poodle who had stopped to sniff her feet. The man walking it quickly glanced away as I caught him trying to peek down her shirt. "Tell me everything," she said as the dog pulled the man towards a Canada goose.

I groaned.

"That good, hey?" She laughed.

"Two weeks ago, I met a guy for coffee who, as soon as I sat down, asked me if I was wearing underwear."

"Ew! What did you do?"

"I got back up and left."

"Good for you!" she said. "That's my girl."

We got up to continue our walk.

"A guy I'd been out for coffee with a couple times invited me over for supper and it turns out he lives in his mom's basement. And they share a kitchen."

Julie choked out her water.

"She was very nice though. She cut his meat up for him. And also mine. Then she asked me if I wanted to bring my laundry over on the weekend."

Julie actually guffawed. "And?"

"I respectfully declined."

"Sounds like a wise choice."

"I had another date last week. This was a reschedule of a date we'd made a while back, but he had to work so we rebooked. In the time between, we'd touched base a few times. Mostly it was him texting me that he 'just wanted to say have a good day!' I mean, that's super annoying, but whatever. Monday morning, I texted him to make sure we were good to go and he was all, 'You bet!' and I was sort of disappointed because I was really tired and hoping he would cancel, but this is what I signed up for, right?"

"I have a feeling I know where this is going." She rolled her eyes.

"Wait for it," I said. "We had initially planned to meet at seven p.m., but he texted me that he could likely be there earlier and he would text me when he left. I was pretty happy about that because, as you know, I like to go to bed when most people are getting home from work."

"So, how did it go?"

"I texted him at six fifteen." I stopped walking, stepped off the path and read from my phone: "'Hey, I haven't heard back from you so I'm going to assume we're meeting at seven p.m.?' Nothing. I then text him again at six thirty: 'Are we still meeting?' Nothing. Seven p.m.: 'So... I'm not going to leave my place until I hear from you. It's too hot to go out unless I have to. Ha-ha.' Seven fifteen: 'I'm guessing we're not meeting. I hope you're okay.' But I didn't hope he was okay because the only excuse I would have accepted for standing me up would have been severe illness or death."

"Did you hear from him again?"

"No!" I exclaimed. "I didn't. I didn't hear from him ever again. Which is so bizarre because we had been talking back and forth for weeks. And, I mean, I was kind of bummed. And not because I really wanted to meet this guy—I was actually pretty pumped to put on my pyjamas—but more because I got stood up by a guy I met on the *internet*."

"It happens," she said quietly, pulling on my arm to get me to keep walking.

"So, then I got to thinking," I said, following her. "If I can't even get men who are on online dating sites to meet me or even respond to my emails, then am I not just fighting a losing battle here?"

"Well, that's not really fair," she said. "Just because a guy is online doesn't mean he's of diminished quality. I have lots of friends who have met great partners online."

"But that's exactly my point. There actually aren't any quality guys online anymore. Because they're married to all of our friends."

She nodded, which I took as a sign to continue.

"Because there are so many women on these things,

all the great guys our age are snapped up in about five seconds. And if I'm not lucky enough to be online for the brief window of time when a great guy is also online, I completely miss out.

"So, I keep trying, I keep biding my time, all the while being rejected by people I don't really care about, mostly so I can say that I haven't given up."

"That's good that you haven't given up though," she said, which was more of a question than a statement.

"Why?" I asked. "Why is it good? I don't even know why I'm doing this anymore. Why do I need a guy to do things with? I have friends. We do things. And if we don't do things, that's okay. Because I also enjoy not doing things. I wish I hadn't told so many people about this stupid napkin thing. If it was just me who knew, I would have given up a long time ago."

"So, give up," she said, like it was the easiest thing in the world.

"I can't," I said. "I have to do it. I have to prove that I can. I don't want people to think I'm a failure. I don't want people to think I quit just because things got hard."

"Listen," she said. "I told you before, you're not your mom, but you're also not your dad. Quitting something isn't necessarily a sign of weakness, often it's a sign that you know how to take care of yourself. I've told you before, you can't please everyone. No wonder you're tired. You need to get better at weeding your garden."

"Is that a euphemism?" I smirked and she smiled. "I know I promised, but I feel bad when I don't answer. I don't want to be a jerk."

"Well, that's very big of you, but do you think men feel bad when they don't answer you?"

"Yes?" I tried.

"No. No, they don't feel bad. The only reason a lot of them are on there is because they want sex but don't want to sacrifice anything. They want to have their cake and eat it too." She raised her eyebrow. "*That* was a euphemism."

"Gross. But isn't that why you're online?" I asked, knowing that was exactly why she was online.

She paused; a flash of something I couldn't read flickered in her eyes.

"Sorry," I said. "I didn't mean for that to sound judgemental."

"No biggie," she said, immediately regaining her composure. "It's true, that is why I'm online. But I only pick guys who I know are on there for the same reason. I don't talk to those who want a relationship and I know how to tell if they do. Guys know how to tell that too, but the difference is they don't care. They'll sleep with anyone who'll let them." A smile rested on her lips but didn't quite reach her eyes.

I felt like I'd stepped over a line, but I wasn't super clear what that line was.

I tried to step it back. "And that Facebook guy Cody wanted to set me up with never materialized. The guy who wanted to meet someone like he did in the 'good ol' days.' You know, when you didn't get to see what people looked like or know anything about them, even their name apparently, until you actually met?"

That did it. She laughed and I breathed a little easier.

"That didn't really sound like a good idea to me anyway," she said.

"I thought so too, initially, but then I realized that maybe he was right. I'm really getting discouraged with the superficiality of it all. Maybe we do need to go back to basics."

"What if he turned out to be a psycho?"

"Well, Cody said he was a good guy," I said.

"That means literally nothing."

"I know." I paused. "He has a thing for you, by the way."

"I know."

"Oh. Well. Good. Did you want his number or anything?"

"Sure don't." She absentmindedly pulled her hair up in an elastic she was wearing around her wrist.

We walked in silence as I tried to think of something else to say.

"Jesse asked me about you recently," she said, saving me. "He wanted to know if you'd achieved your napkin goal."

"Oh. Well, that was nice." I paused and tried to make my voice sound casual. "So, how often do you go in there anyway?"

She took a sip of water. "I don't know, once or twice a week maybe."

"Oh. I didn't realize you went that often without me."

"Does it matter?" she said with a bit of a bite. "You've been busy lately."

"No. I know. Just wondering." Time to change the

subject. "Speaking of being busy, I haven't heard anything from Ben lately. Is he, I don't know, is he mad at me or something?"

"I don't think so." She looked at her phone distractedly. "Have you tried calling him?"

"No. I mean usually we just text."

"Maybe try it." She smiled. "I'm sure he's fine."

I slapped at a mosquito on my arm. "Ugh, mosquitos are out, want to go get an iced coffee?"

"Excellent idea," she said. "This 'walking around the lake' thing is getting old."

Chapter 44

July 1st

"Let's sit here." I pointed to a small patch of grass that hadn't been taken over by lawn chairs. We squeezed past strollers and coolers, trying not to tread on blankets as we quickly spread ours out.

"Relax," Julie said as I frantically smoothed the corners. "The fireworks don't start for another twenty minutes."

"I know," I puffed, wiping beads of sweat from my forehead with the back of my hand. "But I like to be here at least one hour early so we can find a good place to sit. And we're not. And it's hot and sticky and I think I have mosquito repellent in my eyes." I dabbed at them with the bottom of my maple leaf T-shirt. "So I'm sorry if I seem a bit stressed."

Julie sat and sipped from her travel cup of wine. "I know, and I'm sorry we're late, but we did make it and we did find a place to sit and here..." She handed me a bottle of water and a tissue. "Better?"

I took a deep breath and let it out slowly, took a sip

of water and blotted my stinging eyes. "Yes," I breathed. "Better. Thank you."

Normally I loved sharing my birthday with the birth of our nation; me, Julie and Ben hanging out in the park all day, watching free bands and filling our faces with corn dogs and mini donuts. Then we'd all go home and nap and meet at the park again after dark for the amazing fireworks display. It was always perfect. Except this time it wasn't.

"So… Ben's not coming?" I asked as Julie settled in.

"He had to work. Or something. I can't remember," she said. "I'm sure it was important though; I don't think he's ever missed your birthday."

"He hasn't," I said. "Ever."

"Did he at least text you?"

"No."

"Oh. That's kind of weird, actually. Do you want me to call him?"

"No," I said, now embarrassed. "That's okay. I'm sure it's fine."

"Want some?" She held out her smuggled wine.

"No thanks." I took another sip of water.

"You're quiet tonight," she said.

"I'm just tired." I forced a smile, not wanting her to see how upset I was that Ben hadn't come. That he hadn't even acknowledged it was my birthday. My Canada Day birthday was something we had always just shown up for. It was an unspoken, unbroken commitment. Until today. I really did need to call him. But now I was a bit scared. What if he was mad? What if I had done something that had upset him? I wouldn't be able to live with myself if that was the case. He was one of the most important people in my life. Maybe I should have told him that at some point. But how could I have, given I was just realizing it myself?

My mood lifted slightly as the fireworks started and a collective sigh spread through the park as everyone settled in to watch. They were beautiful; every burst of vibrant colour vibrated in my chest and took my breath away. I looked over at Julie who was smiling wide, joy softening her face in a way I hadn't seen in years. I reached over to grab her hand but stopped when something tightened in my chest. A gasp escaped my throat, eclipsed by the booms of the fireworks and the awe of the crowd. As much as I wanted my best friend to be sitting beside me, for the briefest of moments, an ache fluttered through my throat. I had wanted that hand to be Ben's.

That night, as I sat on the side of my bed, performing my nightly ritual of rubbing really expensive lotion into my hands and elbows and pretending it would protect them from aging, my phone vibrated. I jumped. I thought I had already turned it to silent for the night. Who was texting me this late? People knew when I went to bed.

You awake?

It was Cody.

I hesitated before answering. I was tired and it wasn't like he could tell if I was reading his texts. But what if he could tell? What if he saw I'd read it and I didn't respond? I hated technology.

Yup, just going to bed though.

Quick q: is July 8th cool for your date with my friend?

Sure.

He replied with a thumbs-up.

I waited ten more minutes to see if he was going to give me any more information and, when he clearly wasn't, I turned my phone off and went to bed.

Chapter 45

July 8th

July 8th arrived without fanfare. The only time Cody had mentioned the date was to give me the time and location—7:00 p.m., mini-golf at Games 'n' Giggles. His friend, who still didn't have a name, apparently thought it would be fun to do something different. Get to know each other without the pressure of staring at each other's faces.

I liked the idea. It would be nice to do something fun. For the rest of the week, however, I'd alternated between thinking it was a terrible idea and being completely apathetic about it. I no longer felt like my next date could be the one. I mostly just wanted to get it over with.

I arrived home from work to find that Mittens had puked all over the mat in the entryway. I found it because I stepped in it. Mittens sat back and looked at me like he was saying, "Maybe stay home every once in a while and I'll stop doing this," and also, which I found out later, "I pooped under your bed."

I cleaned up the mess, washed my hands and dragged

myself into my room to change, exhausted before the date had even started. This had to be some sort of record.

My phone buzzed in my hand and I almost dropped it. I tipped it up, thinking (hoping) it might be Ben, but it was just a text from Julie:

Good luck tonight!

At least someone was excited.

I needed to shake this off. If I went into every date with a shitty attitude, it was going to turn out shitty. I needed to at least try, or why bother? A flutter of panic tightened my chest. It was now July. Autumn was just around the corner. And then what? I was running out of time.

"I can still do it, right, Mittens?"

Mittens didn't care.

I took a deep breath and smiled at the mirror. If I was going to make more of an effort, I should probably look in my closet for an outfit instead of finding one on the floor.

I decided on faded jeans and a rose-coloured, long-sleeved tunic blouse that tied in the back. I looked pretty good actually. After touching up my make-up, I felt a bit better. Turned out it did help if you tried. I didn't want to get my hopes up again, but I was a bit more optimistic. Maybe this time it wouldn't suck.

Games 'n' Giggles was a large, warehouse-type building just outside the city. It had been a roller rink back when people actually roller-skated but had since been turned into a fun, mostly-for-kids birthday destination with two mini-golf courses, an arcade and a giant, room-sized bouncy castle.

Normally, going to a place like this would have been

my worst nightmare. Kids and I didn't jive unless they were well-behaved and silent, and places like this were typically full of kids who were neither. Tonight, however, was the second Thursday of the month—adults-only night—which made it the only night I would ever enter this place willingly.

I braced myself and walked inside, still expecting a screaming child to run into me, even though they weren't allowed. The sticky smell of buttered popcorn and sugar triggered memories of simpler times. It was surprisingly quiet. I could hear the bells and buzzes from the arcade.

As I walked further, I was met by a perky teenager with dyed-black hair and a tasteful nose ring who gestured for me to follow her to the counter. "Do you have a reservation?" she asked in a bubbly voice.

"I don't think so." I looked around. "I'm meeting someone. At the elephant? I think he said to meet him at the elephant." I didn't see an elephant.

"Oh, of course." She pointed to her left. "Just follow the arrows to Jungle Golf. You can't miss it."

"Should I pay here or…?" I rooted awkwardly in my purse for my wallet and dropped my keys on the floor.

"There's a place to pay there. It'll depend on how many rounds of golf you play."

"Cool. Great. Cool." I smiled, deliberately stepped onto the Jungle Golf arrow and walked down the hall. I was way too old to be here.

Sure enough, I arrived at a large room, which appeared to be Jungle Golf, and just inside the entrance there was a large blow-up elephant.

I looked around to see if my date had arrived and, seeing no one else by the elephant, I settled onto a bench and people-watched. This actually looked like it could be fun. I hadn't mini-golfed since I was a kid, but I'd always liked it. Ben had told me it was good to do things that reminded you of your carefree childhood days. It was supposed to help with anxiety. My stomach sank as I calculated how long it had been since Ben and I had spoken. I really missed him.

But maybe this was just what I needed. Soon I was fully absorbed by an adorable senior couple halfway through their round. He kept kicking his ball closer to the hole when she wasn't looking and it was hilarious.

"Kate?" A familiar voice I couldn't quite place. I looked up and my stomach hit the floor.

"Justin." It came out as a whisper. I couldn't find my breath.

"I haven't seen you since—" *Since I had a meltdown on your front porch.*

Chapter 46

I was living one of my worst nightmares—staring into the face of a man I was once desperately in love with. The man who had watched me from his bedroom window twenty years ago while I made a fool of myself in front of his whole neighbourhood. The drummer who had promised to love me forever. I'd lost myself so deeply in that love that it had taken me years to find myself again.

He looked different; older obviously—he'd aged well, as men tend to do—but the younger man I knew was still there. I could still see the sun-bleached blond streaks in his receding hairline, a hint of freckles across his nose, the tiny wrinkles at the corners of his mouth from the crinkly smile I'd known so well. He wasn't smiling now, however.

He recovered from his shock quickly, forcing his startled features into something more neutral. "It's been... a while. What are you doing here?"

"I'm waiting for... someone. A date. I'm waiting for—"

No.

"You're waiting for me," he said, clearly disappointed. This couldn't be happening. "I guess that's what happens when you prefer to remain nameless," I said, attempting a joke but falling flat.

He shook his head. "I didn't even think—"

"Me neither."

I swallowed and stood up. "Well, it was nice to see you again, you look well," I said like I was leaving a job interview I had totally bombed.

He watched me walk by. "You're leaving?"

"Obviously you were expecting someone else," I said, my eyes on the floor. "And so was I. I can't see this being comfortable for either of us, can you?"

His lips turned up into the beginnings of a grin. "Well, I was actually expecting it to be uncomfortable; all first dates are. This isn't quite what I had imagined, but I was really looking forward to playing mini-golf. And I've already reserved our spot. Why don't we stay and play one game?"

I met his gaze, the blush fading from my face. "Sure, why not? I drove all this way and, honestly, I have nothing else to do."

"I'm flattered," he said dryly, his grin widening into a full smile.

I decided to take a shot at a joke, knowing that the tone of the evening would depend on how it landed. "I promise not to break down crying if I lose."

Silence. Shit.

And then he laughed. Loud, long and full. "Oh, man, your dry humour always gets me."

"Too soon?" I smirked.

"Probably." He smiled and led me over to the counter.

We picked out our clubs and golf balls and he handed me a cardboard card and a little pencil. "Can you keep score? I'm still not good at math."

And then we played mini-golf. And it was really fun. Neither of us were great. I was less great, but we laughed a lot and talked a lot and, once we got over our initial awkwardness, we had a genuinely good time. After each hole, another layer of awkwardness fell away.

On hole one, we got the "so what do you do now" talk out of the way. I told him I worked at a PR agency and got the usual "cool" and I left it at that.

"What about you?" I asked.

"Finance."

I laughed. "Perfect job for someone terrible at math."

"I just fell into it somehow," he said, laughing along while setting down his brightly coloured ball.

"What about the band?" I asked half-seriously. "Still together?"

"Nah." He chuckled. "I still play the drums sometimes, but just for fun."

I set my ball down at the second hole and got ready to swing. "Didn't quite reach your goal of opening for Pearl Jam?" I teased.

"Nope," he said. "Turns out we weren't very good."

On hole three, we talked about why we were online dating and how we liked it. He told me he had just gotten out of a seven-year relationship. He didn't offer a reason and I didn't ask. He explained how lonely he felt and how he wanted to be a part of something again.

"I detest online dating though." He grimaced. "The

superficiality of it all, the clinical dismissiveness. It's like I'm trying to choose a pair of shoes," he said bitterly.

"That's what I said!" I yelled a bit too loudly. "It's slowly killing me."

"Why are you doing it then?" he asked. I opened my mouth, ready to go through my whole "someone to kiss" spiel, ready to pull out the napkin, but after a couple of seconds, I closed it again.

"Honestly?" I said after I took my shot. "I don't even know anymore."

At hole five, I told him that I actually hated my job and he told me that his ex had cheated on him. And not just once as a drunken mistake, but that she had been in another relationship for years.

"How could I not have noticed?" he said. "I feel so stupid."

At hole seven, I realized I was having a really good time. We paused to let some twenty-year-olds go ahead of us and fell into a normal rhythm of chatting, joking and laughing. He told me about his terrible online dating experiences and I told him about mine. It surprised me to learn that some men had as tough a time as we did. I'd thought they had it easy.

By the time we got to hole nine, I'd worked up the nerve to ask him why men online always went for younger women when there were so many great single females who were their age. He smiled in a way that told me he'd been asked that many times before.

"In all honesty," he said, leaning on his golf club, "I think it's because they can. A lot of men who are newly single just want something easy. They want looks over substance. They don't want to fight. They don't want to talk about kids or the future or responsibilities. They don't want someone telling them what to do. They want to be the boss and they want to take care of someone. And with younger women they can often do both those things. In that kind of relationship, the men are the experienced ones. They're the ones who know the answers. The older a woman gets the stronger she gets, the more sure of herself. She has a better idea of what she wants. Some men don't like that. Others are scared that she's going to figure out that what she wants is not him."

"So, it's not that they just don't like saggy parts and wrinkles?" I asked.

"No, it's that too." He laughed and ducked as I swatted his arm.

"Are you that type of man?" I asked, suddenly serious.

He looked up and smiled his crinkly grin. "No. I'm not."

At hole twelve, we took a short break while a group played through and he went to get us bottles of water. I watched him walk to the concession stand and remembered how terrible I'd felt when we were young and he'd walked away for good. I tried to bring back that feeling. To feel sad, lonely and embarrassed. But it was gone; it was finally gone. I could think about that time of my life and not feel ashamed. In fact, I felt nothing.

I felt nothing.

And I was okay with that. A slow smile spread across my face.

Justin walked up and handed me a bottle of water; the surprising coolness of it made me shiver. He picked up both of our clubs. "Shall we?"

We had so much fun playing the rest of the holes that we were done before I knew it. I couldn't remember the last time I'd had so much fun on a date. We talked, laughed and teased, just like we used to. There was no pressure to impress, no pressure to decide if I wanted to go on a second date. I could just relax and be myself for once.

I could relax because I knew.

"I had a lot of fun," I said as we sat down at a metal table, each with an order of fries smothered with ketchup and gravy.

"Me too." He squirted mayo on top of his already saturated fries.

"That's disgusting." I wrinkled my nose. "You're going to have a heart attack."

He smiled and dug in with a plastic fork. "Then I'll die a happy man."

"I'm sorry for the way things ended between us when we were young."

His forkful of fries hung halfway between his plate and his mouth. "I know. Me too." He shoved them in and started chewing.

"I was so young and insecure and I didn't know what to do. I thought losing you was the end of my life."

"Well, I could have handled it better myself. We were both young. It just wasn't working out."

"You knew way back then we weren't meant to be together. How?" I leaned forward on my elbows, narrowly avoiding a splat of hardened ketchup.

He shrugged. "I just did. You were great, we had fun, we were really good friends, but I didn't see it being more than that. Neither of us did anything wrong. It's just how it was."

"I thought you hated me. For years I tried to figure out what I had done."

"I didn't hate you." He smiled and gestured at me with his fork. "But even if I did, isn't it more important what you thought about yourself? You're the only person you are guaranteed to live with for the rest of your life. You're the person you should be trying the hardest to please. If you're truly happy with yourself, it doesn't matter what anyone else thinks about you."

I silently poked at my fries. "Thank you," I said after a few moments. "I think I really needed to hear that."

He smiled and nodded. "You're welcome."

"What a story it would have been if we'd ended up rekindling our relationship twenty years later on a blind date at Games 'n' Giggles."

"You always did like the story better than the reality," he said, taking another mouthful.

"I did. But I like the reality better now. I'm glad we got to hang out and make a better farewell memory."

"Me too," he said, stealing a forkful of fries off my plate.

"We're literally eating exactly the same thing," I said.

"Sometimes I need a mayo break," he said with his mouth full. "Cleanses the palate."

We finished eating and carried our empty paper plates to the garbage on our way out.

"You know," I said as I put on my coat, "despite how this started, and despite the fact that it ended up not really being a date, I had way more fun tonight than I've had on any of my real dates. Thanks for asking me to stick around."

"I'm glad I did. You turned out to be way less crazy than I thought you'd be." He laughed as I punched him in the arm. "Seriously though, if you're not having fun or enjoying any of it, why don't you just stop?"

I didn't have an answer. *Because I need to hit a random goal I set for myself when I was drunk* didn't seem to be a good one.

He held the door open and we walked outside. The warm breeze blew my hair into my eyes and I ran my hands through it, settling it back into place.

We hugged our goodbyes and walked in opposite directions to our cars. Just before I got to the corner, I turned back and watched him walk away one last time, smiling with the knowledge that sometimes the best things happened when they didn't go according to plan.

I slid into my car, still warm from the heat of the day. I sat with the windows down, letting the fresh summer air stream in, and I made a decision. A heavy weight lifted off my chest, dissipating out the window along with the stuffiness of the car. For the first time in six months, my body relaxed.

My phone vibrated and my heart sped up—maybe it was Ben. Maybe he felt awful for not coming to my birthday and was texting to apologize. This was the longest we'd ever gone without seeing each other. Maybe he was going to say he missed me too.

I swiped my password in and my heart sank. It was just my mom. Sending me an e-transferred birthday present. A week late, as usual.'

Thanks, I typed in and pressed send.

I steadied myself to drive home, my throat tight with unshed tears. I refused to let my mom's forgetfulness ruin my night. It had never bothered me before, I thought as I put the car in drive. But why else would I feel so sad?

Chapter 47

July 17th

I lay in bed Saturday morning, Mittens' fuzzy warmth cuddled into the curve of my side, still thinking about Thursday night. "You've always liked the story better than reality," Justin had said. Was that true? Did I want the perfect story so much that I ignored what was actually happening? Did I want someone to want to be with me so much that I just went along with things so I didn't, as Julie had said, "rock the boat"?

I reached for my phone and texted Julie:

Remember Mark?

Oh, man. Please don't tell me you're talking to him again.

After Peter left me in my late twenties, I had rebounded solidly into Mark. He wrote a hilarious blog that I followed like a stalker. He had a picture of himself on the sidebar, staring broodily into the camera, and I would stare at it as I refreshed his page over and over again, hoping to see a new post pop up.

I desperately wanted him to follow the blog I had just started, but I was too nervous to post a witty and noticeable comment on his blog, so I posted a comment on a blog I knew he read and tried to make it as funny as possible. Miraculously, it worked. He visited my blog, commented on a post, and our relationship blasted off from there.

From blog commenting, we worked our way up to emails and online messaging, and what started as messaging every so often morphed into chatting online for hours a day. I remember almost vibrating with anticipation at work, not being able to wait until I got home so we could talk again.

We got along extremely well. He thought I was funny; I thought he was funny; he thought he was funny. We both liked music. And TV. We shared so many interests.

One thing we didn't share, however, was the city we lived in. Who cared though, right? Who needed face-to-face interaction when you could develop a fully functional relationship by typing all your thoughts and feelings into a little box? Neither of us liked talking on the phone and video chatting wasn't even an option back then.

After four months of typing about how well we got along, and how perfect we were for each other, we finally got up the collective nerve to meet in person.

I don't think I've ever been as nervous as I was during the three hours I waited for him to arrive. I changed my outfit four times, each time almost sweating through the one previous. What if he didn't like the way I looked? What if he didn't think I was funny in person? Or what if he did but in a bad way? What if I started to hyperventilate when I saw him?

I needn't have worried.

When he finally arrived, over two hours late, he looked so different from his picture that at first I thought he was a delivery guy.

He looked nothing like I had imagined. Nothing like the image of the confident, ruggedly handsome artist I had created in my mind. He must have seen the confusion or possibly noticed the small gasp I emitted when I realized who he was.

"Not quite what you expected?" he said, trying to laugh it off.

"Of course not," I lied, hastily arranging my face back to neutral. "Come in. It's so great to finally meet you in person."

We actually ended up having a really good time. He was still the funny, smart person I'd been talking to online for months. He just wasn't exactly as I had imagined. He wasn't confident by any means. He didn't seem to have a job. He lived in a bachelor basement suite and slept on an air mattress. There was something else though: despite having chatted with him for months and reading his blog for over a year, it seemed as if I was hanging out with a complete stranger. The connection we shared online was virtually non-existent in real life.

I didn't let that stop me though. I mean we had a great connection online, so I was sure it was only a matter of time before that connection magically appeared in physical form. Besides, he was the only guy I could be myself around. He knew me. Really knew me. And still wanted to be with me. I would never find that freedom again.

After spending the day together hanging out in coffee

shops and walking around the city, we ended up back at my place. As we said our goodbyes, I waited patiently for him to kiss me, just like I had imagined. This was where the sparks would start to fly, I knew it.

I'm not going to lie; I had been waiting all day for that moment. And not because I wanted to kiss him that badly, but because I thought that was obviously the natural next step. Of course we would kiss. We were meant to be together. So, when he didn't appear to be making even the slightest attempt, I kissed him. Why wait for the guy to make the first move, right?

His eyes widened comically—I had definitely caught him off guard—but then he relaxed and kissed me back. Like one would kiss their grandma. Quickly and awkwardly. I assured myself that next time it would be better. He had probably just been surprised. I would make him want to kiss me if it was the last thing I ever did.

After the visit, we settled back into our regular online conversations. The connection was back; it had probably never left. I determined we had both just been so nervous about meeting in person that the awkwardness had covered up all the spark. We continued to talk every day about taking our relationship to the next level.

We reasoned that, if one of us were to move, it would make more sense for me to go where he was, rather than him moving to my city. He had pets and couldn't get out of his lease; I didn't love my job and wanted a change. I jumped in with both feet. Taking a risk, living life the way it should be.

The next time we planned to meet was Valentine's

Day. He would come to visit again and we'd firm up our plans.

It had been months since we'd met in person for the first time. We'd made plans on two previous occasions, but the first time his car had broken down and the second time he had to take his dog to the vet. Valentine's Day was better anyways, I told myself. It was more romantic.

For weeks I agonized over planning the two days we were going to spend together. Everything had to be perfect. I decided on a cozy, candlelit table for two. I marinated a pork roast for days, planning the perfect meal. I bought a new outfit, got my hair done, and gave my apartment the deepest clean it had ever known. I even shaved my legs. I knew our time together was going to be special.

I woke up that morning with a buzz of excitement I hadn't felt in years. This was going to be the beginning of our new life together. I had proactively quit my job as a production assistant just before the break so I could move whenever we decided. My stuff was mostly packed—I figured it would be more efficient if he could take a few boxes home with him so I didn't have to take them all when I drove there. I was planning to sell all my furniture.

That morning, I sat down at my table, opened my laptop and smiled when I saw an email from him, knowing he was going to send one when he left. A flush of excitement warmed my face. I was ready to giddily start counting down the hours until he arrived.

But it wasn't an "I'm so excited to see you tonight" email or a "Just leaving and will be there soon" email. It was actually an "I'm not going to be able to make it because

I'm not feeling very well" email. A "Maybe we should slow things down" email. And an "It's not you, it's me" email. He was "super sorry" though and still wanted to be friends. I guess he figured that would make everything okay.

At first, I was confused. Was this a joke? Had I missed part of the email? Had I missed an entire sequence of emails?

The flush that had warmed my face deepened into a sweaty panic and started spreading through the rest of my body, pushing the air from my lungs and settling in the pit of my stomach.

After emailing back and forth a couple of times and realizing that he did, indeed, intend to carry on with his life without me, I sent a final email telling him it would be too hard for me to be friends right now. I was too shocked and too hurt and, still, too confused. I hoped he understood.

He didn't.

A few weeks later, I received a large package of all the things I'd ever given him, including a Christmas card and a congratulatory letter I'd sent after he'd completed his creative writing certificate. I guess he felt the postage was worth it to make a point.

I had always wondered why it had taken me a long time to get over Mark, but now I thought I knew. It was hard to remember what I had felt more strongly: devastation because the relationship was over or stupid because I had lost myself so deeply in a relationship again. A relationship with someone who, really, I had barely known.

Because I hadn't known him. At all. I had created an

ideal version of him based on our online conversations. Conversations that were easily editable. I had wanted so badly to be with someone that I had draped the fantasy over a real person like a cloak, never bothering to pay attention to what was underneath.

I hadn't cared that he'd never invited me over to his place. I'd let it slide that he'd never opened up about his past. I'd made excuses for his excuses. Just like Justin had said, I'd let myself fall for a story that I'd created and had agreed to whatever Mark wanted so the story wouldn't end. It wasn't his fault that he couldn't live up to my expectations. No one could. They were based on a figment of my imagination. Maybe he'd just seen that before I could.

Chapter 48

July 10th

Hi Ben, it's Kate. I, um, well, I'm leaving this message because I, well, because you haven't answered my texts. Are you... are you okay? I... I really mi— Please call me back.

Chapter 49

"I've decided to delete my online dating account."

Julie looked up from her phone and raised her eyebrows. "What happened?"

We were sitting in Beans 'n' Brews at our usual table while Jesse alternately sat with us and waited on customers. It was a lazy Sunday and the cafe was barely a quarter full. The people who were there were sitting quietly at their tables, nursing their coffees and reading or working on their laptops. No one was making out. No kids were screaming. Just how I liked it.

"Nothing." I took a bite of my oatmeal and raisin cookie. "I just decided I'm done."

She put down her phone and looked at me. "But what happened though?" She picked off a piece of my cookie and popped it in her mouth.

"My blind Facebook date was with Justin," I said and then added, "they're raisins, not chocolate chips."

"Holy shit, *Justin,* Justin? Drummer Justin?" She delicately spat the cookie into her napkin.

"Drummer Justin. Except he's not a drummer anymore."

"Wow, you sure buried the lede on that one. What happened? Why didn't you tell me? It's almost been two weeks! Tell me everything now." She looked angry. Understandably. We always told each other everything.

"I didn't tell you right away because I needed time to process." I held my hands up in defence. "I didn't want to talk about it until I was sure. But after the few mediocre dates I've been on over the past week and a half, I'm ready to process it with words. Out loud. To you!" I opened my arms like I was giving her a gift. "And the date with Justin actually went really well."

She raised an eyebrow. "Please don't tell me you've rekindled your relationship. Or that you're pregnant. Are you pregnant?" she almost shouted.

"It's been ten days; I don't think human biology could tell me that quickly. And no. Nothing has been rekindled."

She visibly relaxed.

And then I told her about the night. I told her how awkward it was and how I almost left when I saw him. And I told her how fun it ended up being but how we both knew we wouldn't see each other again. I told her about the closure.

"I told him how much I hated online dating and he asked me why I was doing it. I didn't have an answer. I mean it's been seven months and I've been on dozens of dates and I haven't found anyone I'm even remotely attracted to."

"Maybe you just need to give it more time," she said, clearly not believing it herself anymore.

"Remember that guy with the Elantra I went out with a few weeks ago?"

She nodded.

"Well, he was a great guy. He took me to that awesome Nepalese place on Winnipeg Street for lunch and gave me chocolate for no reason and, really, there was nothing wrong with him. He was cute, we had a lot in common, he was a good conversationalist, he made decisions and he had ambition and good values. But, for some reason, I was not attracted to him in any way. It was almost like I was wishing he were someone else."

"Who?" Julie asked, eyes wide.

"I don't know." I waved my hand dismissively. "Probably just some mythical great guy who doesn't actually exist."

Jesse sat down and started to speak, but Julie waved him quiet and whispered, "Kate has decided to stop online dating." He leaned forward as I continued my rant.

"And, yes, everyone has told me I shouldn't expect to feel a spark immediately and, yes, I do agree with that, but I didn't feel anything at all. Not even the smallest desire to see him again. In fact, I dreaded it."

"Been there, sister," Jesse said. He held out his hand for a high five then lowered it with a silent "Ouch" when Julie punched him in the leg.

"So, I thought about this. And I thought about what Justin said."

"Drummer Justin?" Jesse mouthed and Julie nodded.

"And I realized that what I've been doing is going out on dates with a bunch of men, many of whom are perfectly fine, and spending the entire date not trying to enjoy myself and get to know them but trying to figure out what's wrong with them so I can go out and find this non-existent Mr. Perfect." I paused and sipped my coffee. "And when I do find something wrong with them, whether it's that they talk with food in their mouth or I don't like their T-shirt, it's always a deal breaker. Then I can finally relax and leave the date with a justifiable sense of relief that I'll never have to see them again."

Jesse turned as a guy with a ball cap on backwards walked up to the counter for a refill. "I'm on a break," he yelled and turned back with rapt attention.

Backwards Hat stood there with a confused look on his face.

"Just go back and pour one yourself." Jesse waved at him dismissively. Backwards Hat shrugged and did.

"I'm surprised you still have a job," Julie said and was quickly shushed.

"Please continue," Jesse said as he ate the rest of my cookie.

"Sometimes, though," I started again, "I can't find anything wrong with a guy on our first date. Which you'd think would be good, right?"

They nodded, completely in sync.

"So, when they ask me out again, I say yes because I can't think of a reason to say no. And after I say yes, I keep trying to think of a reason to cancel because I don't want to go. But I can't think of a reason. So I go. And it sucks. And the whole process starts over again." I sighed and then added, because I had just thought of it myself, "It's like I'm always hoping for someone specific to show up and that person never comes."

I took a deep, shaky breath and a sip of my coffee, finding it hard to swallow. "I think I'm the one with the problem, not the men I've been dating. And I've decided to accept that this is the way it is and stop trying to feel things I don't. No pledge written on a crumpled napkin is worth being miserable all the time. I'm done."

They were both silent while I took a deep breath.

I sighed. "I really thought this was going to be fun and it's turned out to be a job. A job I hate even more than my real job. And you both know how much I hate my real job."

Julie sipped her coffee. "I totally get it. Online dating isn't for the faint of heart. It's hard and it takes a lot of patience if you want to get a relationship out of it. And I don't want to beat a dead horse, but it really is especially hard for women."

"And especially, *especially* hard for women our age," I added. "I know many great single women our age who are online dating and failing at it and I know zero men who are our age and are both single and great. They're either one or the other."

"Hey," Jesse said, pretending to be offended.

"As much as we love you, you know you're not our age, sweetie." Julie patted him on the head like a puppy.

He grinned and ducked his head away. "Well, maybe that's your problem. Maybe you shouldn't be thinking of age. Maybe age is relative when you find someone you really like."

Did he just wink at me?

"Yeah, I get that." Julie slid her empty cup over to him for a refill. "And I've hooked up with many a younger guy, but for a relationship? I don't know." She leaned back in her chair. "I once had a guy ask me if I was the kind of older woman who wanted to have a twenty-year-old as her 'dirty little secret' and I was like, 'Frankly, no.'"

Jesse abruptly got up to refill our coffees.

"What's his problem?" I said.

Julie looked up from her phone, which she'd dug out of her purse halfway through the conversation. "I didn't notice anything."

"Probably because you were looking at your phone."

"Probably." She shrugged and put it back on the table. "Anyway, I'm really proud of you."

"Really? I thought you'd be disappointed. You kept telling me not to give up and I did."

"You didn't though. You gave it a good shot and you tried really hard. And, most of all, you know yourself. You knew it was doing you more harm than good and you knew it was time to get out. Honestly, I wish I knew myself that well." She looked down at the table, uncharacteristically modest.

I knew these were the times that I had to stay silent. The rare occasions when Julie revealed something personal. When her secure exterior briefly disappeared and her real self shone through.

She looked up and the moment was instantly ruined by Jesse bringing us back our coffees, which he plunked on the table in front of us.

"What the hell?" I said, mopping up the spill with the

napkin that had once held my cookie. "Why are you so cranky all of a sudden?"

"I'm not," he said, his arms crossed at his chest and his face contorted into a pout.

"You look like a three-year-old ready to have a tantrum," Julie said, laughing.

He tried to stifle a grin but the cuteness couldn't help but poke through. "Well, if you must know, I'm just disappointed, that's all."

"You're disappointed I'm not online dating anymore?" I asked. "I didn't realize you were that invested."

"No, the café is hosting a singles night in a couple of weeks and I was going to ask you both if you wanted to come. It would help having a couple of nice-looking ladies like yourselves there. And I thought it would be fun to hang out. Oh well." He sighed, hanging his head like a little boy, a curl falling into his eyes.

"Why would you think we're not coming?" Julie looked at me. "We would be jerks if we didn't do something that would help out a friend."

I rolled my eyes. Super subtle as usual. "Sure, we'll come. I said I was giving up online dating, not giving up on leaving my house. It could be my last hurrah. Before I give up dating completely."

Jesse grinned like a guy who was used to getting his way. "Great." He looked at me and then quickly looked away, his mood instantly improved. "I guess I should probably get back to my job."

"Those tables aren't going to clear themselves." Julie smiled.

"Feel free to help out if you want."

Why did he keep staring at me?

"Nah, my table-clearing days are over," I said, lowering my eyes and emptying my cup. "I prefer to sit at a desk now and nurse an ulcer for a living."

"You are an adult, after all." Julie stood up and put on her coat.

"A much *older* adult." Jesse winked and I blushed.

I watched him as he walked back to the counter.

"You like him, don't you?" Julie said.

"Of course I like him," I said quickly, abashed to be caught. "He's my friend."

"You know what I mean. I get it though. A cute little bum like that, who could resist?"

We both laughed. "I used to have a huge crush on him," I said. "But now... now I'm not sure. He's so young," I said, trying to brush it off. And then, "Do you think he likes me?"

She paused and watched him cleaning up behind the counter. "Who wouldn't? You're great."

"But what about my age? What if he wants kids?"

"What if he doesn't?"

She bent down and picked up her purse, which had fallen on the floor. "In any case, I think it's a bit early to think about kids."

"I know." I sighed. I was conflicted. And confused. I honestly didn't know what to feel anymore.

"If we ever were to get together, I would have too much respect for him for it to be a fling. And if we did get serious, the subject of kids would be bound to come up.

It would be so much easier if we were dudes and didn't have to think about our ticking time bomb wombs. I bet you a million dollars that when a guy's thinking of dating someone younger, he doesn't automatically wonder if they want kids."

"They don't think at all," Julie said as we walked towards the door. "They just do it."

"Lucky bastards."

We both waved goodbye to Jesse as we left. "Get ready to mingle!" he yelled.

"Can't wait!" I said, my words dripping with fake enthusiasm.

He laughed as we walked out the door.

Chapter 50

August 6th

On the day of the singles night, I woke up with the same lightness that had been greeting me for some time now. It had been three weeks since I'd deleted the online dating app and it still felt great. When I'd first started online dating, I'd wake up feeling excited, eager to find out if anyone great had liked me or sent me a message while I'd slept. Who would I be matched with today? Would today be the day I found Mr. Right?

Towards the end, though, I'd wake up and all I'd feel was dread. I hadn't realized how much online dating had been weighing me down until I'd stopped. Each time I checked the app and saw that a guy had viewed my profile and hadn't contacted me (or, even worse, had viewed my profile after I'd contacted him and hadn't contacted me), each time I'd read a profile that said a guy had a "Masters in kissing and was working on a PhD," each time I would get a message from a nineteen-year-old who wanted to "fulfill his life to the fullest" and was "looking for someone with experience," each time some guy had asked me if I preferred "wieners or bratwurst," I would feel just a little bit heavier. Not enough that I noticed it at the time, but just enough to eventually suffocate me in my sleep.

Now, as I lay in bed, watching the sun start to peek through the break in my curtains, all I felt was relief. Relief that the app was off my phone. Relief that I didn't have to hear from any more men who made me doubt the goodness of humanity. Relief that I didn't have to check and I didn't have to respond and I didn't have to decide. Now I could just live my life and be grateful for what I had. Because, really, I had a lot to be grateful for. And I didn't need a man to help me appreciate any of it. After tonight, I would never have to think about dating again.

I sat up in bed with one big stretch and slipped on my fuzzy slippers, ready for the day. I was actually looking forward to the event. No pressure to find someone or make a good impression. Just hanging out with friends and having fun.

And because I hadn't lain in bed for half an hour hating my life, I had time to have a coffee and get ready for work in a leisurely manner. Maybe I would even read a bit. I shuffled into the kitchen and started a pot.

Mittens slid across my feet with a contented purr and looked up with what I'm sure was confusion, considering I was awake and mobile and he didn't have to poke me in the eye. "Yes, that's right," I said as I scooped him up and kissed him on his little pink nose. "We're going to have a little hang-out this morning before I go to work."

He mewed a "thank you" and jumped out of my arms and over to his food bowl.

I filled up his dish and walked back into my room to pick out my casual Friday wardrobe: dark jeans and a burnt-orange V-neck sweater, dressing to match the autumn colour palette that had just started to appear outside my bedroom window.

As I sipped my coffee, I noticed again what a great mood I was in and how relaxed I felt. It was funny how you often didn't know how miserable you were until you weren't.

I won't even let my shitty job bring me down today, I thought as I flipped through the pages of my new Emily Henry book. *Bring it on, Terry. Bring it on.*

Of course, I should never have tempted fate like that.

Terry was in fine form when I arrived. The receptionist looked like she had been crying, which was happening more and more lately. I pretended I didn't notice as I waved good morning. The last time I'd walked into the bathroom to find her crying on the floor, screaming at me to get out, was the last time I would ask her if she was okay.

Cody was waiting for me at my desk and looked behind him quickly as I walked in.

"What's up?" I asked as I sat down and turned on my computer.

"Terry's on the warpath," he whispered, cupping his hand around his mouth.

I looked around to see who could possibly be reading his lips.

"Why? What happened this time?"

"We didn't get any nominations for award season this year."

"We didn't get any?" I was shocked. We normally cleaned up at those things. We were well known in the PR world for being very creative with the pieces we put out. Or we had been well known. Come to think of it, because of the high turnaround we'd had lately, our creativity had kind of tanked. I hadn't heard any positive feedback at all this year. The only feedback we'd been getting was how much of an asshole Terry was.

"None," Cody confirmed. "Terry is tearing a strip off the creative team right now. He already yelled at Stacey"— our receptionist—"for not getting our submission packages in on time."

"Shitty." I anxiously looked over Cody's head.

"Yeah, to say the least." He turned to leave and then changed his mind. "How's the napkin crusade going?"

"I deleted my online account."

"Really? Wow. How do you feel about that?"

"Awesome." I smiled. I really did.

"What's so awesome? I'd love to hear something awesome after all the fires I've had to put out this morning."

We both snapped our heads in the direction of Terry's hostile voice and saw him standing off to the side, hand on his hip, red-faced.

Cody looked at me with a mixture of bemusement and fear.

"I've, um, quit online dating," I said. I could very easily have said, "Nothing," but I'd tried that before and it made things worse. Given that Terry was the centre of everyone's universe, we couldn't possibly have been talking about anything but him. And if we wouldn't tell him what we were talking about, that meant it was something bad. There was always a lot of "Tell me, I can handle it" until we told him what we were actually talking about and then he didn't believe us. It was fun.

"Oh," he said. "Well, I guess that's great for you. Congratulations." To be clear, he did not say this in a way that conveyed that he thought it was great for me, nor did he feel it deserved to be congratulated. "I guess you didn't bother giving any thought to those who have invested all their time and energy into an online dating project and might need your support?"

And there it was.

"Please tell me you found someone and that's why you no longer need to partake in any online services." He looked up at the ceiling like he was trying to hold back an onslaught of emotion.

"No," I said as Cody backed away, trying to disappear. "I just decided I didn't want to do it anymore."

"Kind of selfish, but whatever," Terry said as his eyes met mine. "And speaking of not doing things, I'm still waiting for the workout you're supposed to be creating for me." Cody's eyebrows shot up. "When do you think that will be coming?"

Shit. I'd forgotten. "Soon, for sure," I said. "I'm almost done. Is that a new shirt, by the way? I really like it."

"Don't patronize me," he spat and turned on his heel to leave. "And *by the way*," he mimicked, "we have an important meeting in thirty minutes. Don't be late." He stormed out, almost knocking over a stand of industry magazines as he left.

Cody had somehow managed to escape, so I was finally alone. And despite the fact that Terry had started my day on an aggressive note, I still felt pretty good. Great, actually. The incredible relief I'd felt that morning still hadn't worn off. The fact that my stomach still didn't turn when I heard an alert from my phone, or any phone, told me I had definitely made the right decision.

So, what was I going to do after my last dating hurrah? Well, I was going to enjoy sleeping in a queen-sized bed all by myself every night and love every second of it. I was going to watch TV, read books and play with my cat and not dread leaving the house to go on dates that I knew would ultimately suck. I would only leave the house for things I wanted to leave the house for. Things that were going to be fun. Maybe I would join a book club this fall or something.

Most importantly, I was never going to shave my legs again. Nah, I would—but now it would be just for me.

Chapter 51

Thirty minutes could go by pretty fast when you were waiting for a meeting you didn't want to attend. Before I knew it, I had to set aside my joyful feelings and make my way into the boardroom.

Normally for staff meetings, everyone showed up five minutes early and the first ten minutes were spent hanging out, laughing and joking about a difficult client or something someone watched on YouTube. This time, however, everyone was sitting at the boardroom table in complete silence. I felt like I was disrupting a funeral when I walked in. In a way, I kind of was.

I sat in one of the few chairs left and rolled myself around so I could face the front where I was sure Terry was going to make his grand, angry entrance. I caught Cody's eye and smiled, but he just looked at me with an exaggerated bug-eyed expression and turned his head back to the front. He actually looked scared. Everyone looked scared. Everyone but me, for some reason. I was a bit disgusted though. Some of my colleagues really needed a shower when they were terrified.

I could hear people breathing like I was in a meditative

yoga class. No one dared speak lest they should disrupt the somber mood.

And then we heard him. The clippity-clop of his expensive leather shoes on the tiled hall floor. The whole room collectively took in a long, shaky breath like it was their last one before drowning. Everyone's head moved as one to the opened door and then they all looked down to their laps as Terry walked in, turned around and shut it behind him.

Here we go. I settled into what I was sure would be the performance of his life. I wished I had popcorn.

He walked to the front, took off his glasses, and set them on the table. He knew people were scared. He knew we were all waiting to see if we were fired, waiting for the fury to be unleashed.

"I'm sure you're all aware that we didn't get any nominations this year," he started.

No one moved.

"Well, are you or not?" He glared at us, arms out, palms to the sky, his face an exaggerated question mark.

We all nodded vigorously.

"Well," he said, satisfied, "you also may have heard that I'm not happy about it."

We all nodded again.

"As you can imagine, I was not my usual, fun-loving self this morning. I was, in fact, furious." He paused for effect, got no reaction, and carried on. "As you know, I'm a very positive person. But today, today I just couldn't find the strength. And you know what? I was going to come in here and take it out on all of you fine folks." He gestured around the room.

Everyone was confused and trying to look at everyone else while at the same time not turning their heads. It was quite comical.

"I was going to come in and rant about all your failings and how you'd let the company down. About how your laziness and lack of professionalism and slowly declining creativity have contributed to the sub-par quality of what we've been producing this year. I was going to say, while I know many of you are new, you're not new to PR and we hired you for your PR experience."

This was false—several of the people in this room had been hired right out of school because they were the only people who would accept the incredibly low wage and lack of benefits.

"I was going to yell and scream and make you beg for forgiveness for contributing to the *only* year this company has not been nominated for several awards and won most of them."

By this point, most of the room was either bewildered or close to tears. If he *was* going to tear a strip off of us then what logically followed was that now he wasn't. But then why did we all feel so bad?

He took some time to compose himself, hanging his head and taking several deep, cleansing breaths. "But then I thought, *You know what, Terr Bear?*"

(He was the only person who called himself that.)

"Their failures are not their fault. Your staff failed—" he paused dramatically "—because of *you*." He turned and pointed to his reflection in the window, his voice cracking on the final word, then looked back to us with tears in his eyes. Real tears. I had to give him credit for that. Not everyone could cry on demand in a staff meeting.

"It's my fault that I coddle you so much you can't live up to your potential. Rather than let you make your own mistakes, I do your job for you. I'm a giver and want to help, but it's clear that my help has made you sloppy."

He looked out the window again and sighed wistfully.

"It's my fault that I'm too nice, that I try to be your friend *and* your commander. I'm too light on you because I know what you're going through and I feel your hardships deeply. I'm an empath, you know." His eyes swept across the room. "You don't know this, but I've been sheltering you from things our clients say. I take so much abuse every day so you don't have to." He paused, his clenched fist held to his lips. "I thought I was doing you a favour. I thought I was protecting you from what clients say about your work. I take all of this on, every day, for *you*.

So now, even though it pains me so much, I know in my heart that I'm going to have to be stricter with you. I'm going to have to stop being your friend and focus on being your captain so I can right this ship. I'm going to have to step back and let you fall and not catch you on your way down. And I will make that sacrifice. Because I love this company. And I love the work we do."

What the actual fuck?

He stayed silent for a full minute while he looked around the room.

"We need to work together. We need to be—" he took a deep breath "—a family again. I won't let you down, my friends. I will lead us to victory." He stood up straight, wiped an imaginary tear from his eye and waited for... applause maybe? I wasn't sure.

Everyone looked around, not knowing what to do. Should we leave? Should we slow clap? Should we thank him for being such a great leader?

And then it happened.

"That is the biggest load of bullshit I've ever heard." A collective gasp rose from the room. Terry's eyes widened. I looked around with everyone else to see who had said it. Turned out it was me.

"What did you just say to me?" he sputtered, his face a mixture of anger and shock.

I stood, never breaking eye contact. By any sense of reason, I should have been shaking or crying, but I'd never felt so calm in my life. If I was going to end it, I might as well go out like a firecracker.

"Terry," I began, quiet but firm, "I have worked at a lot of places and had a lot of bosses in my life, but never have I had a boss so aggressively emotionally manipulative as you. You make it seem like you take on so much work and do so much for everyone, but the only person you do anything for is the person you give the wink and the gun to in the mirror every morning."

He opened his mouth to speak and I cut him off.

"No, actually it's my turn to speak for once. I have never met anyone who was so self-involved, so arrogant, so unnecessarily dramatic and so single-mindedly cruel in my life. You keep saying how empathetic you are and how much you feel other people's feelings. If that were actually true, you would see how much I can't stand you. How tight my chest gets when I hear your voice. How the energy in the room drastically decreases when you walk into it. You know what people who are actually empathetic never have to do? Constantly tell everyone how empathetic they are."

A prickle of stress sweat started to bead on my body, but as soon as it sprang up it melted away and I settled deeper into serenity. The whole room was both silent and fearful. I could feel people looking at me, begging me to stop but wanting me to keep going. They could see what I saw: the shock that was turning to anger and then to hatred in Terry's eyes. I didn't care. I kept going. I needed to do this.

"You are a misogynistic sociopath who should never have been promoted to a management position. Your leadership skills are non-existent. The mere fact that you brought us in here to tell us we didn't get any awards because of how shitty we all are, and *not* because you keep rejecting all of our creative team's ideas in favour of your own, shows how unaware you are of what's going on around you."

It was now just me and him. Everyone else had faded into the background. We were face-to-face, eye-to-eye. I could smell him, the bitter stench of fear. He knew what I was saying was true. I knew he knew. But I couldn't stop. I was tired of pretending—of trying to be the person everyone wanted me to be. And the past eight months of online dating had pushed me over the edge.

Eight months of dating and trying desperately to be someone men would like, of hiding my true self, of questioning my worth. Eight months of giving others the power to dictate my happiness—taking whatever they'd

272

thrown at me. Caring so much about what they'd think if I presented myself as anything but a delicate, agreeable little lady flower. Eight months of all this bullshit had come to a head. And I wasn't going to do it anymore.

"Have you not noticed how much turnover we have here? Have you not noticed how many people turn in the other direction when they see you walk towards them? Have you not noticed how many people have taken multiple sick days because of burnout? This place is toxic and has sucked the soul out of dozens and dozens of talented people, and that's not okay. If you and upper management cared as much about the people who work here as you do about winning awards and trying to make this place look cool, we *would* win awards because we'd want to work here and do a good job. And the work would be amazing. We would be working hard because we cared, not because we were scared. Not because we were trying to churn something out as fast as we could so we could go back to our online job search."

His face slackened into understanding. And almost acceptance. I knew that I had taken his biggest fears and confirmed them, thrown them down his throat, and they had settled in his stomach like undigested food. He moved forward to speak, but I took a deep breath and held out my hand, not quite finished.

"And you know what else is not okay? Massaging women's shoulders when you come up to talk to them. Or leaning in behind them to look at their computer screens when you're really smelling their hair. Or making sexual comments and justifying it by saying you're 'old school' and that people just need to 'get to know your humour better.' None of that is okay."

I looked around, surprised that there were still others in the room. Cody looked at me, raised his eyebrow and grinned. He started to clap, and at first, I thought, *No, stop, I don't want you to be fired too*, but then someone else joined in, and then someone else. And then everyone was clapping and shouting things like, "Yeah," and, "You go, girl," and, "It's about time," and my heart exploded in my chest. I was so touched and proud, and I felt so much love and admiration and support. I knew I'd been right for finally, *finally* doing what I should have done a long time ago.

Terry looked like a Terry I'd never seen before. He actually looked kind of ashamed. "Is that really how everyone feels?" he asked.

One by one, everyone started nodding.

His eyebrows furrowed and his lips turned down into a scowl. But then, all of a sudden, his features relaxed. Like the façade was breaking. Like he was becoming a real person.

"Guys, I know I'm hard on you. I know I come across as an asshole," he started. "I go home every day and look in the mirror and I see what you see and I vow to be better the next day. I vow to treat people with kindness and respect. I vow to stop talking about myself and really listen to what someone else has to say. But every day I fall back into my old habits and I hate myself for it. I'm really not a bad guy. I just act like one because I'm scared." He hung his head. "I make sure that I'm feared when really my only fear is that I will never have anyone to love."

"Terry," I said as I walked towards him, "before you can really love someone, you need to love yourself."

I put my hand on his shoulder and he put his hand on mine.

"Thank you," he said. "Thank you for finally being honest and calling me out on my poor behaviour. I know I need to be better. I know I can be better."

The whole room had tears in their eyes, me included, and we passed a box of tissues around as everyone got up and gave Terry both a hug and their forgiveness. There was now a lightness in the room and everyone was smiling and laughing. It had been a bumpy road, but as a ray of sun poked through the clouds outside and streamed through the windows, I knew it was finally going to be okay.

Of course, that's not what happened.

What really happened:

"Is that what everyone actually thinks?" Terry looked around the room, his lips curled over his teeth in such a vicious sneer I thought he was going to start growling.

Everyone glanced at me, a flicker of apology on their faces, and shook their heads.

I closed my eyes, deflating like a party balloon forgotten behind a bookshelf. I got it. Everyone was scared. The job market was less than stellar right now and Terry was well known in the industry, even though he was well known as an asshole. I got it, but there was a part of me that was disappointed. I had kind of wanted a slow clap.

I opened my eyes to his smug grin, his face red with rage.

"Obviously you're fired," he said, hands crossed over his chest.

"Go fuck yourself, Terry."

I walked out of the boardroom and headed straight to my desk to pack up my things. I didn't have much. I'd never tried to make my cubicle my own. No pictures pinned to the walls, no framed photos of friends or family arranged on my desk. I rummaged through my drawers and grabbed a couple of pens I'd bought myself and a few pads of sticky notes I hadn't. I took my stress ball and two packs of gum. A roll of Life Savers.

I looked around my area, half making sure I had everything and half waiting to see if anyone would stop to say, "Good for you," or, "That took guts," or, "Sorry I couldn't say anything," or even just, "Goodbye." No one did. Everyone had just gone quietly back to their desks to text everyone else about what had happened. Too scared to have the conversations out loud. I didn't even get a text from Cody.

I wanted to feel like what I'd done would make a difference. That things would change now that someone had finally said something. That I'd made a sacrifice for the greater good. But I knew it wouldn't. I knew people who had complained when they'd left and were told, "That's just the way he is," and, "Don't take it personally," and, "He gets results and, frankly, does the stuff no one else wants to do."

I looked around the office one last time, at the exposed brick and the painted heating ducts and pipes overhead, the random unicycle hanging from the ceiling and the brightly coloured posters all over the wall. At a place that was putting so much effort into looking cool and on trend that they'd forgotten about the people who did the actual work. They'd forgotten that if people loved their work and were proud to work there, the place would naturally look cool. Because it would be full of happy people. It wouldn't be just a dressed-up empty shell filled with soulless drones trying to make it to the end of the day without crying in the bathroom.

I grabbed my phone and charger, stuck them in my purse, turned around and walked out the door for the last time.

Chapter 52

When Julie picked me up at 7:00 p.m. for the singles night, I was feeling slightly buzzed. I had cracked one of the beers I had bought for Ben the night we went speed dating and was finishing it off when she pulled up. I thought having a drink would be a better idea than sitting in silence and thinking about what I'd done. And about not having a job. Or a reference. Or rent for next month.

"I smell beer." She wrinkled her nose as I slid into the car. "Did you drink beer? That's unlike you. What happened?"

"Nothing." I picked up my phone, which had slid to the floor when she'd swerved onto the street. "Oh, except I got fired."

"What?" she yelled, eyes wide.

"Because I told Terry to go fuck himself."

"Holy mother of shit." She sharply pulled over to the side of the road. "Tell me everything right now."

I told her everything, and as I did, I started to feel better. Now that it was over, and I allowed myself to think about it, I felt good. Giddy even. I might not have had a job, but I would never have to go back to that place. I would never have to pick up pens off the floor that Terry had thrown at me. I would never have to get up from my desk and take documents to Terry from the printer even though he was closer to the printer than I was. I would never have to overhear him tell one of my colleagues that I "just don't get it." I would never have to have my ideas shot down and be told my job was to take notes, not talk. I would never have to feel so degraded, useless and undervalued that I could barely get out of bed in the morning. I felt so incredibly free.

"Wow," Julie said as she pulled back into traffic. "That's either super ballsy or extremely reckless, I haven't decided which yet."

"Me neither." I settled back into the seat and looked out the window. "Let's pretend it didn't happen and try to enjoy our night. I'll think about what I did tomorrow."

"Hungover. Good call."

"I'm not going to be hungover," I protested. "I've learned my lesson. I will have one drink tonight and then I'll be sticking to water."

"This is going to be fun!" she said. "It'll be what we make it and I want it to be fun. Even if you don't meet anyone, we'll still have fun, right?"

"Right." I smiled. "We'll just see what happens."

But I already knew what would happen. Julie, with her gorgeous long blonde hair styled into wide curls that framed her perfectly made-up face and her "Oh, I just threw this on" butt-hugging jeans and low-hanging T-shirt, would walk in the door and every guy would turn and sigh in unison, thinking that the night had suddenly gotten better, each hoping she would talk to only them.

None of them would even notice me in my similar, yet somehow dumpy "Oh, I just picked this up off my floor" outfit as I faded into the background. At least I'd have Jesse to keep me company. And, honestly, I really didn't care. Julie could have whoever she liked. I was still trying to wrestle with the confusing feelings I'd been having about Ben. And Jesse. And my life in general.

We parked and walked the short distance to the coffee shop, breathing deeply, trying to pull air out of the sticky heat. Most of Saskatchewan was going through an end-of-summer heat wave and I was not enjoying it.

"I'm surprised Ben didn't come with us tonight. He had so much fun the last time we went to a singles event." I tried to sound jokey.

"I actually asked him," Julie said. "He said he was busy."

"He's always busy, it seems."

"I know. It's weird." She stopped and turned to me, lowering her voice like we were in a room full of people. "I think he might be seeing someone."

I felt sick. "Really? That's great. Good for him." My voice sounded unnaturally cheerful, even to my own ears.

"Yeah, like you said, he's been 'busy' a lot lately." She air-quoted. "He's never home. And when we're over at our parents' place for supper, he's always on his phone texting someone. I checked his phone once when he went to the bathroom and a message from 'Sherri' popped up."

"Well, that's really great. Good for him," I said again. I couldn't think of anything else to say. Ben was dating someone. Weird. And speaking of weird, why wasn't I legitimately happy for him?

"Come to think of it," she added, "he's also started chatting more. Without me having to say something first. It's like he's belatedly come out of his shell at age forty-five. Maybe he's just finally happy."

"Hm," I said distractedly. My stomach churned. Maybe I shouldn't have had that beer.

I was silent for the rest of the walk. I had to admit I was a bit shocked about Ben. For as long as I'd known him, he'd never had a girlfriend. He'd never even talked about girls. Or guys. I'd never thought about him dating anyone. I mean it now made sense that he wasn't hanging out with us anymore. I just hadn't expected to feel so sad. Our little group wasn't the same without him. It didn't feel whole.

Well, I thought, trying out a "glass-half-full" attitude, at least I could place one set of confusing feelings aside; tonight I could focus on Jesse.

He was waiting at the door when we arrived. "Ladies!" He grinned. "Thank God you came. There are only dudes so far."

"Oh great." Julie rolled her eyes.

"I got fired," I blurted.

"I thought you were going to think about it tomorrow?" Julie said as she looked around the room.

"Starting now." An abrupt giggle exploded out of my open mouth. Why was I being an awkward weirdo all of a sudden?

"Why are you being an awkward weirdo?" Julie whispered.

"I'm not. Shut up."

The bells jingled above the door and two other women hesitantly walked in, looked around and turned to walk back out. "Ladies!" Jesse said as he walked toward them, stopping them in their tracks.

Suckers.

We found a place to sit and surveyed the room as Jesse spoke to the group. We had ten more minutes to get a drink, go to the bathroom and chat with people before things got started. He had a few ice-breakers planned and then he would set us all free to do what we pleased.

"Why would I want to chat with people?" I asked Julie. "I only have so much small talk in me; obviously I'm saving that for the mingling part."

I turned to get her response and saw that she was already up at the counter getting a drink. Great. Not only was I the one with the pretty friend, I was also now the one who talked to herself.

Julie held up a glass of wine and raised her eyebrows, asking if I wanted one. I gave her a thumbs-up.

Since we'd arrived, three other groups of women had come in, so I felt a bit better, although the more women there were the more competition I had. I wasn't really looking to find anyone, though, so it didn't matter.

While the women had come in groups of two or three, most of the men were sitting alone. Events like these were a bit like going to the bathroom. Women always seemed to need the support while men were happy to do their business by themselves. Or women just liked to use the time to gossip, which seemed to be the case here. All the ladies were huddled together, looking around and whispering, similar to what I was doing except I was whispering to myself. What was taking Julie so long?

I turned and watched her at the counter, talking to Jesse, throwing her head back with a throaty laugh, her hand on his arm. She sure was giving it her all tonight. The beginnings of a frown creased my forehead. Stuff like this came so easy for her. All she had to do was look at any guy here and they'd be all over themselves trying to talk to her. Why was she wasting all her charm on Jesse?

She finally came over with our wine and I took a big gulp.

"Whoa there, tiger," she said. "You don't want to get sloppy before we even start."

I laughed. "You're one to talk," I said under my breath, suddenly cranky.

A flicker of something crossed her face but was gone so quickly I might have imagined it. She sipped from her own glass and looked around the room.

"Well?" she said. "Have you scoped out our options?"

"Do you like Jesse?" I asked, surprising both of us.

She put her glass down gently and scratched her nose. "Of course I do. He's a great guy."

"No, I mean *like* him."

"Like 'like' like him, more than a friend?" she asked, trying to make light of the situation.

I looked at her with a blank stare and the smile faded from her face.

"No," she said. "Not like that."

We both looked up at the sound of Jesse's voice, telling the group that the ice-breakers were about to start.

Chapter 53

Julie

Something isn't right, Julie thought. Kate seemed off. And it wasn't that she was upset because she'd just gotten fired. It was more than that. She seemed angry. And bitter.

Julie did a quick scan of the room, making sure none of the guys there were ones she'd already hooked up with. Not that she remembered them all, but none of them were looking at her like they knew her, so she should be okay.

They were looking at her though. She was used to that, and she knew most of them would probably come and talk to her, then they'd probably be disappointed. And after that, they'd get angry and think to themselves that it was fine that she didn't want to go out with them because she was a stuck-up bitch anyway.

At least they wouldn't have her contact information. She wouldn't have to block their numbers. She wouldn't have to read their messages, alternately begging for another chance and saying people like her were what was wrong with this world.

It wasn't like she was keeping what she was doing

a secret. She was always very up front about what her intentions were. She wasn't looking for a relationship, just some fun. And if they couldn't handle it, that was their problem. They knew what they were getting into. She couldn't help it if they ended up falling for her or wanting to see her again.

Why was it so hard to believe that women could be like this? Using men for pleasure and not having to talk about going on a proper date? Why was it that when men behaved this way, it was expected, and when women did, it was always a surprise? She couldn't possibly be like this. She just hadn't "found the right guy" yet.

That was what one of her colleagues always told her. The one who walked behind her when she was sitting at her desk and put his hands on her shoulders, so close she could smell the coffee on his breath.

The one who, at a work party, had lain on a trampoline with her in the backyard looking at the stars and rolled over and kissed her gently on the lips. "You smell like you," he'd said as he'd nuzzled her neck.

The one who stopped by her house every so often and stayed until 2:00 a.m.

The one who was her boss.

She knew he wasn't the right guy, not because he was her boss, although that wasn't ideal. She knew he wasn't the right guy because she didn't feel anything towards him except obligation. After it had happened the first time, after too many bottles of wine, he had started to expect it, and she'd felt like she had to give him what he wanted. She hadn't said no the first time, so how could she say no now?

Now it was just tedious and mind-numbing. Like a job she knew she needed to quit but couldn't. She'd hit rock bottom. And she felt nothing. Not even shame anymore.

Chapter 54

"Well, that was a giant bust," I said to Julie as I finished my wine.

"Do you maybe want something to eat?" she asked, eyeing me carefully. I made a non-committal noise, which she took as a yes and walked up to the counter with her purse.

I hadn't known what to expect at this event. I'd known there would be fewer people than at the speed dating event, and for that reason I'd thought the quality of men would be higher.

Maybe all the great ones were too shy to be in a room full of people trying to set a world record. Maybe they weren't into that kind of grandstanding. Maybe something small and intimate was what they preferred.

I'd been wrong. Mostly. One or two hadn't been that bad. That said, there had also been one who was so drunk he kept nodding off and one who looked like he was about fourteen. I'd almost asked him what time his mom was picking him up.

We'd only made it through one ice-breaker event before people went rogue and started talking on their own. Or left.

We'd all gotten a piece of paper with questions on it and we had to go around and ask the questions until we got bored. That took about fifteen minutes.

The questions were things like: "What do you do for a living?" or "What is your idea of fun?" When someone would ask me the second question, I would keep answering, "Not this," as a joke, even though no one ever laughed. I stopped caring by the end.

I officially declared my final dating activity an unmitigated failure after talking to one guy who stood so close to me that I could see his molars and one who stared at my chest for so long I asked him if he'd lost something down there. I sat down, crumpled up my paper and threw it on the ground like a child.

Julie came back with two scones and cup of coffee and set them on the table.

"Who's the coffee for?" I asked, knowing full well it was for me.

"Yours if you want it." She gently nudged it in my direction.

"No thanks." I pushed it away.

She took a breath. I could tell by her face that she wanted to say something serious.

"I brought you a scone," she said instead.

"Thanks." I broke off a small piece and popped it in my mouth.

"Did I do something wrong?" she finally asked.

"What do you mean?" I knew I was being an asshole, but I couldn't help myself.

"You know what I mean."

I did. Something *was* wrong. Something had been wrong for a while. I just didn't want to get into it right now.

"Listen," she said. "If you want to go, we can go, but don't get mad at me because you didn't hit it off with any of these guys. It's not my fault." She sat back and brushed a perfect strand of hair off her perfect face.

Well, here we go then.

"No, that part is not your fault," I began. "But did you ever think that, seeing as this night was supposed to be for me, maybe you didn't have to try so hard to make every guy in the room fall in love with you?"

She looked stunned. "What? I was not trying to do that."

"Well, maybe you're not *trying,* but could you try not trying?"

"What does that even mean?"

"I don't know," I said, aggressively blowing a stray curl out of my eyes. "Like maybe try to look uglier. Don't do your hair or wear a potato sack, I don't know. Although I'm sure if you wore a potato sack, you'd get just as much, if not more, positive attention."

She looked genuinely confused. "I'm sorry, I have no idea what you're getting at."

I leaned forward and spoke slowly. "Do you know how hard it is to live your life with a best friend like you? A best friend who is so gorgeous and perfect that everywhere she goes men stare at her? To not even be second best but to actually disappear when you're around? To have to see the disappointment on a guy's face when you pick his friend? To always be in the background? Always. Do you know what that's like? No, you don't know. Because I'm *your* best friend and you look like you and I look like me and you'll never have to deal with knowing how that feels."

"Kate," she tried. "You know I don't do that on purpose."

"Don't you?" I asked.

She blinked.

"You know I always thought that it was just how you were and guys were naturally attracted to you. It wasn't your fault you were born gorgeous and charming. But lately, I don't know. Lately, I'm not sure that's true."

"How so?" she asked, her calm composure fading.

"I've been watching you recently when we're out. After listening to the tips you've been giving me, I thought I'd pay more attention to an expert at work. And you know what I think?"

She turned her palms up, inviting me to tell her.

"I think you do try. I think you know exactly what you're doing. I think if, for some crazy reason, a guy isn't immediately into you, you'll focus all your attention on him until he is. And it doesn't matter who else is there and who it may hurt, it only matters that you get what you want."

As I talked, I watched her face change from interest to confusion to anger to coldness. I knew I was hurting her, but I couldn't stop. This had been building in me for so long and I had to get it out.

"Like, for example?" she finally said, eyes narrowed.

I paused, not knowing if I wanted to go any further. But then I did.

"What about Jesse?"

"What about Jesse?" she said, shrugging.

I looked around to make sure no one was listening. "You know I like him."

She shook her head like she wasn't following. "So?"

"And you say you don't."

"I don't."

"It seems like you do, though, the way you talk to him," I said, knowing I was travelling into potentially dangerous territory.

"What do you mean 'the way I talk to him?'" she air-quoted.

"I've been watching you all night. How you get super close to him when you talk, how you put your hand on his arm, and how you brush his fingers when you take your coffee from him. And it's not just tonight, you do that all the time." I took a deep breath. "When you figured out I liked him, why didn't you stop? I mean you know how hard I've been trying to find someone. Why can't you let someone else have something for once?"

She looked down at her hands, her face softening. Her cold façade was cracking.

"I mean the number of guys you sleep with, why can't you just let me have one?"

Her head snapped up; the coldness was back. I'd gone too far.

"First of all," she said, her voice tight with anger, "who I sleep with is my business. I don't need anyone judging me for what I choose to do or how I choose to be. I'm so fucking sick of this double standard where men who sleep around are heroes and women who do it are sluts. I thought you of all people understood that."

I opened my mouth to speak but she kept going.

"Second, you've never officially said you wanted to pursue Jesse. You can't possibly expect me to base my behaviour on guessing your back-and-forth feelings all the time. And, sure, maybe I did know you liked him, but the number of times you told me he was too young for you grossly outweighs the number of times you gave me any indication you might have wanted to see if there was anything there."

"But—"

"I'm not done. Third, this is how I am and you know this is how I am. If you don't like it, if you're so threatened by my slutty behaviour—"

"I never said—"

She leaned forward, her face contoured by anger in a way I'd never seen before. She said in a low, barely controlled voice, "If you're so threatened by my slutty behaviour, why do you hang out with me? Could it be because you could never get a guy on your own? That the only way you have a chance at hooking up is with my sloppy seconds? Let's face it, Kate, there's a reason you don't have 'someone to kiss' and it's not because you weren't seriously looking. It's because you want to be with someone so badly that whenever you meet a guy desperation seeps out of your pores. You turn into one of those sad women who would do anything for a guy. A woman who doesn't have any opinions of her own. You want men to like you so much that you turn yourself into an extension of them.

"Why do you think Cody's friend was so anxious to get away from you that night? He was embarrassed by how desperate and awkward and ridiculous you were. We all were embarrassed. And you know what was the most embarrassing part? It was so painfully obvious that you were trying to be me."

She stood, scraping her chair back loudly, and picked up her purse as I sat, gobsmacked, unshed tears filling my eyes. We'd never talked to each other like this. It was like we had both been holding things inside for years and they'd finally exploded in a giant friendship-ending disaster.

I blinked the tears away and watched Julie at the front, saying goodbye to Jesse, all smiles and touches, throwing back her head and laughing.

He nodded toward me, probably wondering why we weren't leaving together. She waved a delicate, perfectly manicured hand dismissively. "She's fine," I heard her say.

As she left, not even turning around to say goodbye, every guy in the room watched. They visibly deflated, their dreams of leaving with her popping like balloons. One by one, they walked up to get their coats.

While Jesse said goodbye to the groups, I slipped into the bathroom to dab away any lingering tears.

I splashed some water on my face and wiped the rest of the eyeliner from under my eyes. I looked and felt exhausted. Julie and I had never fought like this before. I felt like half of me was missing. The half that contained all my energy. It was time to call it a night.

Jesse was wiping down our table as I came out of the bathroom. He looked up when he heard the door shut behind me. "Oh hey." He smiled. "I wondered where you went. Are you okay?"

Just thinking about the fight again made my eyes well up. He dropped his cloth and came over, putting his hands on my shoulders, giving me his full attention.

"What happened? Did one of the guys do something to you?" Worry was etched on his face, his blue eyes full of genuine concern.

"No, the guys were fine," I said quickly. "The event was great. Julie and I had a fight."

"Really?" He turned toward the door as if she were going to walk back in and explain. "She said she wasn't feeling well."

"Yeah. Well, she probably wasn't feeling well because we had a fight."

"That's so bizarre," he said as he led me over to the comfy couch in the corner. "I can't even imagine you two fighting. You're, like, inseparable. Like Batman and Robin, Woody and Buzz—" He stopped, stumped.

"Cagney and Lacey?" I tried.

"Who?"

"Never mind."

"It's just that I never thought of you two as being the kind of friends who fought."

I sniffed, dabbing at my nose with a napkin. "Me neither."

"Can I ask what happened?" he asked as he sat down.

I took a breath and he jumped up. "Wait," he said, holding up one finger. "I think we need some wine for this."

"I've never been so certain of anything in my life." I smiled.

"There it is," he said and rewarded me with one of his crooked grins. "There's that beautiful smile. I'll be right back."

Heat reddened my cheeks. I'd only had the one glass so I knew it wasn't because of the wine. Tiny butterflies fluttered in my stomach and I had to deliberately focus on keeping my breath steady. In a beat, my mood had gone from despondent to hopeful. I felt like a teenager as I placed a hand over my mouth so a giggle wouldn't escape. All I could think about was that Jesse thought my smile was beautiful.

Everyone else had left and I watched Jesse walk to the door, lock it and flip the sign to "closed" before he grabbed the wine. He brought the whole bottle. Perfect.

"I figured why waste time going back and forth, right?" He opened the wine and poured us each a glass.

I took a delicate sip, hoping he couldn't tell how nervous I was.

"So, you think the event went well?" he asked.

"It was okay," I said and told him about the men I'd met.

He listened and laughed and then went to fill my glass again, despite it still being three-quarters full.

"I'm good," I said, holding my hand over my glass. I was starting to get a bit buzzed again and something was telling me that I would really want to remember this. That something was him grabbing my hand and lightly stroking it with his thumb.

"You're not going to make me drink alone, are you?" he asked with puppy dog eyes. "Besides, you still need to tell me about Julie."

My stomach flipped and I almost knocked over my glass as I nudged it in his direction.

"Okay," I said. "But I've warned you, this might get messy."

"Consider me warned." He grinned and filled it up.

For the next two hours, I told him about Julie and our fight, about how online dating sucked, and about how hard it was for a woman my age to find someone normal. I told him about how all my past relationships had been terrible and went into my standard "feeling a bit buzzed *why don't men like me?*" spiel. And he listened, and drank wine and listened, and drank more wine. I didn't even notice when he went and got another bottle. I had been talking so much I was still sipping my first glass.

But I did notice when I got up to go to the bathroom and felt a bit unsteady.

"I think I should probably go." I wasn't drunk, but I definitely wasn't in any state to drive. "I'm going to call an Uber." I turned to look for my purse and found it on the floor by tripping over it.

"Woah." Jesse jumped up to steady me. "Be careful."

He'd had more to drink than me, though, and wasn't that steady himself, so we both fell onto the couch and laughed like it was the funniest thing that had ever happened.

"Are you okay?" He leaned over me, his face almost touching mine.

"I think so," I breathed. I could smell the sweetness of the wine on his breath.

"Good."

He leaned over to kiss me.

And I let him.

Chapter 55

I was in my living room, sitting on the couch. It was 2:00 a.m. and I could see Jesse in the kitchen pouring water into two glasses.

"Thanks for paying for the Uber," I said as he put the glasses on the coffee table.

He laughed. "I probably could have driven, but you're right, better to be safe."

I felt completely sober now. Like I'd just woken up. I shook my head to clear the fog. Things were clear now. Very clear.

I took a long drink of water and rested the bottom of my glass on my thigh. Jesse took my glass, put it back on the coffee table and laid his hand where the glass had rested.

I met his clear blue eyes and melted. The way he was looking at me. The fire in his eyes, his soft smile, his head tilted to the side as if to ask if this was still okay. As if to ask if this was real.

All this time, I had been so worried about our age difference and what other people would think. And all this time he had been right there, his feelings as strong as mine. Why had I been looking elsewhere when the man I had wanted was right in front of me? Why had I even been thinking of Ben?

Hold on, why was I thinking of Ben?

He has a girlfriend now, I told myself as Jesse leaned in and outlined the slope of my chin with his finger. He smelled like cinnamon and coffee. His thumb brushed my lips and I was lost.

"I've wanted to do this for so long," he whispered and lowered his mouth to my neck.

Me too, I said, but only in my head; my words got stuck and came out as a sigh.

Take that, social norms, I thought as he pulled off his shirt and revealed a set of abs that were so chiselled it was shocking.

I tentatively reached forward and flattened my palm against his stomach, not knowing what to think, not knowing if this was real. He sighed as our skin made contact and I decided it was time to stop thinking. This was real. This was happening. I grabbed his belt and pulled him toward me, taking charge for once in my life. I was all in.

Chapter 56

Julie

Julie looked at her phone. The bright, glowing numbers sent a sharp pain through her head as they told her it was 3:00 a.m. She sighed and set her head back on the pillow. Three a.m. and not a wink of sleep to show for it. She turned her head and spied the empty wine glass sitting on her bedside table, red lipstick stains around the rim. She licked her lips and tasted the remnants of the bottle crusted in the corner of her mouth.

She picked up her phone again and scrolled through her Tinder contacts, checking to see if any of them were online. Many were. She exited the app to send a text. "*U up?*" she typed and then changed her mind. She turned off her phone and let it fall on her bed while tears rolled down her cheeks.

She was so tired. Tired of feeling shitty about meaningless one-night stands, of being drunk more than she was sober. Tired of trying so hard. Kate was right: she'd known what she was doing with Jesse. She knew what she was doing every time. But she couldn't help herself. She couldn't stop.

But what if it was time to stop? To stop blaming the past for her decisions and start taking care of herself and taking control. Maybe it was time to be more like Kate. Not to go find a man—she had plenty of those—but to figure out what she wanted and make a plan to get it. Kate had believed in herself. She had believed she was worth it.

Maybe it was time for her to believe that too; to believe she deserved better than meaningless sex and never-ending hangovers. Maybe it was time she stopped being a victim.

But what if it was hard? It was so easy to blame her past, to behave poorly and blame other people for her choices. If it was easy, though, why was she so exhausted?

Was she ready for this? Ready to do the work? Or was it too late? The voids she had created were so deep, so empty.

She picked up her phone, swiped in her passcode and looked at the text, her decision made. She took a breath, wiped the tears from her eyes, and hit send.

Chapter 57

August 7th

It was morning. My chest felt heavy, like I'd smoked a pack of cigarettes. Had I smoked last night? Nope, it was just Mittens curled up on my throat, oblivious to the fact that he was partially cutting off my airway. I heard something that sounded like the shower. Was someone in my shower? Who the hell was in my shower?

Then I remembered.

Jesse. Jesse was in my shower. Jesse, my friend—my very young, very hot friend—was in my shower. Naked. Presumably. How had I let this happen? How had I made such a horrible mistake? But had it been a mistake? Logically, yes, I was still much older than he was. My mind said, *Get up, get up and tell him you made a mistake. Tell him you were drunk. Tell him you don't remember anything.*

But I hadn't been drunk. And I did remember. I remembered it all. And my stomach did a flip that had nothing to do with my mini hangover. I'd known what I was doing. I'd wanted to do it. Because, despite everything I'd thought about being with a younger guy, despite what my friends had told me and society had told me and what I'd been telling myself for so long, I had finally taken control. I had made the choice to be with him.

A smile spread across my face as the bathroom door opened. He walked into the bedroom with a towel wrapped around his waist. Drops of water fell from his still-wet hair and rolled down his shoulders. My stomach flipped again.

"Morning, gorgeous," he said and gave me a peck on the cheek.

"Mm…" I murmured a soft sound of contentment, luxuriating in the afterglow of fantastic sex. "Good morning, Ben."

What?

I bolted upright, sending Mittens skidding across the duvet.

"What?" he said.

"I-I," I stuttered. "I was just texting my friend. Ben. And he… I… I guess I just had his name on my brain." I looked down, hoping he couldn't see how red my face was.

"That's cool," he said, unperturbed.

"Oh. Cool," I said. My mind was racing. "Feel like breakfast?"

"I'll just grab something at work. I don't want you to go to the trouble." He slid on his jeans and sat on the bed to pull on his socks. "Thanks though."

He found his wallet on the dresser, slipped it into his back pocket and walked out the door.

"See you later?" I blurted.

"See ya!" he yelled cheerfully as the door slammed. Oh,

the bliss of youth and the ability to have more than one glass of wine without being hungover.

I reflexively reached for my phone to call Julie and remembered with a sting of regret that we were fighting. Now what? Who could I talk to about this?

You know what? Fuck it, I thought. I was tired of trying to passively figure things out on my own. I was going straight to the source. I was going to call Ben. Since when did he get to decide whether or not we were friends? So what if he had a girlfriend? We'd been friends for decades! This radio silence was bullshit.

He answered on the third ring.

"I have news," I announced before giving him a chance to say anything.

"Hi to you too," he said.

"I did something," I said. "And I wanted to tell someone. A friend. So I called you. Because we're friends. Right? We're still friends? Sorry, are you sleeping?"

"No, I'm awake. What did you do?"

"I found someone, I think. Probably. Someone to kiss. Per my napkin goal." I waited. "So? Any thoughts?"

"That's really great," he said quietly. "Congratulations."

"Are you sure I didn't wake you?" I tried to read his mood over the phone. Was he happy? Sad? Angry?

"No, I'm just tired, not a big deal."

"Well. Okay. Good. Also…" My heart quickened as I mustered up the courage to say what I had really called to say. "I don't know what I did to make you angry, but do you want to maybe meet for coffee? I want to talk to you about someth—"

"Actually," he interrupted, "I need to go. Someone's calling on the other line. Talk later, okay?"

"Oh, sure, I—"

He hung up.

Disappointment vibrated softly in my chest. He didn't care. I didn't know what I had expected—jealousy maybe? I'd thought he would have at least been interested. Or at the very least want to go out for coffee to talk things out. What was going on?

I opened my freezer, looking for something unhealthy to eat for breakfast, and found an old pizza-pop frozen into the back corner.

"Perfect." I scraped the wrapper off and threw it in the microwave.

It was so crazy how tasting something you hadn't tasted for a long time could bring back a memory. The familiar comfort of Ben and Julie and me sitting in the kitchen of one of their shitty apartments, eating pizza-pops at 4:00 a.m. after a night at the club.

As we'd tended to do in our twenties, earlier that night, Julie and I had picked up a couple of guys at Checkers, our favourite bar, and stupidly, as usual, had decided to continue the party at one of their houses. The memory was fuzzy, but I distinctly remembered doing shots and laughing hysterically, looking up at one point and seeing Ben sitting in a chair in the background, trying not to nod off.

"Come join the fun," I remembered yelling. He'd just smiled and shaken his head.

"Why does he even come out?" I'd slurred to Julie,

probably not as quietly as I'd thought. "He never even talks to anyone."

Julie shrugged as we both did another shot.

He'd always been like that, never joining in, always sitting on the sidelines. I mean I'd been glad for the ride and the company, but he'd never seemed to have any fun. Why hadn't he just gone home?

And then it hit me. He had never had fun because he hadn't been there to have fun. He'd been there to make sure we didn't get into trouble. He'd been there so we could get drunk and have fun and never have to worry about being taken advantage of. He'd been there to take care of us and make sure we were safe.

In a flash, everything made sense. The pieces of the puzzle started fitting together. Ben always being around. Him never thinking any guy I dated was good enough for me. Comforting me every time they inevitably proved his point. Always being my shoulder to cry on. Always being on my side. The way he wouldn't look at me when I talked about all my dating experiences. And the way he did when he carried me to the car after our speed dating disaster. The look of disappointment in his eyes in the pub.

The truth was I'd had my perfect person. I'd had my someone to kiss for years. I'd just been too self-involved to notice. Too wrapped up in whatever drama was going on in my life that I didn't see what was happening right in front of my face. I'd missed the trope. And now it was too late.

Chapter 58

I parked my car in front of Beans 'n' Brews, my stomach tightening at the thought of seeing Jesse. Hopefully it wouldn't be too busy and we could sit and chat. As hard as it was going to be, I had to tell him we couldn't see each other anymore. I now knew I had feelings for Ben and, even though I'd missed my chance, I didn't think that would be fair to Jesse.

I walked up to the door and reached for the handle then quickly pulled away. I saw him through the glass, serving a group of younger women, big smile, pouring on the charm. All of a sudden, I felt old. Maybe I should have made more of an effort with my appearance. In my haste to get here, I hadn't even showered.

I started to walk back to the car and then stopped myself. You know what? Who cared what I looked like? I was going in there to break up with him not ask him to prom. And just because I wasn't twenty didn't mean I didn't belong. If I wanted men to treat me like I was worth something, it was time I started feeling that way about myself.

I reached for the handle with purpose this time and

confidently pulled it open. He was now alone at the counter, absorbed in his phone, but looked up when he heard the door. He smiled, big and wide.

"Hey, you," I said, trying not to look too sympathetic.

"Hey, yourself," he said. "Your weekend regular?"

"Yes, please."

He rang up my total and I tried to hide my surprise. Shouldn't the person you'd just had sex with get free coffee? Rude.

"Are you staying or going?" he asked while he foamed the milk.

"I was going to stay, but if you're too busy…" My voice faded, waiting for him to interrupt.

He gestured to the sitting area. "Nope, not too busy, there are still seats." He grinned.

Not quite what I was expecting but, sure, obviously he wanted me to stay.

"To stay then," I said with what I hoped was a smile that said, "Come sit with me when you're not busy," but just in case it wasn't, I said, "Come sit with me when—"

"If you'd like to have a seat, I'll bring it out when it's ready," he said and turned to face the espresso machine.

"Oh. Okay." I grabbed my purse off the counter. "I'll be, um—" I awkwardly pointed to a corner full of people and then to another, also full of people, and then "—at that empty table by the window," I said to no one because he was back at the counter helping someone else.

I pulled out a chair from one of the two-person tables and put my jacket on the back. I hadn't brought a book with me and I didn't want to push through everyone again to go look at the books that were there. What was I going to do? Just sit there like an idiot? Maybe I could read something on my phone. I hadn't thought of a back-up plan if Jesse had been too busy to sit.

I looked up and saw my latte sitting on the counter ready to go. I tried to catch Jesse's eye to see if he was going to bring it over, but he was busy making more coffee. Had he even remembered I was here? I stood up to go get it and then saw him coming over.

"Sorry about the delay," he said with a wink. "Super busy."

He put the latte down. "Can you sit?" I asked.

"Maybe later," he said as he turned back, "when it dies down a bit."

"Okay, see you t—" He was gone.

It didn't die down for another hour and a half.

And I waited. Sipping my latte. Wondering if I should just leave. Getting a refill of regular coffee and then sipping on that. Reading a tiny, crappy book on my phone.

Jesse waved and smiled once or twice and then came over to ask how I was doing and if I wanted anything else. I asked him again if he could sit, but he had to run back to the lineup of customers.

Finally, after I'd drunk more coffee than I'd ever had in my life, and I'd been to the bathroom four times, he came and sat down.

"Man," he breathed as he collapsed onto the chair. "What a wild morning. It's been like this since I got in, I'm beat. You must have really needed some alone time. You never stay here this long by yourself."

I didn't say anything right away. Couldn't he tell I was here to see him?

"I came to talk to you," I said, grabbing his hands.

His smile faded but he recovered quickly. "About what?"

"I had a great time last night," I started.

He looked at me, tilted his head, and breathed out a puff of exasperation. His mouth curved into a sad, pitying grin.

"Listen, Kate…"

Fuck. Me.

Chapter 59

"Listen, Kate," he began. "Last night was super fun, but I'm not really looking for anything serious right now."

"What?" It was all I could manage. This wasn't how it was supposed to go; I was supposed to be saying these words to him.

"I mean you're really fun and stuff, but I can't see this turning into anything," he finished, pulling his hands away. "I really like you, but just as friends, you know?" He grinned and sat back as if there was nothing more to say.

"But you knew about the napkin pledge," I finally said because I couldn't think of anything else.

"Oh, right, yeah. But that was for someone serious. We were just having fun."

"Hm." I said. "Well, funny thing, I was about to tell you the same thing."

He laughed. "Sure you were."

My head snapped up. "What does that mean?"

He leaned back and casually rested his arm on the back of the chair. "I mean look at me." He gestured at his face. "If you knew how many women asked me out, your head would literally explode." He then (horrifically) lifted up his shirt. "Have you seen these abs?"

I looked around the room, embarrassed for both of us, and leaned over and yanked his shirt down. He giggled.

"My God." I shook my head in disbelief. "What could I possibly have been thinking? I was so caught up in obsessing over our age difference and wondering if you could possibly like someone like me that I completely overlooked the fact that you behave like a child."

"Don't be such a sore loser," he scoffed. "You're hot, but I'm just not interested in dating older women. Sorry if you misunderstood." He got up to leave.

"Me too," I said. I packed up my stuff as he walked away. "But I'm mostly sorry I ever had feelings for a guy who doesn't know the meaning of the word 'literally'," I yelled as my final clever parting shot.

I grabbed my coat and pushed past the empty tables, bumping chairs and knocking things over in my wake. So much for making a graceful exit.

I opened the door and speed-walked to my car. Even now, I still naïvely half expected to hear Jesse call my name behind me, running to apologize, saying he wasn't himself, saying he really did have feelings for me but he was just too scared to admit it. I was an embarrassment to womankind.

I slid into the car and turned it on, laying my head on the steering wheel.

I was sad; I was angry; I was embarrassed. But I was mostly exhausted. I had been trying so hard to find someone that I had ignored and then destroyed everything in my wake. I'd lost my best friend, I'd lost my other best friend, and now I'd lost whatever dignity I'd had left.

"Ugh!" I groaned out loud as a new realization hit me. "And *now* I'll have to find somewhere else to go for coffee!"

I drove home in a fog and dragged myself up the apartment building's stairs like I was moving through quicksand. I didn't want to go inside my place. I didn't want to see the empty wine glasses and the tangled sheets. I didn't want to see the napkin pledge that I had crumpled up and tossed on my dresser.

I pushed open the stairwell door, ready to take the walk of shame down the hall, when I noticed a stranger was sitting on my door mat.

Except it wasn't a stranger. It was Julie. "You didn't answer my text," she said. And then she started to cry.

Chapter 60

I was speechless. She looked absolutely terrible. Julie, who looked beautiful after puking her guts out after twenty-four hours of partying. Julie, who never left the house without perfect make-up and the most flattering outfit and every hair in place. I'd thought it was just natural— that she never had to try—but it turned out she did. Because now she looked like death.

"What the hell happened?" I unlocked the door and let her in, my own troubles forgotten.

She didn't move, except to wipe her runny nose with her hand. Her usually flawless face was streaked with make-up and she looked like she hadn't slept in a week. Her blonde hair was tangled and matted; bobby pins hung from loose curls. She was wearing black leggings with tiny pieces of Kleenex all over them and a faded Cotton Ginny sweatshirt full of holes, with pieces of chips on the chest.

"You didn't answer my text," she said again.

"What text?" I pulled out my phone and held it by my side. I wanted to check my texts, but I couldn't pull my gaze away from her face. It was like a car accident. No matter how horrific it looked you couldn't turn away.

She grabbed my phone, swiped in my password, and shoved it in my face. "This text."

"U up?" I read out loud. "Sorry, I didn't get the alert. Also, isn't that a booty call thing?"

"Are you sure?" she yelled and I jumped back. "Are you sure you didn't get the alert? Or are you ignoring me now? And I know it's a booty call thing, but I didn't think you knew. And that's all I had the energy to type."

I reached my arm behind her and gently nudged her inside, closing the door. "Why don't you come in and sit down?

I honestly didn't get the alert," I continued as I closed the door. "Sometimes that happens. I was actually up though. What did you need?"

"I needed you," she said as she deflated, tears sliding down her cheeks. "I needed to tell you the secret I've been keeping. I needed to tell you the truth."

Chapter 61

Julie sat on my couch under a thin blue blanket my grandma had crocheted. I placed a glass of water in her hands. Mittens lay in her lap, his cat intuition attuned to the fact that something was wrong. When she'd first arrived, I'd been shocked, but now I was worried. I'd never seen her this upset. She looked scared.

"Do you maybe want some wine instead?" I asked, turning back towards the kitchen.

"No, thanks," she sniffed. "I've stopped drinking for a while."

"Pardon?" I literally stopped in my tracks.

"Come sit down," she answered. "Please. This is going to be hard and I don't want to wait any longer."

Now I was scared.

"First," she started as I sat down on the opposite end of the couch, "I want to say I'm sorry."

I resisted the urge to say "pardon" again.

"You were right about what you said," she continued. "I did know what I was doing with Jesse, even though I knew you liked him. I guess I just wanted the attention."

"*You* wanted attention?" I said. "You get the most attention of anyone I know."

"Can you let me finish?" she said. "Please." She took a breath, paused and put her mug on the coffee table. "I'm sorry, this is really hard."

"No, I'm sorry," I said, knowing talking like this was a struggle for her. "Go on."

"The thing is…" She shifted uncomfortably, pulling the blanket tighter, trying hard to hold back tears.

I grabbed her hand and squeezed it, hoping that would provide her with some amount of comfort. No matter what we had said to each other, she was still my best friend, and I hated to see her in pain.

"The thing is," she continued, "I always know. I always know what I'm doing." She looked up to see my reaction.

"Like with guys? The flirting and stuff?" I asked, even though I knew. I didn't know what else to say.

"Yes. With guys. With the flirting. I always know exactly what to do to get their attention. My hand on their arm, compliments, laughing at their stupid jokes—they're all things I do on purpose, things I do for attention. I've been doing it for so long I hardly even know I'm doing it anymore."

"Why though?" I asked. "You're gorgeous, kind, funny and smart; you could get their attention without doing all those things."

"I don't know why. It started as a way to feel better about myself when I was in a bad mood. And it worked. When I received that kind of attention, I always felt better. So, I'd do it again the next time. And the next. It got to the point where I'd crave it. It was like a drug. The feeling of being noticed, of being admired, of being wanted. It was like a high. When it was over, I couldn't wait until I got my next hit."

Her voice cracked and she paused to sip her water.

"And it didn't matter who I hurt. The guys who thought they had a chance, the girls who were with them." She cleared her throat and looked down. "You."

I looked down at the floor.

"It wasn't until we had our fight that I realized how bad it was," she continued. "After knowing how much I hurt you and realizing what would have happened if you hadn't called me out, I knew I'd hit rock bottom. I knew it was time to change."

"What would have happened?" I asked, even though I already knew.

She looked me right in the eye. "If you hadn't said anything, if you had just let me continue, I would have slept with Jesse."

"And our friendship would have been over," I added, my mouth suddenly dry.

"I know," she said and started to sob.

We both sat in silence; minutes felt like hours. I didn't know what to say. I had always thought of myself as the one who suffered. The one who carried the weight of the world on her shoulders. It had never occurred to me that Julie was feeling the same way. I had always thought things were so easy for her. Maybe things weren't that easy for anyone.

"Well," I finally said. "You didn't sleep with him."

YOU didn't, I thought. "And maybe you wouldn't have. Maybe you would have stopped yourself."

"Maybe." Her voice cracked. "I don't know. I'm so sorry. I'm so sorry for what a terrible friend I've been. I never want to hurt you. I couldn't be me without you. I love you so much. I hope you know that." She broke into fresh sobs.

"No, I'm sorry," I said and placed my hand on her leg. "I'm sorry for all the things I said. I think you're so brave and so strong and an amazing, fierce, independent woman who I will forever admire. I was just being a jealous asshole, selfishly caught up in all my own stuff. I should have known that things weren't right and I should have been there for you. I'm glad you told me the truth and trusted me with your secret."

She looked up, her eyes exposing an ache so raw my breath caught in my throat.

"That wasn't it," she said. "That wasn't the secret."

Chapter 62

I'd never fully known why Ben had come home early from college. I knew something had happened, but neither Ben nor Julie would tell me what. I'd always figured it had had something to do with Ben's anxiety. Maybe he just hadn't been able to function when he was away from home and he'd been too embarrassed to tell me. Eventually, I'd stopped asking.

It turned out, the night before Ben had come home, he'd received a call from Julie.

"Start from the beginning," I said gently as Julie blew her nose and straightened up. Her eyes were now dry, she was all very matter-of-fact.

"Remember Oliver?" she started. "The guy I used to work with?"

I nodded. It had been a long time ago, but I remembered meeting him a handful of times. Nice guy, always smiling. Always with his wife, who was also really nice. The few times I'd talked to him, he'd shown me pictures of his two kids. I remembered them being very cute.

"The beginning was Oliver."

It started with flirting. He would always stop to talk to her in the hall. He would stay late if she stayed late. They'd sit in her cubicle, talking for hours. She had initially thought they were just good friends. He couldn't be flirting with her. He was married and, by all accounts, a real stand-up guy.

One night, at a work party, she'd caught him staring at her, and when she'd stared back, he hadn't looked away. Later, he'd sat beside her and, when their legs had bumped, neither had moved them back into place.

"Would it be okay if I kissed you goodbye?" he'd asked at the end of the night, his face close, his hand on her cheek.

She was flattered but also shocked. How could this guy, who everyone thought was a stand-up guy, think it was appropriate to kiss her goodnight? She said no, of course. But she wanted to.

At work, things were normal. They never talked about the party, both of them pretending it hadn't happened. *He was probably just drunk,* she thought.

At the next staff meeting, he put his hand on her thigh under the boardroom table. She went to remove it but then didn't, loving the burst of adrenaline that shot through her. The danger of getting caught was intoxicating. She had to focus on slowing her breathing so she wouldn't give anything away.

It went on like that for months. Nothing, and then a brush of lips on her neck when he was trying to see something on her computer. Weeks would go by and then he'd stop her in the hall and gently slip a piece of hair behind her ear, tracing the line of her jaw with his thumb. He was toying with her and she knew it, but she didn't care. She knew it was wrong, but she loved every exciting second of it. What was the harm? It wasn't like anything had really happened.

But then something did happen. One night, at another staff party, she stepped out of the washroom and he was waiting. She smiled and tried to slip past but he blocked her path.

"No one's around," he said. "How about that kiss?"

She knew she shouldn't. This was going too far, but she was drunk (not a good excuse, she knew) and he was so close she could smell the rye on his breath.

At first, she demurred, lowering her eyes. "We really shouldn't," she said. But she desperately wanted to.

He reached up and softly slid his fingertips across her cheek and into her hair, his hand cupping the back of her head, lightly pushing forward.

"I know you want this," he whispered, right before his lips brushed hers.

That was it; she was gone. She completely gave in. Not caring how wrong it was. Pushing all awareness of the right thing to do away for this one moment of something forbidden. It was wrong, but it was thrilling.

They were almost caught but broke apart at the last minute, both flushed by the kiss and the close call. The person they saw never suspected a thing. Oliver was a good guy. And Julie wasn't the Julie she was today.

It happened a couple more times over the next few months. The secret kisses at parties, the thrill of almost getting caught, the exhilaration of getting away with it. He would make the first move and coax her until she agreed. They would never talk about it after. They carried on at the office like everything was normal, but Julie always felt terrible and vowed to stop it the next time it happened.

And then she finally did. After a staff Christmas party, a few of them had gone over to Oliver's house for drinks. His wife had left for her parents' early and had taken the kids. Julie thought this would be the last place Oliver would try something, so she allowed herself to drink more than usual.

But he did try something, right outside his bedroom door. And despite the fact that she was well into her fourth glass of wine, she said no. And she stuck with it this time. The shock that he would try to kiss her in his own home, where his wife and children lived, made it that much more real, and that much more wrong.

"We have to stop," she said. "I can't do this anymore."

He took it pretty well, she thought, all things considered. He smiled and agreed it was not the time or place. He probably realized it was a mistake and that stopping was for the best.

For the rest of the night, her wine glass was never quite empty. Oliver was always there, topping her up, making sure she always had a drink in her hand. She thought it was his idea to do shots, but she couldn't remember for sure. All she knew was that they did several, and the final shot of sambuca was the last thing she remembered.

Until she woke up, on a bed, with someone on top of her, the weight of his body pressing her down. She could feel his hand under her dress, pulling at her underwear, and then heard the tear of the elastic waistband. She couldn't move. She told him to stop.

"I know you want this," was the only thing she heard in response.

When it was over, when he finally rolled off, she pretended she was asleep, or passed out, or whatever she had been when it had started. When she heard the shower running, she got off the bed, dizzily grabbing her balled-up underwear off the floor, trying not to throw up. She could feel that she'd lost a contact lens but decided it wasn't worth looking for. She just wanted to get out. The last thing she saw as she left was the picture of his wife and kids on the bedside table.

She remembered parts of getting home. Crying in the cab, making the driver stop so she could vomit. Twice. Feeling sore and dirty and awful, yet so grateful for the water bottle the driver gave her, pity in his eyes.

By the time she got home, it was light out and she was fully lucid, the magnitude of what had just happened hitting her hard. She walked into her apartment and felt like she was dreaming. Like she was living someone else's life. Like she was walking into a stranger's home, the familiar comforts out of reach.

She went into the bathroom and sat on the floor, trying to piece together the night. Trying to remember the time between the shots and waking up on a bed, unable to move, unable to breathe, living a nightmare. She tried to remember what had happened before the fear.

The worst part about not remembering was that she knew she'd yielded on previous occasions. That was why she always drank when he was around. When she was sober, she knew kissing him was wrong. When she was drunk, she knew it was wrong too; she just didn't care.

But losing her inhibition enough to kiss him was one thing; losing it enough to sleep with him was another. She'd said no earlier in the night—had she finally said yes? Had she asked for this?

When she realized she might never know, she rested her

head in her hands and softly started to cry. Even if she had wanted it to happen, she hadn't wanted it like this.

She lifted her head and looked at herself in the mirrored shower door. She didn't recognize who she saw. She'd been acting like a stranger, like someone she didn't know, and, if she was being honest, someone she didn't particularly like. She'd been fooling around with a married man. Maybe this was what she deserved.

The pain and the wretchedness, the feeling of being violated and unclean, the soreness and shame—she deserved it all. She was a horrible person.

After three hours, when the tears wouldn't stop, she called Ben.

"It wasn't your fault," I said gently, resting my hand on her back as she sobbed.

"Yes, it was," she cried. "I was drunk. I led him on. I shouldn't have kissed him that night. I shouldn't have kissed him at all."

"It wasn't your fault."

"I shouldn't have drunk so much. I shouldn't have done shots. I should have left after he asked me the first time. I shouldn't have flirted so much."

"It wasn't your fault."

"I should have said no."

"You did say no."

"I should have said it louder. I should have said it more."

"It wasn't your fault." I reached over and gathered her into my arms so her face was resting in my lap. I stroked her hair like she was a little girl. And I let her cry.

Chapter 63

We spent another two hours on the couch talking. She told me that, after that night, she had started drinking more and more until, over the years, she had eventually lost control. How the constant numbness of alcohol had fueled her days for two decades. How, over the years, she'd had to keep increasing the amount of alcohol to find the same sedated relief. She told me about how much she really drank now and how she often drank alone.

"How could I not have known?" I said, dumbfounded.

"Functional alcoholics are very good at hiding their illness," she said without emotion. "That's what makes them functional."

After we had talked, after we had cried and hugged and she had said everything she had wanted to say, I made up the spare room and tucked her in, pulling the blankets up to her chin. She fell asleep immediately.

I sat on my couch with a mug of tea and tried to gather my thoughts. I was glad she'd told me—it explained a lot about her behaviour and also why she'd quit her job back then, seemingly out of the blue. But I was also angry. When a woman said no, she meant no. No matter how drunk she was and no matter what she'd done before. When she said no, whatever was happening needed to stop.

Julie didn't deserve this. No one did. Before I left her room, I'd looked at her peaceful, sleeping face and felt the prickle of tears in my eyes. "It'll be tough," I'd said quietly. "But we'll get through this together."

Now I was alone and the impact of everything that had happened that day really hit me, the tears came with a vengeance. I cried because of Jesse and how stupid I felt. I cried because the only man who had never left me now had a girlfriend. I cried for Julie and all the horrible things she had gone through. But mostly I cried because I'd missed something so important. I'd been so bitter and resentful of all the attention Julie got, so preoccupied with trying to get the attention I thought I deserved, so certain about how our lives were and how they had always been that I had missed the incredible pain and heartache that my best friend had been carrying for twenty years. A pain that might very well have caused her to drink herself to death if she had let it.

I'd had no idea how much she'd been drinking, how many risks she'd been taking. She had always held her liquor well. If I'd been paying more attention, would I have seen that it had become a problem? At what point did "drinks a lot" become "drinks too much"? I wanted to think I would have woken up eventually, but what would have happened if I hadn't?

I was just about to go in and check on her again when the buzzer rang.

It was Ben.

Chapter 64

"She's asleep," I said as he stepped into the apartment.

"Is she okay?" he asked. "I just got your text."

"I think so. I hope so."

"She will be," Ben said. "She's very strong."

"I know," I whispered. Tears filled my eyes.

"Hey," Ben said, lifting my chin with the crook of his finger. "She'll be okay. I promise."

I looked up and met his eyes and my heart skipped several beats. I couldn't believe I had missed this for so long. This feeling. This connection. Even though he wasn't here for me, I had to say something. I knew he had a girlfriend now, but I had to tell him how I felt.

Instead I said, "What's that?" and pointed at the paper bag he was holding.

"Oh," he said like he'd forgotten he was holding it. "I brought food."

He handed me the bag and my stomach growled in anticipation. I hadn't eaten since yesterday.

I put the bag on the table, glanced at the familiar yellow-and-green logo, and peeked in. "Is this—?" My eyes widened in delight.

"It is," he said. "Takeout from Humpty's." He handed me a coffee from the cardboard tray he'd set on the floor and closed the door. "I stopped by Beans 'n' Brews and you weren't there. Then I got your text and Humpty's was on the way. I figured you guys would be hungry," he said as he put a couple of containers in the fridge for Julie.

Humpty's was the old diner we used to go to in our twenties after the bar. The Hangover Killer we'd called it. Greasy eggs and bacon, a perfect end to a long night of partying before we'd go home and sleep the day away. I hadn't known how good we'd had it back then. No worries, no responsibilities. Sleeping all day and not giving it a second thought.

I stuck my face into the bag and breathed in the cloying scent of fried food and squeeze cheese. It instantly took me back. I could almost see the three of us sitting in a corner booth, drinking endless cups of terrible coffee, Julie and I laughing loudly about something stupid we'd done, Ben quietly smiling, taking it all in.

I sat down at my kitchen table, peeled back the plastic tab on my coffee and sipped the foul-smelling brew. Still terrible.

I finished unpacking the paper bag and my stomach growled again. As much as I wanted to know why Ben had been at the coffee shop, I wanted something to eat even more.

I opened the cardboard container that had my name written on it in black sharpie and grabbed a plastic fork. He'd remembered what I used to order all those years ago.

"Chicken and waffles with a side of bacon, right?" He smiled as he opened his own.

"Wait, don't tell me." I held my hand over his container. "Big Breakfast with sausage, rye bread and eggs over easy."

"Obviously," he said as if there were no other option, opening the lid and stabbing a sausage with his fork.

I wondered how hard it had been for him back then to stay at parties and deal with all the people and the uncertainty of panic attacks. While unclear about the extent, I'd known back then that he'd been dealing with anxiety. But I'd still never asked him how he was doing, never wanting to have to take care of someone and ruin my fun.

All this time I'd thought he was someone who needed to be taken care of. And all this time he'd been the one taking care of me.

I knew what I had to do.

"It's my turn now," I said out loud.

"Hmm?" he mumbled, mouth full of food.

"You and Julie have been taking care of me my whole life. When we were kids and my parents fought and I basically lived at your house after school. When they got divorced and I needed somewhere to cry. When my dad left and never looked back. All of my shitty boyfriends and shitty dates and questionable nights at the bar. You both were there for me. You both took care of me. You both never left. And now it's time for me to be there for both of you. It's my turn now."

He smiled, his typical Ben, gentle, kind, crooked grin. "We didn't take care of you because we had to, you know. We wanted to. We… we both really care for you, Kate. I know Julie will be grateful for your help."

"Of course I will always be there for her," I said, taking

a gulp of coffee. My mouth had suddenly gotten dry. Probably because all the moisture in my body had pooled to the palms of my hands. Was this what taking control of your life felt like? Because, if so, I was not completely on board. I wiped my hands on my pants and continued. "But I'm not just talking about Julie."

He looked up, eyes questioning.

"I need to tell you something," I said. And then, "Wait, why were you at the coffee shop? You never go with us. I didn't think you liked it."

"Oh," he said. "That. Well, I'd had a feeling the guy you called me about was Jesse," he said. His eyes dropped but then purposely rose up and held mine. His stare was intense, but I didn't feel uneasy. I had never noticed the flecks of gold in his eyes before.

"But you said you didn't want to meet," I said, my eyes never leaving his.

My stomach growled loudly but I couldn't eat.

"I know," he said. "I wanted to make sure you were okay." He paused and put his hand on the back of his neck, looking like he couldn't decide if he should say what he wanted to say next.

"Just say it," I said softly.

"I never really liked that guy." His gentle face contorted, not used to saying anything unkind. "I could tell who he was the first time I met him. You probably didn't notice, but he treats men a lot differently than he treats women."

I hadn't noticed.

"Didn't you ever wonder why there are always so many women at that place and barely any men?"

I hadn't wondered.

"I'll give him this though. He sure knows what he's doing." He shook his head.

I looked down, shame colouring my cheeks.

"Sorry, shit, sorry. I didn't mean… sorry." He reached for my hand and the spark that jolted up my arm shocked me to my core.

"But it's true, isn't it?" I said, not taking my hand away, feeling comfort in its warmth. "He played me like he plays all the women that go in there. And I fell for it."

And it all rushed out, everything that had happened. The singles night, the fight, Jesse at my place last night, Jesse at my place this morning. Julie's pain. My negligence.

Ben listened without interrupting, handing me his napkin when the tears spilled over and started falling onto my plate. He ate his food without taking his eyes off my face.

"Julie's pain is not your fault," he said when I was done. "When people try that hard to hide what they're feeling, their success isn't anyone else's failure."

"I can't believe it took Julie telling me about her trauma to realize how self-involved I was being. How lost I was in my own world. I could have helped her." I sniffed.

"You can help her now."

I nodded, not fully convinced I should be let off the hook.

"And by the way"—he frowned—"this was completely Jesse's loss. He might 'literally' have abs of steel but"—his eyes softened—"you're beautiful, Kate."

And just like that, my heart was full. I didn't know what

to say. No one had ever told me that. I opened my mouth to speak, but he beat me to it.

"Listen," he said, putting down his fork. "I know what it's like to live in Julie's shadow. I know what it's like to always be second. I came to the realization long ago that she'll always be the golden child in our parents' eyes."

"That's not true," I said. He raised his eyebrow. He knew that I knew it was. I smiled as he continued.

"I know you think I'm just the quiet guy in the background not paying attention, but, Kate, all I do is pay attention. I watched you try so hard to match Julie's personality when you both were young."

"Young*er*," I said stubbornly.

He laughed. "Yes, young*er*. I watched you grow and realize that you're never going to be Julie. I watched you turn into your own person. A great person. But lately, I've been watching all that growth and greatness start to disappear. In your search for someone to be with, you've started to lose parts of yourself.

"You started drinking more and flirting with strangers and making decisions that were, no offence, a bit questionable."

I blushed, remembering the night of the speed dating event.

"You stopped talking to me after the speed dating event," I said, finally connecting the dots.

Now it was his turn to look down.

"Do you know what an SSRI is?" he asked.

"Um, no." That was random.

"It stands for Selective Serotonin Reuptake Inhibitors. It's the medication I take for my anxiety."

I sat back, ready to listen. He'd never talked to me in much detail about his anxiety before.

"I used to feel uncomfortable around people all the time. Because of my anxiety I had panic attacks. Sometimes I couldn't go out in public, and when I did, I rarely enjoyed myself. My anxiety kept me from doing a lot of things. And it caused the people I love a lot of pain—mostly Julie, who I will be eternally grateful for. For so long, just like you, I felt that no one would want to be with me. Because I was different. Because I was damaged.

"But then, when I was in college, I started learning more about what was happening to me and why my brain reacted the way it did. Eventually, after I'd started to get things under control, I realized that I enjoyed going out and I met a lot of great people. I met one woman who was especially great. She liked me for me and she accepted me the way I was. I had thought I would never find that."

I'd had no idea Ben had dated someone in college. Turned out I'd had no idea about a lot of things. "What happened to her?"

"We broke up when I came home."

"I'm sorry," I said, now knowing why he'd had to come back.

"It's fine," he said, dismissing it with a wave of his hand. "That's not the point. The point is that I did find someone. And I didn't have to pretend to be someone different. I could just be me, faults and all."

I nodded, taking it all in.

"We wouldn't have lasted even if I had stayed; we were

better as friends, but I'm so grateful I met Sherri." I perked up at the name.

"Your girlfriend?"

"What? No." He laughed. "Well, yes, I mean, back then, I guess. I still talk to her from time to time if I'm struggling. She not only accepts me for who I am, but she teaches me so much. She taught me to enjoy the simple things in life. And she taught me that I needed to give up trying to control everything." He looked at me knowingly.

I smiled. And then I smiled some more. I literally (correct usage) couldn't stop smiling. Ben didn't have a girlfriend. *Ben didn't have a girlfriend!*

"I noticed you were different after you came back," I said. "Is that when you started taking the medication?"

He nodded. "Is your face okay?"

"Yes, sorry." I put my hand over my unwavering smile. "Please continue."

"I do still have bad days sometimes, but the medication has helped quite a bit. I even started pushing myself to do things that made me uncomfortable. Things that in my twenties would have been so terrifying that I would never have taken the risk." He paused and swallowed. Sipped his coffee. Wiped his top lip. Sipped again.

"And you're right," he finally said. "I did stop talking to you. Not because I wanted to, but because I knew if I didn't, it would go against everything I'd learned about self-care, about self-preservation. I couldn't keep watching you trying so hard to meet someone." His eyes lowered, but not before I saw the pain he'd been holding behind them.

This was it. My chance to take control. My chance to

stop being a victim. My chance to get out from under the heaviness of all the stories I'd created about my life and start living it without blaming everyone else for my misfortunes. This was my life. It was time to write my own story. "Ben," I said, "I need to tell you something."

He put his hand on mine and cleared his throat. I could tell he was struggling with what he wanted to say. But I could also tell he needed to do it. And for once, I didn't put my needs first. For once, I gave him what he needed. I closed my mouth and let him talk.

"You know sometimes when you see something or think of something, like a sunset or a birthday party, and all you feel is warm and happy?" His eyes sparkled. "Even when you're feeling down. And it just surprises you. Out of the blue. You're just unexpectedly happy, even for a second?"

I nodded, tears filling my eyes.

"I rarely felt that way before. But over the years I started to feel it more and more. Even from little things. Sunlight streaming through the trees, a dog wagging its tail, the smell of fresh-cut grass. Out of the blue, I would feel happy and full of hope. Before, there was only one thing that would make me feel like that."

I held my breath. And everything fell into place.

"It was you, Kate. It will always be you."

Chapter 65

I will remember Humpty's takeout with fondness for the rest of my life. That one moment at my kitchen table when everything changed. The lingering smell of greasy food and terrible coffee. The comfort of Ben's hand on mine. The absolute terror in his eyes. My deep desire to make him feel safe. It was my turn now.

I pulled my chair closer and brought my hand up to his face, brushing my thumb over his day-old stubble which, surprisingly, was a pretty sexy look on him.

He breathed in quickly and looked down at my chin. "You don't have to," he whispered. "I just wanted… I thought you should know. No more secrets."

"No more secrets," I whispered back.

He looked up and met my eyes, begging me to tell him how I felt, begging me not to hurt him.

I leaned forward, wondering what it would be like, wondering if it would be weird.

Our lips met and we melted, falling into each other with the desperate relief of a thirst finally quenched, fitting together like we were one.

"Are you sure?" he breathed, pulling away and resting his forehead on mine.

"I've never been surer of anything in my life," I said. "Literally."

He smiled and closed the gap, his fingers sliding up my back and into my hair, cupping my head and deepening the kiss.

And now I knew. It wasn't weird; it was amazing. Of course it was—it was Ben.

We came up for air just a few minutes later. Both of us knew Julie was in a fragile state and that seeing her brother and her best friend making out in the kitchen might just push her over the edge. Julie came first. We both agreed she was the most important.

For the rest of the afternoon, we took turns looking in on Julie and we talked, holding hands on the couch like we were in grade twelve. Now we had taken the first big step we knew we could wait before we let things get serious. We knew we had to wait until Julie started getting better. And we had to make sure this was something we both wanted to do. The last thing we wanted was to destroy our friendship.

"It might take months," I said, stroking his hand with my thumb.

"I've waited thirty years," he said. "I can wait a few months. I will never leave you, Kate, even when things are tough."

I settled my head on his shoulder and closed my eyes. I knew the wait would be worth it.

Chapter 66

September 14th

Kate: How is she?

Ben: Not great today. She's been in bed all afternoon.

Kate: One day at a time, right?

Ben: Right.

Kate: I'll see you tonight when we swap.

Ben: You bet.

Kate: Miss you.

Ben: Miss you too.

Chapter 67

October 6th

"I can't believe it," Julie said, her hands curled around a pumpkin spice latte. She looked at Ben and then back at me and tilted her head. "But I kind of can, you know? I'd never thought of it before, but it kind of makes sense." She smiled.

Ben and I exhaled in unison. "So, you're okay with it?" I asked.

"Because if you're not…" Ben added.

"Of course I am!" Julie laughed and grabbed both our hands. "You are my two most favourite people in the world. I want you to be happy. And as weird as it is, looking at you both now, I honestly feel like you belong together."

"Oh, thank goodness," I breathed, placing my hand on Ben's thigh. He turned his head and smiled, the love in his eyes matching mine. Whether or not we wanted to do this wasn't even a question anymore. If the last couple months had taught us anything, it was that being together was the only thing we both wanted.

Julie looked at us, eyes moving back and forth. "Could you not make out in front of me right away though?" she said. "I think that's something I'm going to need to be eased into. Or, like, never see."

Ben grabbed my hand and smiled. "I think we can manage that." He looked at his watch and turned to me. "When do you have to go interview for that freelancing gig?"

"Not until two p.m.," I said. "We have plenty of time to hang out."

"Also," Julie said, "you're right, the coffee is much better here. Cheers to 13th Avenue Coffee House, our new favourite place." We raised our mugs in unison.

As we drank our coffees and talked, my heart filled. I was so grateful to have such a great best friend. I hadn't been sure how she was going to react, but after she'd given us her blessing, I realized I'd always known she would. All she wanted was for us to be happy. I was so lucky.

Since Ben and I had kissed I had discovered that the flip I had gotten in my stomach whenever I'd seen Jesse wasn't really due to attraction—at least not completely. It had been more nervousness and uncertainty and perhaps a bit of fear.

I'd wanted to find someone so badly that I'd tried to make the only man I'd been even remotely attracted to into the man I wanted him to be. The butterflies in my stomach hadn't been fun, new-relationship butterflies. They'd been butterflies fueled by anxiety. I hadn't felt the good flip in my stomach for so long that I hadn't been able to see the difference. I hadn't felt the good flip until Ben.

Now I knew that the good flip felt like a quiver of joy when you saw the face of the person you loved and that you couldn't help but smile when their name came up on your phone. It was the heat of your heart beating faster when they were around and missing that warmth when they weren't. It was giddiness and hopefulness and knowing that you could just let yourself fall. It was pulses quickening and losing control and not even noticing that your stomach wasn't sucked in because all you could feel was the electricity of lips touching skin. It made you feel happy and safe. It made you feel wanted and loved.

When I was in my twenties, love had been anxiety, drama, chaos and insecurity. It had been bouncing from guy to guy, hoping to find the perfect one. It had been never knowing and always being on edge, waiting for the other shoe to drop.

Love in my forties was so different. It was stability, compassion and respect. It was passion and excitement and celebrations and being together but also feeling secure enough to do things apart. It was good days and bad days, growing and learning. It was thinking about the future and knowing about each other's past. It was building a life together and never looking back.

It was Ben. It would always be Ben.

Chapter 68

New Year's Eve
Ben

Ben sat on the couch reading a book, Mittens purring by his side, a piece of leftover tinsel stuck on one of his paws. He gave the cat a scratch behind his ears and the purring deepened. It had taken a while for Kate's cat to get used to him, but he'd finally settled down, accepting that he wasn't going to be disappearing anytime soon.

Ben peeked over the top of his book and watched Kate clicking away on her laptop, absorbed in her work. Ever since she'd gotten fired from the PR agency and had decided to do freelance consulting, she always seemed to be on that thing. But he didn't mind. Telling her boss where to shove it was the best thing she'd ever done. Months later, she still talked about how free she felt, how she'd known the place was toxic but hadn't realized just how toxic until she'd left. "I never have to see Terry again!" she'd still say every once in a while.

As he watched her, his mouth curled into a reflexive smile. He hoped part of her newfound happiness also had something to do with him. He knew it did. He knew his own happiness did anyway. He still couldn't believe how lucky he was. He woke up every day and, before he even opened his eyes, he felt the warmth of her lying beside him and he was at peace. He knew he could face the day. He could do anything with Kate by his side.

He still had challenging days, of course. Anxiety and depression didn't magically go away, but now he had hope. Hope for his future and the knowledge that he didn't have to face it alone. Happiness was always within reach and he knew it always would be.

She looked up and smiled, eyes sparkling. "Ready to go?" she asked as she closed her laptop. "It's a big night."

He placed the silver plastic headband on his head and blew an enthusiastic toot on the party horn, causing Mittens to jump off the couch with a yowl.

"Whoops."

"And just when he was starting to like you." She linked her arm through his and pulled him towards the door.

Life was good.

Julie

Julie walked out of the kitchen with two more bowls of chips and placed them on the dining room table, checking one more time to make sure everything was ready.

I can't believe I'm nervous, she thought with a laugh. This was the first event she'd hosted in years and the first dry New Year's she'd had in, well, probably ever. She wanted everything to be just right.

She'd decided to start slow, just inviting Kate and Ben and a few of Kate's friends from her new book club. Then Ben had invited a couple of people he knew from work, so she'd decided she might as well invite a few friends from her yoga class. It was still manageable though. She knew it would be fun.

She poured another glug of sparkling water into her champagne flute and walked around the room, pushing in a book, straightening a blanket, fluffing a pillow, finding a rogue Christmas decoration behind a chair. *Everything looks great,* she told herself. *Sit down and relax for crying out loud.*

She sighed as she sat on the edge of the couch, ready to pounce if the doorbell rang, knowing Ben and Kate were going to show up early to help set up. She couldn't have been more grateful for the way they'd stuck by her over the last few months, through her several attempts to get sober and her mood swings while she'd gone through withdrawal, both from the booze and the booty calls. There had been bumps in the road, and there would surely be more, but after finally finding a therapist that fit, she'd been two months sober. That was the longest she'd gone without a drink in years.

And while she still wished it were wine she was swirling in her glass, she knew this was what she needed to do to get better. To like herself again. To love herself. To believe she was worth more than drunken one-night stands. She was slowly getting there. She was actually starting to see the light at the end of the tunnel. She knew she deserved happiness, to feel the sunshine, and each day there was a little less darkness.

She stood up as she saw headlights through the window and walked to the door. She welcomed them in as they stomped the snow from their boots on the mat. She gave Ben a hug as Kate placed a bag of orange juice and ginger ale on the floor. "I thought we could make virgin mimosas," Kate said cheerfully as Julie pulled her in for a hug of her own.

Ben took the drinks and a bag of food over to the table and started setting things up as Kate moved the board games onto the counter so they were out of his way.

Julie swallowed a lump in her throat, so grateful to be spending this night with the two people whose unconditional love might very well have saved her life.

"Happy New Year, guys," she said.

New Year's Eve

Ten Seconds to Midnight

"Are you happy?" Ben whispered, his forehead touching mine, the shouts of the New Year countdown in the background.

"The happiest," I whispered back as his lips brushed my neck.

I thought of the gift Ben had gotten me for Christmas. My pledge napkin framed, an inscription on a little gold plaque attached to the front: *You'll always be my someone to kiss.*

It was hard to imagine that in one year I had gone from my lowest point to my highest. That in seconds I would officially achieve a goal I had set in a drunken stupor. A goal that had taken me down a path of hopeful naivety and painful rejection, of anger and disappointment and of awareness and growth. A goal that had ultimately taken me to Ben.

As the countdown ended and his lips lowered to mine, I closed my eyes and relished the win.

It had been so worth it.

About the Author

 Jamie Anderson is based in Regina, Saskatchewan, Canada. A proud Canadian and Saskatchewanian, she wanted to set her first two novels in the place she was born and raised.

She works in content marketing, has a certificate in professional writing and has done a smattering of freelance writing, character development and copyediting over the past several years.

She's been writing for as long as she can remember, and has been reading for longer than that. She lives happily with her mountain of books, her TV and her two plants.

 Sign-up to Jamie's newsletter *https://dl.bookfunnel.com/cxifz0ucfv* for news on her follow up romance novel Love, Julie. You'll also receive exclusive deals, special offers and a FREE copy of Jamie's sweet, uplifting novella Running from Christmas as a welcome gift!

Acknowledgements

1. First and foremost I'd like to thank my publisher Tarn Hopkins from TRM publishing. She took a chance on me when "literally" no one else would. She saw something in my terrible submission and helped me shape it into a book that I'm very proud of, talking me off the wall a few times in the process.

2. Thank you to Johanna Craven for the great editing and Ken Darrow for his excellent proof-reading. All of your feedback, edits and suggestions made the book shine much brighter.

3. Thank you to Spiffing Covers for the amazing cover design. I fell in love with it immediately.

4. Thank you to the podcast *The Shit No One Tells You About Writing*. If you haven't listened to it, I highly recommend it. Without hyperbole, I would not have made it this far without the advice of their excellent hosts.

5. Thank you to Kendall Litschko, Shalya Dietrich, Kristina Waddell and Andy Tate for being my first readers and to Paula Kohl for doing the first edits. Your

expertise and feedback made the book better and your encouragement helped me keep going, even when I would rather be watching TV.

6. Thank you to my BBF (Best Book Friend), Stacy Smith, whose excellent book recommendations helped me fall in love with romances and whose never-ending enthusiastic support made me feel like I could maybe even write one.

7. Thank you to all the beta readers and my excellent street team. To all of my amazing family and friends who have been extremely supportive throughout this whole journey, especially Jack Hilkewich who was the first person who made me believe I might actually have some sort of writing skills.

8. I'd like to thank my dad Kerry, my mom Catherine and my brother Chris. Without your love and support I would not be here. You have all taught me so much: both my parents gave me my love of books, my mom gave me the gift of writing, my dad gave me dedication and perseverance and my brother, despite being younger, will always be the person I look up to the most. This book is for you.

9. Finally, and most importantly, I'd like to thank anyone who read this book. Whether you liked it or hated it, thank you so much for giving it a chance. Writers wouldn't be anywhere without readers, so my wish to you is to always find the books you love.